PROPHECY GIRL

A Five rders Novel

Book One

HOLLY ROBERDS

COPYRIGHT

Published by ToastPig Publishing

Cover Design: Holly Roberds
Editors: Jolene Perry, Allison Martin, & Hopey Gardner

ACKNOWLEDGEMENTS

Most people struggle through their lives with naysayers dogging them every step of the way. I was not one of these people. My endeavors to write books have been met with nothing but wild cheers of support, interest, and unshakable confidence in my inevitable success. I deeply wish the same luxury for everyone who is trying to find their way.

Thank you to my parents who instilled in me a deep love of books. They have supported me emotionally, mentally, and even financially through the years, making sure I have the opportunity and time to pursue what lights me on fire.

To Julia Tetrud, my first die-hard fan who has staunchly believed I would become a successfully published author since our meeting in a college creative writing course. Julia, you are my angel. Without my wicked smart brainstorm group, my weird little dream (yes, literal dream) would have NEVER been novelized much less become a full-fledged series. Brooke Davies and Kim Maclean may we always be creepy and weird together.

To Aidy Award and Lyz Kelley who sat me down and said, "Hey girl, this is how you do it." Hey guys, I did it! These two have never hesitated to share their wealth of information with others, and the world is a better place for their generosity. My beta readers, Tara Vassar, Amanda J Clay, Leah Asher, and Adrienne Torkildson. Imagine my surprise when I meekly asked for help from such talented writers only to met with a chorus of 'yes's.' You are amazing women and writers and I love our bond more than you can know.

Thank you to my friends who showed up in droves to every book signing, party, or gig I've ever had. I am humbled by the quality of people I have somehow managed to surround myself with. I hope I remember you guys when I'm famous. And last but not least, thank you to Christopher Love of My Life Hammond. My husband, you walked out right of a romance novel and make my dreams come every day. I will always reward your faith in me and am working hard to make us billionaires and you a house frau so I can bother you any time I damn well want.

SUMMARY

And just like that, Calan lost his powers and his heart.

Calan lives and breathes the law of the Order of Luxis, never distracted by the modern world or it's temptations. That is until his mission to destroy an unholy dark entity brings him to Emma. With one look, she makes Calan question everything, which may lead to the world's undoing.

Without his powers, Calan must find a way to protect Emma from blood-thirsty creatures, but above all he must save her from himself. But above all else, Calan must fight his new and all-consuming passion for Emma, or all will be lost.

CHAPTER ONE

She inspired my first ever fantasy.

As I stared across the racks of wine bottles at the girl with the blonde hair cropped just at her shoulders and thick pink glasses, something stirred deep in the pit of my stomach, then travelled lower. The book obscuring half her face was bound in bright colors with a man and woman embracing on the cover. Being in here every day this week has taught me that tomorrow she would come in with a different one.

Her name tag read Emma. Emma hadn't taken notice of me studying her, which is exactly how it was supposed to be. I was no one from nowhere.

Looking at her made me ache in places I hadn't known existed before. Like wiggling a loose tooth, I kept coming in here to feel it again. Loneliness. It had taken days for me to recognize the emotion she evoked in me. I hadn't allowed myself the self-indulgent feeling since I was ten-years-old, enduring the trials. Imagining us together both eased and worsened the loneliness, but I couldn't help myself.

The print on the blanket underneath us is covered in small blue flowers. Her eyes fasten onto mine and she can't help but lean forward, toward me, reaching for me.

The refrigerator fans were so loud, I could barely hear the country music playing in the background. The fans also kicked up the smell of wet concrete into the air, which oddly enough, I've developed a fondness for.

I reached for the wine bottle in front of me, all the while watching her liquid brown eyes race across the pages. When I walked in today, she pulled her head out of her book to smile, attempt eye contact, and welcome me into Smoky Badger Liquors. I had pulled the hood of my heavy brown coat up over my head so she couldn't have seen anything but a nod as I entered. My Masters always gave me high marks in camouflage. I'm exceptionally good at disappearing into shadow, so I can watch. So I can hunt.

My Masters trained me harder than the rest because of my bright blue eyes and dark curly hair. They explained the rare features were disadvantageous and molded me with disciplinary force until I was able to master silent movements and veil my presence until I became a ghost in any environment. I seldom removed my hood. In North America, it was easier to blend in, but I still garnered many looks if I left the hood down, especially from women. They would hold eye contact for too long, give me mysterious smiles. It was my understanding women are the keener observers of the sexes. I couldn't help but feel they had spotted something which made me stand out, and I couldn't have that. The hood stayed up.

I take her back to the half-built skyscraper where I spend my nights. The night air sweeps through the large rectangular cuts where floor-to-ceiling windows would eventually be installed, though no worker has appeared since I arrived in town. The white stars twinkle down at us, granting us with their divine knowing. Having Emma here with me is the utmost felicity. Her lips spread into a smile when she sees what I've brought out.

Normally, the numerous pockets on my dark khaki pants would be full of daggers, but I had to leave them behind to get through the metal detector. The first time I entered, Emma apologized for it, saying too many 'yay-hoos' had come in with their guns on their way out to or back from hunting trips. I didn't comment because I was hunting too. Although physical weapons would not be of useful aid to me this time.

I tracked it to this area a week ago. It had been clinging to the shadows, waiting for the perfect moment to feed again. That wasn't going to happen though. Not while I was around.

I pull out a bottle of wine, as well as a loaf of bread and a small block of cheese. In my fantasy, we sit on the blanket and eat to our heart's content. She tells me about the books she reads, though I'm sure their content is too sophisticated for my understanding. In my fantasy, I don't eat alone.

There is a word for what I keep imagining. I'd once seen a picture of two people eating on a blanket together on a massive sign by the road when I was hunting in Ohio. They smiled and waved, their other arms locked behind each other's backs in half an embrace. I still couldn't remember the word. I eat alone and don't talk to humans because I am not worthy. Not yet anyway. But what is that word?

"Did you need help finding anything?" Emma tipped the book away from her face to ask me the question.

I realized then that I'd been holding the same bottle of wine for almost ten minutes.

Then it happened. Emma looked at me. Truly looked at me, so that no matter how expert I am at staying hidden, I was completely and utterly seen. It was both terrifying and exhilarating. My heart tripped over itself in earnest as if waving its arms and crying out, 'Yes, I see you too. I am so pleased you see me.'

I hadn't yet responded and my expression intensified toward her. The only other customer in the store glanced over from the bourbon display and raised an eyebrow in my direction. The man's dirty blonde hair framed a round face covered in scraggly facial hair not quite long enough to be a beard. His eyes were skeptical, looking at me like he knew my every thought about the woman behind the counter. He wore his camouflage trench coat unzipped, showing off a black "Metallica" tee shirt. The coat still managed to nearly swallow up his six-foot frame. I resisted the urge to squirm under the gaze of a lanky young man with bad posture.

"Um." I paused before walking toward Emma. "Yes, actually I'm not sure what I should purchase next." I shouldn't have engaged. It wasn't tactical. There was no reason to do so, but I couldn't help myself with those brown eyes boring into me.

Emma tucked a bookmark in between the pages and set it aside. As I walked over with the bottle in my hands, she straightened the over-sized shirt hanging open over a white tank top. Everything about her screamed small-town, except her eyes. Her eyes spoke of wisdom and worldliness beyond this little Colorado mountain town. I would wager her knowing eyes were the result from all those books she reads.

"What do you think of this one?" I asked, awkwardly holding out the bottle to her, almost dropping it. It's an act. I don't drop things. But it was important I come off like a yuppie. I still wasn't entirely sure what a yuppie was, but it's what a man spat at me in an alley way a month ago when I grabbed him and slammed him to the ground. I claimed I'd slipped, which was a better explanation than why I really threw him to the ground, and how it would have resulted in him losing his head if I hadn't. As much as I disliked having to appear ridiculous and uncoordinated, I know how necessary it is to not appear as what I am.

Taking the bottle from me, Emma's fingers touched mine with the barest brush. Heat shot up my arm then down my back sending a shiver rolling down it with unfamiliar pleasure. Again, the fantasy assailed me in vivid color, and I desired it more than anything I'd ever wanted in my life. Someone to see me.

But it was forbidden. I was not to be seen, certainly not to know affection. I was to follow the missions wherever they took me.

Emma didn't notice my mind wander or my deliberate swallow. She examined the label, biting the inside of her cheek as she thought. "This is a Malbec, so if you want something bolder and spicier, this is your gal," she said with a smile, handing it back.

I wished she was my gal, my thoughts mimicked her term. I took back the bottle, "Oh, okay."

Her dark brows wrinkled in confusion. They were thick and dark, a striking contrast against her honey wheat hair and chestnut brown eyes. It added to the intelligence of her face. "You sure do have interesting taste in wine."

Uh oh. I put on an easy smile, "How do you mean?"

She gestured to the bottle in my hand, then tugged at the bottom of her plaid shirt. "I mean, you never drink the same kind twice. Most people come in and pick the same bottle or at least stick to the same types of wine. You've gotten everything from a cabernet to a dry white, all the way to rosés and moscatos."

Could she guess the small army of wine bottles I'd bought remained unopened, gathered at a corner of the uninhabited building I had made base camp? The fact that I'd never even had a sip of alcohol in my life was probably poking through and making me seem out of place. I'd assumed people would pick out as many different kinds of wine to collect the variety. My Masters would be disappointed in me.

I shrugged and maintained the easy smile, though my back muscles tensed.

One of the refrigerators kicked up a high whine along with a clunky rattle, making the machine sound sick. Emma looked over at it with her brow furrowed. I sniffed the air for burning rubber but detected nothing electrical. Emma stared at it a few long seconds before turning her attention back to me.

"Still figuring out what you like?" Emma asked.

I nodded in agreement, grateful to let her lead the conversation.

She smiled back, clearly pleased to have figured me out. "Well, there's not a lot of good stuff here. Small-town people tend to keep it sweet or in a box. Let me show you the best of the crop here and maybe that will help you decide." Emma came around from behind the counter. The prospect of knowing one of her 'favorites' kicked up the speed of my heart again in hungry anticipation for something that gave me a little piece of her.

The refrigerator next to the first complaining machine loudly rattled and shook now, like it might expire any second. The other man in the store eyed the fridge from an aisle away, edging away from it.

Emma took a few steps toward the refrigerators. "That's weird. At least it's cold out, so if the fridges die, I can nestle the bottles in the snow out back." Casting a shy glance over her shoulder at me, she bit the inside of her cheek in a way that made me feel all at once restless. "I guess I shouldn't advertise where I plan to stash the unsupervised booze." Emma laughed lightly, but I wasn't paying attention to her anymore.

A third refrigerator matched the clatter and screech of the first two. One of my hands fell to Emma's arm, stopping her from moving any closer. I almost didn't notice how good it felt to touch her warm, impossibly soft skin. Almost.

My gaze darted around the store. "You need to go," I instructed in a low voice.

CHAPTER TWO

There wasn't time to try and fabricate a lie to get her to vacate the premises. Then I smelled it. Akin to rotten meat and bad eggs. A marker, telling me that evil was near.

The other customer pulled the collar of his t-shirt over his nose. "Gross, what is that smell?"

Emma covered her own nose. "Ugh, I don't know but it can't be good." Then she noticed me searching the empty space above all the wine racks and asked, "What? Do you think the power is going to blow?" She looked around the store along with me.

"Yes," I said, allowing her to come to her own conclusions again while trying to lead her away from the refrigerators. I couldn't anticipate where it was going to attack from, so I kept Emma close to my side.

Emma broke from my grip and jogged to her register. "Let me grab my phone so I can call the fire department from outside."

"No." I cried out, but I was too late. She raced in the opposite direction of the front doors.

"Travis, you need to get out of here, too," she yelled to the other customer, grabbing her phone from under the counter. All the refrigerators lining the walls screeched and howled like tortured animals.

Before Travis could get far, a scream wailed through the store, piercing through the racket of the refrigerators. The high pitch made the hairs on my arms and the back of my neck stick up like needles. My skin broke out in a cold sweat. This wasn't like the icy single-digit temperature outside, the cold blanketing the store now had an unnatural underlying heat to it that I'd become all too familiar with. While Emma and Travis threw their hands up to protect their ears, Emma's phone clattered to the ground. I whirled around. The screech had come from the front doors.

A mass of energy materialized five feet above the ground. It resembled a dense gray fog, swirling and curling around itself until a shape like the top half of a skull emerged from its center. The eyes were two sucking holes of darkness. A dark mouth yawned out of the fog with another scream. The form swelled with what I could sense as anticipation and raw, desperate hunger.

A soul eater. It appeared between me and the way out. Soul eaters don't appear in human form like benign ghosts. They are twisted and demonic—their only purpose, to consume and destroy souls.

A sharp gasp from Emma behind me told me she saw it just fine too. I prayed to the gods that she wouldn't panic and do anything to hurt herself. Curses streamed out from Travis somewhere behind me.

This was what I'd been waiting for. Throwing back the hood of my jacket, I stepped up to face off with the soul eater. I'd prefer there were no witnesses, but there was no time to protect them from knowledge of the dark. It was more imperative I protect their souls. Squaring my hips, I pressed my fingers together to make a triangle for the Holy Trinity. Taking in a deep breath, I began to chant, "Luminatos treahgo eearhovotas." It was in a tongue strange to Emma and Travis, no doubt. The language was as old as time itself. I poured every bit of belief I possessed into my words to banish the soul eater back to the Stygian, the dark world. It was by a powerful force of sheer will that would banish this spirit away.

The soul eater advanced though I knew it wasn't coming for me. It wanted Emma. It coveted her soul. It would suck her up like sweet honey. Or that Travis guy, although I bet he wouldn't be as delicious.

"Laseto, reinetic, ioenai."

It let loose another high-pitched scream as light gathered between my hands with a comforting warmth. Fear for Emma made my throat squeeze tight. I refused to let anything happen to her, but gods I wished she had gotten out of here. I needed the whole of my focus on the soul eater.

The light from my hands spread, pure rays stretching toward the evil spirit. Sweat broke on my brow as I felt the pushback of its' dark power. I was almost there; my power had almost reached its peak. It was like a wave cresting, preparing to break in a heady rush to extinguish the dark being.

Before my power could reach its zenith, the resistance of dark energy from the soul eater dissipated. I was awash in surprise, and my own unused forced back-splashed without a counterforce to focus it, in a sprinkle around me like sweet raindrops. It had never taken so little effort to banish a dark entity. Relaxing my hands and stance, I realized I hadn't.

The dark incorporeal form was still present, but it was changing, undergoing some kind of metamorphoses. The swirling mist solidified and from it stepped out a very real, very solid foot.

I stared, incredulous. It wasn't possible. Soul eaters couldn't become solid, yet soon it had two legs and half a torso. Formed from mottled gray flesh, the limbs were abnormally long and stretched out. Tendons protruded out from its body in harsh contrast.

Emma cried out from behind me. "What is that?"

I didn't have words as I watched it solidify up over two large arms then up over a head. The monster was now eight-feet tall. Where a face should have been, it was dark and fuzzy, like my eyes couldn't focus. Putrid sulphur and heat pressed down on the store with unrelenting force. Chills wriggled down my spine like a waterfall of squirming maggots. Sweat poured down my face. I blinked. What I was witnessing was wholly impossible. To prove me wrong, the Soul Eater grabbed a rack of wine and hurled it at me.

I dove out of the way just in time, only to hear the rack of bottles smash and shatter against a display against the wall in a tremendous explosion of glass. Shards sliced the flesh across the top of my hands where they covered my head. Something bit deeply into my calf, just above my boot where my pant leg had ridden up, but I didn't cry out. Lifting my head and turning slightly, I saw a jagged piece of curved glass four inches long sticking out of my leg. On my feet again, I reached down and yanked the piece out.

Warm blood trickled down into my boot. Back to my feet, I searched for Emma.

"Emma?" So consumed with fear for her, I didn't notice the soul eater upon me until the cold of its shadow fell over me. I whipped around, my head snapping back so I could look up into its hazy face. The dark sucking holes for eyes and a mouth appeared as it had when it was incorporeal.

"Chevalier," the creature hissed through a mouth never used before.

"Soul eater," I nodded back. I wanted it to believe I was still unafraid, but a soul eater becoming solid went against everything I'd ever been told. It had been a long time since fear had touched my heart.

Reaching into my heavy coat, I pulled out an opalescent moonstone the size of my palm and brandished it out toward the soul eater – the only useful tool I could smuggle through the metal detector. Most people knew it as a symbol of peace and harmony, but I knew it to be an amplifier to my power. I yelled out to the soul eater, "Hominay, regeta, questano."

It threw back its massive head and let out a raspy chortle. Despite the light emanating from the moonstone reaching out toward the soul eater, the beast swept its massive arm, smacking me across the room, my body slammed into another rack of wine bottles. Bottles shattered under my weight. Corks popped with enthusiasm, followed by a hissing spray of liquid.

The breath had been knocked out of me, but my armor-lined clothing protected me from any broken glass. Wine dripped down the back of my head as I sat, gathering my wits.

From my new angle I could see Emma flattened against the floor behind a rack. Her eyes trained on me with a mixture of fear and wonder. Travis was crouched over her. He began to pull her up and toward the back exit, but they were too slow. The soul eater advanced on them. I tried to yell for them to look out, but the words came out as a wheeze after my hard impact. The soul eater hovered over them now. Travis's body trembled, warring with its own fight or flight instinct. Glasses askew, Emma blinked up at the cloud as if she weren't quite sure she could believe her eyes and was trying to wake herself up from a dream.

"Propheros," the soul eater hissed at Travis.

Holy gods of creation. The soul eater just named the Propheros, which could only mean one thing: the time of Darkness was almost upon us.

CHAPTER THREE

It felt like I'd swallowed the moonstone and it had dropped down to the pit of my stomach with a sickening thud. It couldn't be. The Propheros? Here?

Launching myself from the broken racks, I pulled out my moonstone again.

"Illiamos," I shouted, throwing it up toward the creature. The spirit made flesh turned to see the moonstone just as it exploded into pure white light. It wailed as its form exploded with the light of my will, amplified by the moonstone. I shut my eyes against the blast, throwing up an arm to brace against the rush of energy.

When I opened my eyes, I saw it had returned to its incorporeal form. Again, I struggled to comprehend what was happening. If my Masters were here, they could instruct me what to do.

I already felt the dark mist straining to regain its solid form, and without another moonstone I was out of options. Racing to Travis and Emma, I yanked them by their arms to their feet, then ushered them out the back door.

"What in the hell was that?" Travis's voice broke. He kept pace with me but tugged his arm from my grip once we were outside in the frosty glare of midafternoon light.

The pine trees surrounding the liquor store glistened with a layer of frost, their needles tinkling against each other in glassy laughter. The wine coating the back of my head instantly froze, but I ignored the unpleasant sensation. I continued pulling Emma forward as she stumbled. Her panting emitted white puffs in the cold.

"Seconded." Emma lips trembled. "What in the hell was that?"

Her face was now almost as white and clear as the eggs I used to pick out from under the chickens we kept at the Temple. Fear radiated off her. Mindfully, I pushed away her fearful energies away from me. Never before had I been in danger of allowing such pollution to enter my will, but standing in front of Emma, my defenses were weakened. How could she have such an effect on me?

"It's a soul eater," I said. "Come on, we must get you both to safety."

"A soul eater?" Travis screeched. His sweat-soaked hair lay plastered against the sickly pallor of his face. "What the fuck is a soul eater?"

Emma found her footing and kept pace enough that I could release my grip on her. "Pretty much says it in the name, doesn't it, Travis?"

I tried to cover the smile that sprang to my lips as I directed them to the edge of the forest. *That's my girl.*

I corrected myself, no, *not* my girl.

Travis stopped short of the forest's edge and shook his head while pushing his hair back. "Oh no no no, there's no way, man. I'm not going in there with you."

Emma covered her torso with her arms, now shivering in the bitter cold of ten-degrees. Under her plaid-shirt, Emma's white tank top was darkened with sweat stains and bordering on transparent, her hair stringy and wet at her brow and neck. She was probably terrified, yet I still found her to be some beautiful, unearthly creature.

"Travis," she said. "Follow the guy who just saved our asses from the big scary dark mist monster, otherwise you'll end up like every hysterical twenty-something dude in a horror movie."

Travis's posture remained rigid, unmoving.

"You are more than invited to stay and chat with the beast," I offered, though I had no intention of leaving him to the soul eater. Especially not after learning Travis was the Propheros.

Travis paused then said, "I have my truck here. I can just drive away. Way smarter than on foot. Plus my phone is in there, and I can call for help."

"My phone is smashed to bits inside," Emma said quietly, now biting her lip.

I shook my head. "I have a place we can go. It is safe and close by. If you leave my side, it will discover and destroy you."

His back stiffened. "What happens if it gets me?"

Emma stamped her feet in the inch of snow to keep warm, then turned her head in the direction I was originally leading them. "He called it the soul eater, Travis, what do you think? It dines on pizza and donuts?"

"Why aren't you freaking out?" he screamed at Emma.

She dropped her arms to her sides and screamed back. "Because you're doing it enough for both of us. Plus, apparently I have survival skills you freakin' lack."

Travis recoiled as if she hit him, stunned into silence.

Prepared to knock the belligerent man over the head and throw him over my shoulder if need be, I counted to five while he looked back and forth between the forest and his car, mulling over his nonexistent options.

With tight lips, Travis finally nodded when I got to four and followed after Emma. Quickly catching up to Emma, who seemed to instinctually know where I was leading them, I took of my coat and threw it over her shaking shoulders. I was left in a long sleeve shirt that was also armored but not to the same extent as the coat. I already felt better with Emma engulfed in some amount of protection and warmth.

She looked up as if she was about to protest, but then seemed to think better of it and mumbled a begrudging, "Thank you." She wouldn't look me in the eye, and her avoidance gave me a funny twinge in my stomach, reminding me of what it felt like to eat worms.

I'd had to eat them to survive when I was ten-years-old, undergoing the Trials. Even hours after I'd digested the slimy critters, I swore I could still feel them protesting, wriggling around in my belly.

People typically didn't make eye contact if they were afraid of you and the way Emma's gaze only darted to my chest, arms, and stomach – anywhere but my face – meant she must be terrified of me, but she kept in step.

"Glad you two are getting cozy," Travis groused behind us.

Remembering the soul eater had pronounced Travis the Propheros, I dropped back to pace him in case anything should materialize and try to snatch him.

"We are almost there," I assured him, and directed Emma which way to lead us until we reached the small, abandoned church. The crumbling structure probably only accommodated forty parishioners back when it was an active house of worship.

"This looks like it's chock-full of building code violations," Travis said, digging his heels in against going inside.

"Building code violations?" I asked.

Emma gave me a strange look. "Like the building is unsafe and could come down on us if we go inside."

I nodded, understanding. "The structure is sound."

"Who *are* you?" Travis sputtered, still not willing to enter.

I looked around, wondering how far behind the soul eater was. "Someone who is trying to save you. Now get inside."

He snorted. "It wouldn't even work if we did. I'm Jewish. No Christian church is going to save me."

"We don't have time to argue. We must get inside." I could have explained that any place of worship would ward against the dark, but I had a feeling Travis was looking for any reason to dismiss my help.

Already, I missed being the normal nobody who popped into Smoky Badger for a bottle of wine every afternoon as I scoped out the grounds, waiting for the soul eater. I liked being that guy. Now I was back to protector and it was difficult when people didn't want to be protected, which was surprisingly often.

Travis crossed his arms. "No dude, this is ridiculous. I'm going back to my car. I'm not staying in a place where I'll be buried in rubble. You can count me out."

A whisper through the trees spoke to me of flesh being torn from bone. It was a warning, and I knew I was left with no other choice but to use force.

Before I could do anything, Emma stepped up and slugged Travis in the face knocking him out cold to the ground. An impressive feat considering she was five inches shorter than him. She immediately bent over and pulled at his legs to drag him inside the church. She paused to look up at me. "Are you going help or just watch me do all the work?"

An invisible hand squeezed my heart with rapid succession, but I ignored it, scooped Travis up, and took him inside. Emma closed the door behind us.

No sooner was it shut and bolted when a heavy *bang bang bang* rattled the door in its frame.

CHAPTER FOUR

"Is it the soul eater?" Emma asked just barely above a whisper.

Depositing Travis onto a rotting pew that looked like one of the few that wouldn't fall apart on contact, I straightened, closed my eyes, and listened. Not just with my ears but I reached out to listen with the whole of my senses, gently probing at the energy outside the door.

The malevolent presence was almost overwhelming, yet I knew it would not be able to pass the threshold. Then again, the soul eater had already done one impossible thing today. Looking back at Emma I nodded. "Do not go near the windows or doors. It's trying to scare us out into the open. We will wait until its power has dissipated. It cannot stay on this plane for long. Already its energy is ebbing."

Much of my energy had been expended as well, but I pressed on.

Emma shivered despite being engulfed in my warm coat. "Good thing Travis is out cold then. I doubt his anxiety could handle the stress. He'd be running up and out the chimney if it was his only exit."

There wasn't a chimney in the small church. It was one large room with boarded-up windows. Golden light from the late afternoon sun seeped through cracks in the boards illuminating dust particles dancing angrily in the air at our disturbance. The banging echoed throughout the room like thunder, as if it were a sound chamber meant to amplify the knocks. The church smelled like rotted wood, along with the slight vanilla scent of the aging pages of books, reminding me of the Temple. Trash and pine needles littered the floor. Over by the pulpit, an oil drum lay on its side along with an abandoned, gray, tattered blanket. Vagrants had squatted here before.

I glanced down at Travis, the Propheros. If he knew the whole truth of what he was, he'd probably try more than climbing out of a chimney to escape his fate. The Propheros is the true savior, it is foretold that he shall rise to banish the coming darkness. As a

Chevalier, I was bound to protect him with my life until he made the ultimate sacrifice.

"What's a Chevalier?" Emma asked in a low voice, sitting on the edge of the rotting pew across from where I deposited Travis.

A jolt of surprise went through me. *Could she hear my thoughts?*

The heavy *bang bang bang* came again. Emma jerked and closed her eyes against the assault, her hands disappearing into the coat sleeves.

It took a moment to remember she couldn't read my mind despite her bewitching presence. She must have heard the soul eater call me that.

"You're sure it can't get in?" There was a plea in Emma's eyes, begging me for assurance.

I'd do anything to make her feel safe. After watching her for a week, the fantasy life I'd built around her was utterly out of hand. Also, I liked the way she looked bundled up in my coat far too much.

"Yes, I am sure." I nodded. Then to assure her further I walked to the half-broken podium at the front of the church and reaching into its base, pulled out my broadsword. It was best to prepare any potential safe houses near the vicinity of the hunt.

Her lips formed an 'o' as she assessed my blade.

"A Chevalier is a servant to the Light." I wanted to tell her more, but I stopped myself.

I must remember, as a servant, I am of no consequence to anyone and can never be so until I have atoned.

"So you are like super strong?" Her eyes swept up and down my body with interest. My body temperature rose several degrees.

"My physical strength is derived from the same means as a civilian. I train my body every day with the dawn. I have no abnormal physical ability."

Her mouth twisted in displeasure. "While I can't even manage to get my ass to Zumba classes."

I didn't understand to what she was speaking of, but she seemed to say it more to herself anyway.

"But you can do magic?"

The woman was a veritable fountain of questions.

"That is a word for it, but it is the power of my will that held the Soul Eater at bay."

"So I could just will things away if I tried hard enough?" She held her hands up, trying to mimic my earlier movements. I suppressed a smile.

"No. I have been fashioned since birth to be a force of will. I am shaped by belief and with that strong, unerring belief, I can wield great power."

Her eyes grew round and hungry. "You're like some kind of mega manifestor, then. I read the Secret once, so sometimes I try to manifest parking spaces." Her words weren't making sense to me, once again. "How many people can do it like you?"

My heart became leaden. I was not a person, and her referring to me as such caused pangs to shoot through my heart.

"There are very few," I said, trying to keep any emotion from touching my face. "Others who are strong in their beliefs can sometimes use certain objects or passages from a sacred text to generate power that is similar to but not as powerful as a Chevalier. Even then, the believer must be strong indeed. It takes tremendous focus and fortitude to expend the necessary energy."

Even now, weariness pulled at my muscles and mind, insisting rest was necessary. I was conditioned and used to pushing through the chemical warnings. It was also why I did not wish to face the Soul Eater so soon again. I would not last long in my state. I needed some time, and meditation if it were available.

"And a Propheros?" Emma asked, nodding to Travis. "I heard the... mist monster call him that."

"He is..." I trailed off. I shouldn't be telling her any of this. If my Master were here, he would say the girl was of no importance, especially under the circumstances. At the very least, I should drop her off somewhere after this, leaving her with as little information as possible. But the soul eater might find her, and I couldn't bear the thought.

I took a breath. "He is an important figure of a prophecy written over a thousand years ago. He is to protect the world from the coming darkness."

She scrunched up her nose and shot Travis a skeptical look. "No offense, but I think you should nominate a new prophecy guy. I doubt Travis has even killed a spider."

I shrugged as I grabbed the empty oil drum then pulled it into the aisle between Travis and Emma. I didn't name the Propheros. My job was just to protect him.

Another *bang bang bang* and Emma retreated into the coat like a turtle into its shell.

I walked over to her and reached into the pew in front of her. The movement forced me to lean close to Emma. Her eyes rounded like marbles behind her thick-rimmed glasses, and her lips parted. This close, I could feel the heat of her body radiating out from under the confines of my thick coat. The temptation to lean forward and capture those lips in a kiss was so strong it made my entire being ache. It ached like it had when I returned from the trials, broken and bruised from surviving the elements, except this ache had a fire to it. With a jerk, I ripped the rotted wood out of the pew and made a pile of broken wood.

Soon I had a contained blaze burning. Emma removed her hands from the coat pockets and held them up to the fire. "Nice dumpster fire skills you got there."

"Thank you," I said, feeling proud I was able to impress her, but then I realized there was something in her voice I missed, at first. Sarcasm. I was unused to it and ducked my head away so she couldn't see the heat in my cheeks.

"It's weird seeing such a manly warrior type blush," she said, keeping her gaze on me which I avoided. "Especially one who can fight a soul eater, whatever that is."

"It's a kind of malevolent spirit," I explained, bypassing the other comment she made.

"Funny," she said, "Last I checked, spirits weren't supposed to take physical form."

I couldn't help but smile at her this time. "You are smart indeed. It must be from all those books you read. It was astounding to watch you absorb one a day."

She reared back, startled, but I wasn't sure why.

"You've been watching me?"

I shrugged, uncomfortable. I moved to sit across from her, next to Travis. I hunched over the fire. "No, or I mean yes. I mean, I was keeping an eye on the area. I tracked the soul eater to Smoky Badger."

She blinked. "You knew it would attack the liquor store?"

I continued, avoiding her intense gaze. "No," then in a quiet voice I added, "But it was warmer in there than keeping watch on the town from outside all day and night."

She cocked her head to the side. "Warmer, huh?" It was like she knew I was withholding information.

I wasn't lying. Smoky Badger Liquors was considerably warmer than outside, but I had no problems posting up in a pine tree to keep watch. It was sometimes quite cozy perching in a place where I could see everything from a bird's eye view. But I certainly spent more time in the liquor store than I intended, because of her.

"Yes, I like to read. I don't always finish a book every day." She muttered under her breath, "Sometimes it takes me two days."

"You must be terribly wise, consuming that much literature," I said.

Her face twisted up in disbelief and I knew I said something wrong again, but I wasn't sure what.

"Is that a joke?" she demanded, a hard edge to her tone once again.

I sat up and shook my head. "No, it's not a joke. Even the best of scholars I know cannot finish a book in a year. From what I understand, it sometimes takes them years to finish reading one volume. You must be very wise to read so much."

She shook her head slowly and asked, "Where did you come from?"

Travis let out a long groan and brought a hand to the already darkening bruise on his cheek where Emma punched him. "Wha-what happened?" he mumbled before he jerked up as if hit by lightning.

CHAPTER FIVE

Travis's eyes were wild as they rolled around, taking in his surroundings.

"Calm down, Travis," Emma said.

Her mouth turned down at the corners, making me think maybe she was also disappointed he had awakened. I could only assume her displeasure came from having to endure his hysteria again. Whereas, I was disappointed because, as uncomfortable as it was, I enjoyed feeling like Emma and I were alone together.

Bang bang bang.

Emma gave the door a crooked smile. "There now, not nearly as loud or thundering as last time. Just like…" She looked at me as if horrified by some fact. "Oh my god, I don't even know your name." She clapped a hand over her mouth.

"Calan," I said.

Again, I wondered what my Masters would think of my disclosure, especially Master Ylang. I should have only told her I was a Chevalier, a servant. To name myself to a civilian of no consequence in the greater battle was a sin of vanity. The delight on Emma's face chased away my thoughts of coming punishment.

"You look like a Calan."

Travis was still rubbing at his puffy face. "Yeah dude. What, do you like workout every day? Wouldn't know to look at you in that big coat, but it's clear now you're swole."

I nodded though I didn't know what 'swole' meant. "I train every day, yes. For three hours. It is necessary for someone of my position to do so."

Emma's eyes fluttered down behind her glasses to my torso and arms again. This time I recognized the expression. Lust. My stomach shifted hotly.

If Travis weren't here, I couldn't be sure what I would have done. I decided in the end it was good he was here acting as a chaperone.

"So can we go home now?" Travis whined, hope lighting his words. "Haven't heard any banging in a minute."

I shook my head. "No, we must go to my Master."

"Me too?" Emma asked, her voice hopeful.

"The soul eater has your scent now. It will come for you no matter where you are." I added slowly, "If you want to live, I believe it's best if you stay with me."

Travis folded his arms. "How very Terminator of you."

My brows scrunched up. "Pardon?"

"Don't mind him," Emma said, waving him off. "He's just being a baby. But yes, very interested in living."

"A baby?" Travis flailed his arms, bordering on hysteria again. "Something is trying to kill us. A… what did you call it? A soul eater? I think it's totally normal for me to freak out over being chased by a monster."

"It's a spirit," I corrected.

"What?"

"It's a malevolent spirit. Well, it was until it became corporeal, but technically it's still a spirit. Not a monster."

Travis looked like he was sucking on un-ripened berries as he asked in a deadpan voice. "What? Are you telling me there are such things as monsters, too?"

"No, of course not," I scoffed.

Travis gave a watery smile and ran a shaky hand through his hair.

"Demons are very real though."

He blanched.

"They would probably be closer to a monster than a spirit. Demons are obviously solid all the time."

Emma eyed Travis, as if anticipating he might snap. "So Calan, I need to go back to my place to pick something up before we go anywhere."

"No," I shook my head. "As I said, we must immediately go to my Master. He will know what to do. I can create the portal, now that we cannot be trailed by the soul eater and I am strong enough again to do so."

Travis's eyes were round and glazed as he nodded. "Oh yes, a portal. Of course, that's what we should do. Makes perfect sense. Beam us up, Scotty."

"Don't lose it, Travis." Emma snapped.

Travis's ire rose but his hysteria lessened. "Just because we dated a couple weeks in high school, it doesn't mean you know me or can tell me what to do."

Highly uncomfortable with both the friction between the two of them as well as the discovery that they were once romantically involved, I walked to the back corner of the church and knelt. Focusing, I called forth my will to create a portal.

"Sure it does," Emma said. "Believe me, dating you for two weeks, I learned all there was to know. You're just upset you can't hit the bong to solve this problem like you do everything else."

After a couple minutes, I turned around. I had to raise my voice to be heard over their bickering. "It takes a great amount of concentration and energy to create a portal. It would be helpful if you could be silent."

I didn't mean for the edge in my voice to be so sharp, but I wasn't used to being around people, much less their conflicts.

Emma threw her hands up. "Shutting up now."

Travis just folded his arms and glared.

"Thank you," I said with genuine gratitude then turned back to manifesting my will. This time I made a box shape out of my hands to take us back to the Temple.

My will did not flow. I blinked.

"How's that portal coming?" Travis called out.

I shrugged my shoulders back, ignoring him, closed my eyes and focused my will again.

Several more minutes passed in silence before Emma chimed in, "How long does this usually take?"

My jaw clenched of its own accord and my back muscles tightened.

She continued, "Do I have time to take a nap or should we be ready to go here shortly?"

I got off my knees and back onto my feet. Irritation pulsed under my skin, a strange, foreign sensation to me. I was so often in alignment with the Light, I rarely knew of external conditions to break my peace.

"It should have formed by now," I mumbled, reluctant to say it out loud.

"What?" Travis asked.

I spoke louder this time. "The portal should have formed by now. I'm not sure if it's this place, or if I need more rest...."

Emma took a few steps toward me. "Has this happened before?"

I shook my head.

Travis rocked on his heels and slapped an open hand against a fist. "Can't get the old juices working there, eh? I feel ya. I mean not me personally, but I've had some buddies couldn't perform when the time came."

"Travis. Shut. Up." Emma looked like she was close to punching him again.

I felt as though he were alluding to something else but didn't know what. From Emma's reaction, it wasn't a good implication.

Emma sighed, turning to me, "Well, we can't stay here all night. It's getting colder every minute, and there are only so many things we can break and set on fire in here before we bring the whole church down on us."

Trying to focus on what could be done, and not ruminating on my failure to create a portal, I nodded in agreement. "Yes, we must find safe shelter for the night."

Take her back to the building you were staying in. Get the blanket, and offer her one of those wines you bought....

I cut off my own thoughts. This was no time for fantasy. My priority was the Propheros, not sharing a meal with this adorable yet alluring girl.

Lost in thought about where we should take shelter quickly devolved into self-recriminations about not being able to conjure a portal.

Emma's warm hand on my forearm pulled me away from the dark thoughts of what my Masters would do when they heard of my failing. It had never been so crucial to use my abilities as now when I needed to protect the Propheros.

"We could go back to my place," she said softly.

Afraid to move an inch so that it might compel her to take her hand off me, I said in an equally low tone. "It won't be safe. Under no circumstances can we return to your home."

I have never been touched before like Emma was touching me at that moment. It was gentle and caring. I wished the sleeve of my shirt was pushed up so I could feel her flesh against mine. At the Temple, anointment was the closest thing to a gentle touch I'd known. In watching from a distance, I was always entranced by couples who cuddled, or a child who ran into the arms of a parent.

Embrace was something I'd never known and from the outside, it looked... nice. Now I'd had a taste of that touch and found my assumption to be true. It was both gratifying to know as well as dissatisfactory. This was probably the only moment I'd know any such affections and it left me wanting.

Brushing aside my cresting desires, I reminded myself such things could never be for me. Not until I atoned and was deemed worthy. My purpose was the mission.

"Calan," Emma said, and I liked the way my name sounded coming out of her mouth. "Since we can't use your portal, we might as well go back to my place to figure things out."

I shook my head. "Absolutely not."

Her hand slipped from my arm, and I immediately missed it. "It will take two seconds."

"Two seconds?" I asked quizzically.

"Not literally," Travis said when he saw my expression. "Geez, you act like you popped straight out of the dark ages."

Emma's eyes widened. "Wait, are you from the past? I mean your clothes are modern, but he is kind of right. You're kind of old fashioned."

My lips tightened. "No, I am not a time traveler." I didn't offer further explanation as to where I came from. "We cannot go back to either of your abodes," I insisted, hoping that would be the end of such ideas. "We need a more long-term safe house."

Emma smiled brightly and gave my arm a squeeze. "Actually, I know just the place."

CHAPTER SIX

Fifteen minutes later we were hurrying back out in the frozen, dark woods.

Through chattering teeth, Travis said to Emma, "You think you're really clever, don't you?"

I didn't know what he meant.

"Did you have a better idea? You want to take him home to your parents' house and show off the basement where you live?" she shot back at him. When he didn't respond, she added, "That's what I thought."

"We aren't far now," I threw back at the two of them. As they tried to keep pace, I had to remember to slow down. Soon we arrived back at Smoky Badger Liquors. The windows of the shop had been blown out, but no one was around. The soul eater had returned to the Stygian to regather its energy, but would no doubt come back to the physical plane to destroy the Propheros and Emma. I knew I must inform my Masters but I counted on my magic to relay information as well as transport my physical body. I had no such way to do so now that my magic failed to flow to my will.

"Where was the portal supposed to lead to anyway?" Emma asked. Her eyes remained fastened on me as if avoiding looking at the store's wreckage.

"It is to the Temple where I was trained. It is where my Masters are. They will help us."

"Maybe we could just grab a plane to this Temple?" Emma asked.

I frowned. I'd never been in an airplane and had no intention of climbing the sky in an oversized metal bird. It was unnatural. "I've only ever used portals to return to my home. I wouldn't know how to use any other transport system to get there."

"But where is this Temple on a map?" Emma asked.

"I don't know." I shrugged, uncomfortable with her continued persistence to find another route. The only one we needed was by way of my magic. I was sure I would be able to generate a portal soon. "My masters told me once we lived in a world between worlds. Where we could protect the old ways. The true ways."

"So it *could* be another planet." Emma's mouth fell into a small 'o.'

They were confusing me. "No, it is in the World, on Earth. It is hidden in a jungle, far from humanity's reach."

"That explains a lot," Travis said, his tone dry.

"What does it explain?"

He threw his hands in the air, "Why you don't get what we are talking about half the time. You're like some kind of warrior Rain Man."

Emma shot Travis a glare.

I straightened, taking Emma's look to mean I'd been insulted. "My missions take me all over the world, but I do not interact with civilians longer than duty calls for. I speak over fifty languages, not all of them well, but I can navigate any terrain. So no, I do not stay long enough to familiarize myself with eccentricities of any one culture. I show up, I adapt, I hunt, and then I return to the Temple."

They quieted, seeming to process. I stalked toward the vehicles, feeling foolish. I'd never exposed myself in such a way. It felt like I'd roll over to show them the soft underside of my belly, like a pig unaware it was ever in danger of being slaughtered.

After a brief discussion, we piled into Emma's black jeep over Travis's rusted truck, which had only two seats in the small cab. Travis complained that he got carsick and should be allowed to sit in the front. However, I pressed the necessity of my being in front to watch for any impending threats. Plus, it was tactically optimal for him to sit in the back where he would be most protected. He begrudgingly got in the back but only after Emma threatened to slug him again if he didn't get into the vehicle.

As Emma drove, Travis slumped back and crossed his arms, sulking. "Always believe a pretty face, do you?" he asked me. "Safe house, my ass."

Before I could ask him what he meant, Emma put her hand on me again, silencing my thoughts with a pleasurable heat that was only intensified by her smile. "Don't listen to him, he's just upset he has to sit in the back."

Travis let out a snort but didn't say anything else.

After ten minutes, Emma drove up to a three-level brick building. Unbuckling her seatbelt, she said, "It's just upstairs."

Pleased to know she also had safe houses at the ready, I followed Emma into the building and up two flights of stairs, Travis trudging behind us. On the stairs, a mother in a long red coat passed us. She held the miniature hand of a child bundled up in a pink and purple coat and snow pants so that the child waddled more than walked down the stairs. I realized what Emma had done.

After we exited the stairs to a hallway, I grabbed Emma's arm to slow her down, though a small part of me knew I was using any excuse to touch her. I harshly whispered, "We should also not be in a place crawling with civilians in case we come under attack."

"Don't worry." Effortlessly shaking off my grasp, she stopped in front of an apartment door with the number 301 on it and unlocked the door.

"Emma, have you taken us to –" I didn't get a chance to finish the question before I was interrupted.

"Who's the stud, roomie?"

A young woman, Emma's age, was sitting on a charcoal couch, her long, pale leg perched on a dark-wood coffee table. While she struggled to pull on a knee-high boot, her predatory eyes raked me up and down. From her cropped black hair to her revealing purple skirt and low-cut top, everything about her was downright indecent.

The living room she sat in was connected to a small galley kitchen with a large cutout so you could see between rooms. Paintings decorated the beige walls. They were strange, merely globs of color with little form and nothing recognizable to me. Multiple jars of lit candles filled the apartment with the smell of baked goods.

Travis pushed past me to get inside. "Didn't know you thought I was a stud, Krystan."

"Didn't mean you, dick-head," Krystan said flatly, her disappointment evident with his entry.

Travis put his hands in his pockets and rocked back on his heels. "Didn't know you were still so obviously desperate for attention. Thought maybe it was just a high school phase."

Krystan gave him a smile that was anything but friendly. "Better to be in the spotlight than stick to the shadows like some spineless little wallflower. By the way, who did you take to prom again, babyface?"

Travis ground his teeth, "We've been out of high school for four years Krystan." Then he added in earnest, "My mom was a teacher so she was a chaperone. She wasn't my date."

Krystan went back to pulling up her boot as if disinterested now. "Sure, because all the teenagers took a turn dancing with the Prom chaperones."

Having had enough of this interlude, I cut in. "Emma," I said as neutrally as possible through my clenched jaw. "Could I speak with you in private?"

"Oooh, can I come?" Krystan asked, then shimmied her shoulders and licked her teeth.

Travis leaned toward me and nudged me in the ribs with an elbow. "Told ya the pretty ones will mess with you."

I couldn't get my brows to unfurrow or wipe the scowl off my face. None of this was helping my focus or calm so I could create a portal that would take us to my Masters.

"Come on Calan, we can talk in my room," Emma said. I followed her to the room straight back from the entrance. She held the door open for me, so I went in first. She shut the door behind us.

CHAPTER SEVEN

Emma's bedroom was a concentrated wave of her intoxicating scent. It rolled over me, nearly sweeping me away. It was a mixture of vanilla and the inviting salt of her skin. It instantly fogged my mind and made my mouth water, so I switched from breathing through my nose to shallow breaths with my mouth.

The walls were painted a shade darker than lavender and the bedspread was a light heather gray. The bed swallowed up most of the space so there was barely room for both her and me to stand with any comfortable room between us. A slim, white oak desk was pushed up against the far wall. Photos of

Emma with Krystan were scattered about in ornate frames. Piles of books with broken spines were on the floor, on the desk, and bursting out of the seven-foot bookshelf in the corner by the small window. Almost all had pictures on the front of muscular men holding women in some kind of embrace.

"How could you?" I found my incredulity once more.

Emma shrugged. "You weren't going to let me come home and I told you I needed to come back here before we went AWOL."

I didn't bother asking was AWOL was. "You lied to me." For a moment I was at a loss for words.

Seeing how upset I was, Emma stepped in and put a hand on my arm. Her face was now full of regret and sorrow. "Calan, I'm sorry. I just knew it was the only way —"

I brushed off her touch, stepping back. My voice was cold to my own ears. "No, it wasn't the only way. I believed you. I believed you, Emma."

She threw her hands up in surrender. "Calan, I get it. Lying is a big deal to you, I see that now. I'll never do it again. But I'm having a hard time believing a pit stop is the worst thing to happen. For crying out loud, you act like no one has ever lied to you before me," she said, resting her hands on her hips.

My lips tightened of their own accord and I kept my hands fast against my sides.

"Oh my god," her mouth fell open. "This *is* the first time anyone has lied to you."

I didn't respond.

"No, that can't be. Someone has surely lied to you. You're something like twenty-two, right?"

"I am twenty-five-years old," I said, not dignifying the rest with an answer. The way Emma was reacting made me feel out of place again. It was more evident than ever I'd been fostered in a gap between worlds.

"But surely you were at least lied to about Santa Claus, or the Easter bunny? Or someone told that you did a good job on something when you were really awful at it? It's how people operate."

"I wasn't brought up observing such celebrations, and where I'm from, honesty is the most important construct and gift one can give. I built my faith from the bricks of truth my Masters gave me. Their word is my bond."

Emma didn't respond right away, seeming to absorb what I just said. She still didn't understand the severity of her error, so I had to explain. "Emma, because of your lie, I am responsible for not only yours and Travis's lives, but the lives of everyone in this building. I am at a complete disadvantage. The soul eater becoming corporeal is something I've never encountered before. I can't ensure the safety of those around us."

Emma's face cleared of expression. "You're right. It was selfish. I wish I could say it wasn't, but I wanted a change of clothes... and this." She reached to her desk and grabbed a pocket-sized black, leather-bound journal. She opened the book and out slid a silver necklace. The thin chain coiled messily into her palm. "The necklace was my mother's. My dad gave it to me after she died." She slipped the necklace over her head and I caught sight of the charm on the end of it. "Five years old, and I was petrified to wear it. Even as I got older, I was always afraid I might break the chain or lose it, like I do with all the rest of my jewelry." Emma's cheeks flushed, and she avoided my gaze. It took a moment to recognize she was embarrassed.

"How did she die?"

From the way her eyes fluttered up in surprise, I realized I had asked the question too brusquely. I'd observed before that when people spoke of the dead, they often spoke quieter, softer, and more slowly. I wasn't sure why they did so, but I knew I did it wrong.

She toyed with the pendant and studied the design as if she hadn't laid her eyes on it in a long time and was re-familiarizing herself with its curves using the pad of her thumbs. "Car crash."

I didn't know what to say but I stepped in so close that I couldn't help but inhale her scent. I suppressed the shudder that swept through my body. Emma shivered too but it wasn't cold in here. With my index finger, I lifted the ornate pendant off her breastbone and my fingers warmed at its touch. It was in excellent condition, but it felt old. The silver circle was divided in half horizontally by metal bar, a crystalline white gem stone sat just above where it was divided. The bottom of the charm had four more little bars separated the lower portion of the charm into five segments.

"It carries power," I said. Though I didn't recognize the design, there was something familiar about it and the energy humming from it.

"Oh," she said softly, but I wasn't sure she heard me. Her eyes moved back and forth between mine and I felt the warmth of her breath through my shirt. I suddenly wanted to slide those glasses off her face. Emma's pink tongue slid out and licked her lips, leaving a sheen across them.

My heart tightened, and my blood rushed downward. It was like my body was preparing itself for a fight, but nothing like that at the same time. Until a week ago, I'd never known these sensations.

Emma reached up and pulled her glasses off. Blinking up at me, Emma's hand drifted up to the side of my face but hovered just above my jaw. Lightning bolts of sizzling sensation shot down my body into a coil of electricity at the base of my stomach. She gave a small gasp then her fingers clenched into her palm, and she dropped her hand. I almost groaned in frustration but kept still.

"I'm sorry I lied to you, Calan."

I gulped a deep breath of air and broke my gaze with her. What was I doing? I was a Knight of the Light and was simply not worthy to touch such an angel, much less think of doing so. I needed to remember my mission. Protect those from the darkness and the Propheros above all else.

This time she did grab my chin and brought my gaze to her, though she was almost six inches shorter. "I mean it. I'm so sorry to break your trust when obviously it's something you value so much. Especially when you are trying to protect us. I promise to never lie to you again."

A lump formed in my throat where there hadn't been one a moment ago. "Thank you." The words came out hoarse. Her eyes were drawing me in like the wave of an ocean until my body wanted to drown in her. Gravity begged me to fall upon her with all the hunger I possessed.

Stepping back, I said, "You might as well change into more appropriate clothes since we are here."

It was hard not to notice the rapid rise and fall of Emma's chest as she tried to blink away the glassiness in her eyes. "Okay."

"I'll be just outside," and gave a slight bow of my head, dismissing myself. Getting past her back to the main room required body contact to squeeze by her as there was so little room. In a moment, her entire body was pressed against mine and my manhood, which was already stiff, my head was dizzy from the blood rushing away from it. Emma's hand instinctually fell to my chest. Her face was so close, I saw flecks of gold around her irises.

"Calan, I meant to thank you."

I could only mutely nod. Emma's head lifted up and as if in slow motion she pressed her lips against mine. My thoughts scattered while reality came into sharp focus. Though I'd never kissed anyone before, I matched the pressure and suction she gave.

It was one thing to speculate what kissing was like, but I hadn't considered what it would be like to swallow her breath, to discover the curvature of her lips, to know flesh on flesh. The already hot hum of my blood exploded into a fury of desire I'd never known. It demanded I wrap her in my arms, grasp and touch every part of her, and taste every corner of her delicious, sensual mouth.

I didn't, of course. I was more disciplined than to give into base urges. For the first time in my existence, I resented my position, my duties, my mission.

My fingers firmly wrapped around Emma's shoulders to gently pull her away from me. When we broke apart, she was panting, her lips already fuller, and wetter than they'd been a moment ago.

"Emma, I can't." Though I was certain I was only telling myself, trying to command myself into listening to reason. "I am a Chevalier. I am a servant, not a man."

Her eyes narrowed. "I don't understand. Of course you're a man." Then she looked me up and down hotly. My skin broke out in goosebumps wherever her eyes landed. "More man than I've ever seen before, that's for damn sure."

I shook my head. "No, I'm not. My only purpose is to protect life from the dark. I can't...." I didn't know how to finish.

Before she could say or do anything else, I moved past her and out of her bedroom, shutting the door behind me, feeling both frustrated and relieved to have a physical barrier between us so I could focus. I ran my hands up over my flushed face and smoothed back the hair dipping over my forehead.

I have no soul.

That's what I should have told her. Emma would understand why I couldn't continue to kiss and touch her, if I'd explained. I was a servant, repenting for the soul I lost. In my last life, I had done something so heinous and unforgivable that the gods took my soul. Until I atoned through service to the Light and earned it back, I would be forever damned. But another part of me didn't want to tell her. I wanted to pretend I was ordinary and that I could bring my fantasy to life. I was ashamed to tell her I was a soulless being and why.

"Now that's what I call a quickie."

I looked up, startled. I'd forgotten my surroundings, another blunder. Travis had thrown his legs up on the coffee table and had his head back, letting out a slight snore from where he dozed on the couch. Krystan, however, was in the kitchen, pouring a glass of something clear that smelled sharply like something I used to disinfect wounds with. She looked at me pointedly through the cutout of the wall.

"Might want to wipe off your face there, sport," she said again in that deadpan manner. "That shade of rose really isn't your color."

It took a moment for my mind to process what she was saying, then I brought my hand up to wipe away at my lips. Sure enough, a rose color now tinted my fist. I looked back up at Krystan, embarrassed. She threw me a wink.

CHAPTER EIGHT

"So you *aren't* coming with me to Denver to go clubbing tonight?" Krystan asked Emma. Her arms were crossed and her toe rhythmically tapped the floor. Her boots were ridiculously tall, both up her leg and at the heel. I wasn't sure it was safe for her to be wearing such things, but she strutted around the apartment as if they were an extension to her already long legs.

"Krystan," Emma said, trying to shove more clothes in a messenger bag. "We have some baddies coming after us, and I'll be gone for a while, but I'll be alright."

Emma didn't look at me. Since she reappeared from her bedroom, she kept her gaze diverted, focused on her small pack for the trip. She now wore thick leggings and an oversized cream turtleneck sweater. Her hair was pulled back in a short pony-tail and her glasses were gone.

Krystan looked first at the still-snoring Travis then at me with an arched eyebrow. "With these two yahoos?" She uncrossed her arms. "And what do you mean baddies? You make it sound like the Russian mafia is coming after you."

"Something like that," Emma said under her breath. Having clipped her pack shut, she threw the strap over her shoulder so the satchel lay at her hip. "Just do me a favor and if anyone asks, tell them I had to leave town for a family emergency."

Krystan's long arms began to flail in agitation. "That's great, and what if they ask me —"

Emma had walked over to Krystan and put her hands on Krystan's shoulders, though her roommate was considerably taller. "I have absolutely no doubt in your ability to fabricate stories, Krystan."

A smile quirked the side of Krystan's mouth but refused to fully express. "I suppose that's not wrong. Though I still think you should drop these crazy dudes, come with me to Denver for the weekend and crash at my cousin's till whatever sitch has blown over."

"Another time," Emma said, and gave Krystan a hug. Then she turned to me. "Okay,

I'm ready." She looked over my shoulder rather than right at me as she held out the coat I'd lent her.

A spike of pain needled at my heart. I took back my coat and slowly put it back on, realizing it now smelled like her. I tried to resist, but I couldn't help but inhale deeply. Her scent was both sweet and deeply intoxicating, like a ripened peach.

"Travis," I addressed the still-sleeping man, trying to forget about forbidden fruits. "We need to go."

He didn't stir, just kept on his sawing snore.

Krystan smiled too brightly. "Allow me." She walked over next to Travis and used her booted foot to kick the coffee table out and away from his feet as she screamed, "Fire, fire, fire."

Travis's legs dropped to the floor hard and his body jackknifed up as he screamed. When he realized there was no fire, Krystan leaned over and pinched his cheek. "Hey haircut, time to get out of my apartment."

I did not understand why she referred to Travis as haircut, when he looked rather in desperate need of one.

He jerked away from her pinch with a deadly scowl. "Thank god for that. I'm scared I'll catch one of your skanky diseases."

She tsked then said, "You wish you were that lucky."

"It's time to go," I said, my voice coming out rough. I wasn't sure if it was because their friction made me uncomfortable or because I was too aware of Emma keeping her distance from me.

When exited to the parking lot, Travis was still insisting that since Emma got to retrieve things from her home, he should get to do the same.

"Seriously, she gets what she wants because she lies to you and has a pretty face? How is that fair?"

He couldn't see me send my eyes toward the heavens in silent prayer. Long had I been told of the great Propheros that would save the world, but never in my dreams did I imagine the Propheros to be so whiny.

"We will acquire new clothes for you on the way," I said. "For now, we will go to one of my safe houses. It is a farther distance than I would like but security is imperative. I have objects there to help rejuvenate my magic, so we can travel to the Temple." I didn't bring up the fact I'd never had to 'recharge' my magic before. However, in a truly safe place I could delve into my deep meditations without fear of Travis or Emma being under attack. It was the best way I knew to train my will.

"What exactly is a farther distance?" Travis asked.

"About eighteen hours."

Emma said quietly, "Guess we're road tripping it."

Travis stopped in his tracks. "Eighteen hours? We are driving eighteen hours with a dude we just met to, what? Get away from some soul eater that wants to kill us?"

"Travis," Emma said in warning while adjusting the strap of her bag over the shoulder of her heavy black coat with the white, fur-lined hood.

"Hey, I know. Okay? I was there too," he said, then shook his head. "But this is ludicrous. Maybe it was all in our heads. This can't be real, and I am not going along with this." He pointed his finger at the ground, taking his stand once more.

The urge to rub at the pressure building at the bridge of my nose was overwhelming, but I resisted. "Travis, as hard as this is to believe, you are an important figure of prophecy and I need to keep you safe. Now that the soul eater has spotted you, the Dark will send more agents to come for you. They won't stop until you are dead."

Travis snorted and crossed his arms.

It is the great and terrible thing about belief. It is so powerful it can overcome what you have witnessed with your very eyes. Most people poured their belief into protecting whatever reality they knew, and soul eaters were not a part of Travis's reality.

Emma came closer and put her hand on me, her voice carried a strange tone. "Calan, what's that?"

I was about to ask her to specify when I heard it too. It was the unmistakable sound of flapping wings. Except these wings were not that of a bird. The time between flapping told me the wings were far larger than any fowl I knew of in these parts.

Travis was oblivious. "Seriously, prove to me you're magic and all this is real, or I'm leaving."

"Oh my god," Emma said under her breath as she saw them too. Three of dark shapes descended from the sky, one dive-bombing straight for Travis

I leaped onto Travis, smashing him into the ground just as the knobby hands reached out to get him.

"What is wrong with you, man?" Travis sputtered. I rolled off him and jumped to my feet.

"Stay down," I commanded. Emma was already on the ground, having ducked before I jumped on Travis.

I ran the few paces to the Jeep, threw open the back door, and grabbed my long sword before running back to Emma and Travis. Another demon flew straight toward Emma. I sprinted across the frosty asphalt in time to hack off the outstretched arms just as it closed its fingers around her hair.

"What in all that is holy are those?" Travis screamed when he finally got a look at what was attacking us. Their dull green flesh spanned out into a wingspan of six feet. Their bodies resembled that of a human baby's except their arms and legs were much longer, with knobby joints, spindly hands, and pointed ears. Their faces were permanently set into evil grins which displayed sharp teeth. They drooled something black and viscous.

"They are the Crib. Now crawl under the jeep." I ordered.

Travis scrabbled to his feet but a Crib swooped down and grabbed Travis from behind, jerking him off the ground. The Crib flew up and away with a screaming, flailing Travis. My heart stalled. The whites of his eyes cried out for me to help as the massive wings flapped, flying him away, and out of my reach.

Despair threatened to swallow me whole. Without the Propheros, the world was lost.

CHAPTER NINE

*N*o. I was trained to not feed the doubtful thoughts which leave one impotent and helpless. To do so would be turning against the Light. I would not fail the gods in this life.

I raced after the Crib carrying the Propheros away from me. Travis weighed it down so his feet brushed against the car roofs in the parking lot as its wings flapped hard, trying to gain more momentum to propel it upward.

Sprinting after it, I followed until I was close enough. I leapt onto the hood of a van, then up and over the roof. I surged off the van with all the power I possessed, flying into the air. I got my shot. I took a swipe at the Crib. Its wing tore under my blade. The demon shrieked and lost air as black blood spurted from half a wing. Travis fell onto a car with a hard thud and metallic clang. He rolled off with a guttural groan and crawled under the vehicle.

Good man, I thought with relief.

The Crib's descent was slow but sure. Then it smacked across several cars like a pebble skimming a pond before it dropped out of sight. It wouldn't be getting up anytime soon.

"Thank the gods," I said to myself in a prayer of gratitude. Yet my body was stiff with an unnamed urgency.

"Calan," Emma called out.

I turned around to see her running for her life, two Cribs gaining on her.

"Emma, run toward me," I shouted, racing straight at her.

I was six feet away when one spindly mottled hand grabbed ahold of her hood and jerked her back and down. Emma gagged and choked as she was slammed onto her rear. A few more steps and I cut off the arm holding her hood. The Crib howled and flew away. The other Crib dive bombed me and clawed at my face with its dirty jagged nails, digging into the flesh of my cheek and scraping up until warm blood seeped out of my stinging wounds.

I couldn't get a good swing at it as the Crib hovered just over my head and behind me. It pulled out a chunk of my hair out and aimed to drive those same jagged, dirty fingernails down at my eyes this time. I had no leverage to stop it from blinding me.

The body of the Crib jerked with a pronounced *thump,* slamming into the back of my head. A *thwack* this time and the demon tumbled mid-air over my head into a large silver truck, cracking the windshield on impact.

Turning, I found Krystan, now in a bulky zebra, faux-fur coat that hit the tops of her high boots, panting. Her eyes looked like they might pop out of her head. She wielded a baseball bat tarnished by a smudge of black ichor. Demon blood.

"What in the hell was that? Am I dreaming? Is this a dream?" She looked dazed, and a pitch of hysteria wavered in her voice.

"Krystan, duck," Emma screamed just as the Crib with the amputated arm dropped from the sky and grabbed Krystan's hair. On instinct, she dropped the bat and reached for her hair as it abruptly pulled her several feet off the ground.

I had it this time. I jumped up on the nearest car and plunged the sword straight through the Crib's chest. It screeched in agony. Krystan dropped the two feet back to the ground, landing in a crouch. She rubbed the top of her head. The Crib spewed black blood from its mouth. I dodged most of it but some of it spattered against my ear. It fell back onto another car, wings spread out as it took its last breath.

From behind me, I heard the same thwacking sound as before, only to find Emma had picked up the bat and was mercilessly beating the last Crib into a bloody black pulp on the asphalt.

She yelled with every swing of the bat. "Don't you ever come after my friends, you big, ugly baby monster. I'll show you who you're messing with."

Krystan came to stand next to me, still rubbing the top of her head. She watched Emma with me for a moment as we stood in awe of her fury. Then Krystan shrugged at me as if to say, it should have known better than to mess with Emma. I returned a look of silent agreement.

Krystan's boots hurriedly clip-clopped over to Emma. "Sweetie, sweetie, that's enough. The big bad baby is dead. Ya done good." She gently tried to extract the now ichor-covered bat away from Emma whose shoulders heaved up and down from the exertion of the beating she just gave.

"Travis," I yelled. Seeing that Krystan and Emma were okay I realized I had to make sure the Propheros was unharmed. "Travis," I ran back toward the car I'd seen him disappear under. Spotting his unmoving feet beneath the vehicle, an icy block of fear weighed down my chest.

Dropping down to the ground, I found Travis looking up at me with bug-wide eyes from under the car, still breathing and seemingly unharmed.

"Okay," he said softly, "So I think I'd like to stick with you. If you don't mind me tagging along."

A laugh of relief escaped me as I dropped my head and reached to pat him on the shoulder before helping him out from under the car.

We walked back over to the girls. Krystan's arm was thrown over Emma. Krystan said in a shaky voice, "Okay, so when you all let me believe you were running from the mafia, we all meant to say...."

Emma looked up at her apologetically. "We are being chased by evil spirits and demonic forces."

"Ah-huh, so this has nothing to do with all the psychedelic drugs I tried last month. That's reassuring. Sort of-" Krystan muttered to herself while pressing the heel of her palm to her forehead. "I need a drink. I need many drinks. I need enough to drinks to kill all the little brain cells that just witnessed and retained what happened." Then she glared at Travis. "And this is all somehow Travis's fault."

"What?" Travis said, throwing his hands up and waving them in fierce denial. "I did not do this. I just wanted to try a new whiskey today and took too freaking long to decide. Some mist-like ghost thingy came after us. I think its superman's fault here." He pointed at me.

Emma's words were sharp. "Yet again, Travis, not a great way to treat the guy who saved our asses twice in one day."

"Yeah, Travis," Krystan said, eyeing the now soiled broad sword I still held at my side. "Don't forget to give me props for saving your greasy ass too."

Travis ignored her and looked at me, nervous now. "You know what I mean, man. Seriously now, I'm gonna be like white on rice with you. I will do whatever you tell me to, Yoda."

"Yoda?" I asked.

"Is he for real?" Krystan asked, her head rearing back and looking at me like I'd grown another appendage.

"Believe it," Emma said with a sigh.

I suspected I was being insulted again.

"Travis, you need to know the truth," I said, turning away from the feelings that arose at having Emma tease me. "They were indeed coming after you. I've never seen demons attack so openly. This is unprecedented."

Krystan eyed the damage that many of the cars sustained in the fight. "No joke. It's gonna be impossible blaming this on a hail storm."

I continued, ignoring her. "You are the Propheros. The soul eater claimed you to be so back at the liquor store. You are a figure of great importance and the object of a prophecy written a thousand years ago that says you will prevent the coming darkness."

Travis's face emptied of emotion and blood. Then he leaned over and threw up. The girls stepped back, though they were already out of range. I went to his side and patted him on his back until he was done.

When Travis straightened, he wiped at his mouth, his body shaking from more than the cold now. "How in the hell am I supposed to do that?"

With the ultimate sacrifice.

I couldn't tell him the truth though. It wasn't my place.

"Only my Masters can direct you to fulfill your destiny. I am only here to protect the Propheros as well as the innocents from the manifestations of the Stygian."

"The who from the what?" Krystan interrupted.

"The manifestations, like the soul eater and the Crib we just fought." I explained. "The Stygian is the dark realm from whence they came."

Krystan looked at Emma, mouthing the word 'whence' silently. Emma shrugged.

I went on, ignoring their silent communication. "It is best compared to what you would know to be hell."

Emma swallowed. "Flying demon baby creatures, yeah I could see them being from a special kind of hell." She didn't notice that splotches of their ichor had flown up onto her face and hair.

It was distracting. I wanted to wash it off her. Take her away from the darkness and put her back in the light where she belonged. But it was too late.

Emma caught me staring and returned my look with an unreadable expression.

Krystan put her hands on her hips. "Wait, so why is my girl involved in Travis's prophecy crap?"

I didn't look away from Emma. "We were attacked by a soul eater. It has her scent and it will come for her no matter where she goes now, like a bloodhound. Just like Travis, it's best she stays under my protection."

Krystan scowled and floated her fingers around in the air. "So, do I need to come be under your protection, too?"

Turning to Krystan, I said, "No. The Crib are dead and the soul eater does not have your scent. Just lay low and keep an eye out for anything strange."

Krystan saluted. "Aye, captain." Despite her strange, casual response, her eyes were wide enough to swallow the rest of her face, and her hands shook. "On that note, I'm going to visit a more densely populated city where there are far slower meat snacks lumbering about than me." She laughed, but it was only

to cover up the clacking of her chattering
teeth.

I'd seen it more times than I cared to
count. Krystan was going into shock. The
totality of what she witnessed slamming into
her, breaking down her mind and the rules of
her world.

Emma gave Krystan a big hug. "Thank
you."

"It's what I do, boo. Love you," Krystan
said, holding Emma tight, her eyes clenched
shut for several long minutes. When she
released Emma, she whipped around, heading
to her vehicle at the far end of the lot. She
threw up a middle finger for Travis as she
walked away. He seemed disgusted by the
gesture. I didn't understand why. I'd ask later.

I wondered if Krystan would be okay.
Often, I left right after having done my part as
people devolved into the throes of shock after
they witnessed the unexplainable. I was told
not to linger after a mission was complete and
to immediately return to the Temple for
further instruction. Why now did I care how
Krystan would process information?

I shifted my weight to catch Emma
looking after Krystan's retreating form, one
hand gripping the other while worry tightened
her face. As if sensing my observation, Emma
dropped her hands and forcibly relaxed her
shoulders back.

"So," Emma said, now eyeing the still
oozing bodies of the Crib. "Road trip?"

CHAPTER TEN

The car drifted lazily into the next lane, then lurched as Emma jerked the wheel.

"Do we need to pull over?" I asked gently.

Emma had been driving for just under an hour when I noticed her eyelids droop with fatigue. Travis was already snoring loudly in the back once again. I was learning his stress response was to pass out.

She trained her bloodshot eyes on the road ahead. "Um, no. Maybe if you could just switch me in about half an hour."

I had been dreading this moment. I toyed with the hilt of the sword which stood between my legs. "Emma, I can't drive."

"Why? Because it's hard to protect us and drive at the same time?" She sighed. "I guess that makes sense."

I kept my eyes on the hilt as I traced the designs of stars and ornate circles on it with my thumbs. "I mean I don't know how to drive. I never learned."

I felt her stare but didn't meet it. It was just one more thing I lacked. I didn't drive, I'd never tried the wine I bought from her, I didn't understand most of the references she and Travis made, and I didn't have a soul. Before now, I'd never been self-conscious of what I was. I'd always known I was less-than. Unworthy. But being around Emma brought it into a whole new light and it blinded me with its harsh glare.

"So magic and sword play, that's what you're good at," she said as if trying to make sense of me.

I wasn't a puzzle though. Far from it.

"Yes." I was surprised by the bitterness of my tone.

"And taking people at their word," she added with a side-long look.

I didn't respond to that one, unsure of what she meant by it.

"Not everyone does that you know," she said quietly. "Most choose not to trust anyone and assume everyone is always lying to them. Hell, some are even hoping to catch people in their lies just to prove themselves right for shutting everyone out. People can find a perverse comfort in proving to themselves they are alone and others are only out to get them."

"Having faith in others is imperative when cultivating faith in the greater good."

"What do you mean?" she asked.

"To avoid suffering, we must have faith in our place, in the people around us, in the greater design."

She shrugged. "Yeah, I guess that's why organized religion is so popular. We all want to avoid suffering and everyone tries to find different ways of doing it. Except everybody gets hurt in life at some point, then we begin to build walls around ourselves." She cast another curious look at me again. "Except you. You don't seem to do that."

I frowned. "That's not self-preservation. It's separation. People separating from each other is like turning away from the Light."

"Maybe," She shot me a look. "But sometimes someone *is* out to get you."

Emma pulled the jeep over to the side of the road and flipped off the lights. Unbuckling her seat belt, she twisted her body so she could face me. The blue glow from the radio illuminated her as she studied me. Again, when she looked at me it was like truly being seen and my heart pounded with excitement.

"You don't have walls or protection around you. You're guileless and open yet..." she bit on her lip a moment, as if chewing on a thought instead of her lips. "Somehow separate."

I swallowed hard. "I am a Chevalier. I am a servant." Emma had turned the engine off and with it the heater, but the air seemed to warm around me under her intense stare.

After a few moments, she replied, "So you've said." Before I could respond, her eyes batted away from mine. "Why are you making yourself separate from me?"

I lurched forward. "I'm not."

She looked up through her lashes. "Yes, you are." She picked at the fingernails on her left hand. "I thought maybe you liked me from the way you'd been staring at me all week. There is something here. It's undeniable no matter how much I try. Something draws me to you like a magnet, and all I can think about is you. I feel like I'm going out of my mind, but I can't stop this attraction. Like my mind won't rest until I can get close to you. And yes, before you ask I don't have a filter. I just say whatever it is that I'm thinking." She ducked her head away as if embarrassed.

I turned my head to look out the passenger window. It was a clear night. The full coin of the silver moon cast its bright light onto the expanse of fields covered in a layer of glittering snow. They led to the dark looming mountains beyond. Only one vehicle passed by since Emma pulled over.

It was undeniable for me too, and a force unlike any I'd known. I wondered if the gods were laughing from up high as they cast temptation before both of us like bait on a hook.

Emma continued. "When I kissed you, I sensed you wanted more but then you stopped."

An abrupt snort halted her words. Travis then released a whooshing breath and went back to a steady respiration.

I could hear Emma resume picking at her cuticle. "Is it me?" Her voice came out strangled.

My hand raised of its own accord to the soft skin on her jawline. "No. Of course, it's not you."

She furiously tucked her hair behind her ear. "Oh man, this is embarrassing. I just met you and already I've thrown myself at you and been rejected. It's not like I haven't dated before it's just," she cocked her head to the side. "I feel such an intense attraction to you. Like you're a magnet built just for me and I can't help but be drawn to everything you are. Even if I'm not sure what that is."

I dropped my hand and held my hands together in my lap to keep from touching her again. "Emma. You're right. I am separate. I can't be with you."

The word came out just above a whisper. "Why?"

I closed my eyes. "Because as a servant, I am meant to protect humanity from the forces of the Stygian. I am not to belong to anyone or anyone to me. I belong to the gods until they deem I am done with my mission."

"You mean until you're dead." It came out flatly, not as a question at all.

The word no was on my lips, but I stopped before answering.

Tell her. Tell her that one day you'll earn your soul back and then you can belong to anyone. Even to her.

I couldn't do that to her. I could earn my soul back tomorrow or the gods could deem me worthy in fifty years. Either way, it wasn't fair to keep her waiting. She had her path and I had mine. Our meeting was by chance and my mission was to secure the Propheros.

"When I have vanquished the soul eater, you'll return to your life and forget all about this." I tried to smile but it felt like ice on my face.

Emma snorted. "Vanquish. You sound like one of the guys in my romance novels." She ran both hands over her hair to tug at her ponytail, tightening it, and took a deep breath before exhaling dramatically. "Okay, officially hitting the reset button on my crazy run-away emotions. It's probably all the stress of being attacked by evil spirits and demons making my feelings all cuckoo toward you." Then she grinned at me. "It just doesn't help that you are wickedly attractive."

"Wickedly attractive?" I asked, unsure how wickedness could possibly be attractive.

"Oh yeah," she said with a seductive, sly smile. "Those baby blue eyes set against the chiseled jaw and slightly curled hair? I have never seen a real man with a face sculpted like a Greek god."

It was like she was trying to make me blush. Knights of the Light didn't blush.

Seeing my discomfort, her grin widened. "You also got a warrior body, all lithe muscle with some bulk and build, but not too much." Her eyes darkened as she ran them over my body. "Perfectly shapely. And did you know you have this little perfect dimple right here?" She reached out a slim finger to press at the middle of my chin where I was aware of a permanent indent. "I mean, total babe-magnet." She crossed her arms, relaxing back in her seat with a light chuckle. "Krystan says I read too many bodice rippers, and right now, I'm beginning to see what she's talking about. But for the record, I don't feel sorry one bit for trying to take a pass at you."

No one had ever described me in such a way. My Master only served to point out my failings so that I could better strengthen them. Never had I received such praise, no less for features that I viewed as a disadvantage.

Her grin widened and she released her arms. "Handsome, you better stop blushing because I might try to kiss you again." With that she pulled a lever to lean her seat back several inches and nestled up to the driver's side window. Crossing her arms across her body, she dropped her chin to her chest and closed her eyes. "Wake me in fifteen minutes. I'll have some more driving juice in me then, and I'll be better able to fight my urge to kiss you silly."

The pounding of my heart from the image was the drum that kept me more than alert for the next hour while Emma and Travis slept.

CHAPTER ELEVEN

"Who orders a salad at a diner?" Travis asked in disgust.

Emma shot a scathing look at Travis from where she sat next to him, in the bright red booth. The garish seats squealed whenever I moved. The sun had not yet revealed itself from behind the mountains, but the sky grew lighter by the minute. Thankfully, the diner only had a handful of patrons this early in the morning. Though I tried to convince my companions we could eat in the car or out in a nice snow-covered patch of field, they both dismissed my suggestions.

Emma glibly answered Travis's question. "A guy who's got a body that won't quit and who can vanquish demons from hell." She turned and gave me a cheery smile over parroting the use of my term 'vanquish' last night. I tried not to smile, but it was impossible.

"Maybe you should try a salad sometime yourself, Trav," she drawled out the nickname.

Instead of shooting back yet another barb, Travis rolled his eyes as he took the first bite of a burger so big it barely fit in his hands. Grease dripped down his wrists and onto his plate with alarming speed. A tomato slipped out and plopped on the plate next with a loud splat. I suddenly felt queasy.

With his mouth still full, Travis asked, "So how much longer until we get to your safe house?"

I had to break my focus away from the half-masticated bread and cow-parts in his mouth. The sight of Travis eating was fascinating as it was revolting. Concentrating on my own food, I attempted to brush off any feelings of self-consciousness. This was the first time I had ever eaten at the same table with others.

"About half a day," I replied to his question.

I let Emma sleep for an hour before waking her up, putting my coat over her body for warmth when she began to shiver in her sleep. She could only drive for another hour before she became too groggy. She cursed herself for sleeping with her contacts in. She kept mumbling something about 'damn vanity,' before she pulled the car over to shake Travis awake. He managed to drive for a whole forty-five minutes before he started vigorously complaining about hunger pains.

Emma tucked into her grilled chicken sandwich more delicately, but pieces of lettuce, tomato and avocado as well as the large hunk of chicken kept slipping out of the sandwich and occasionally out of her mouth. She kept furiously looking to see if I was watching whenever it happened. Instead, I kept my attention to my salad. I had silently blessed my food and theirs even though they'd already started eating.

It was strange to eat with other people, especially coupled with casual conversation. At the Temple, I ate alone in my quarters while everyone else took their meals in the dining halls.

It took less than ten minutes for Travis to finish his burger and fries. He slouched down in the booth moaning and holding his stomach. "I think I ate too fast."

Our waitress, an-ample bosomed, dark-skinned woman with braids, came over with a hand perched on her hip and a knowing smile. "Didn't save room for pie did you, honey? That's a shame because we have chocolate silk, cherry, and a special honey custard pie today."

Travis's face brightened. He straightened in earnest only to contract in pain once again. "Give me a minute." He grasped the booth and propelled himself out of the seat, headed straight to the restroom. The waitress walked off chuckling.

I stared after him. "Do you think he needs my assistance?"

"Definitely not," Emma said in thinly veiled disgust. "I'm sure he'll be out in fifteen minutes, asking for two pieces of pie. One of these days his binge eating is going to catch up to his skinny frame. He's already gotten a paunch started in the last couple years. I remember in high school he once had three pizzas delivered to the cafeteria and ate all of them in one sitting for a five-dollar bet. The idiot spent far more on those pizzas than he got in the end." Putting down the second half of her sandwich, she asked, "Did you want to split a piece of pie?"

My instincts told me to agree with anything she wanted. "No, thank you. I don't eat such things."

Her eyes swept up and down me over her coffee cup. "Yeah, I figured."

I shifted in my seat causing it to obnoxiously squeak again. "The body is a temple. It is important to feed it with respect and nutrients." I was talking too much. Why was I still talking?

She straightened in her seat, setting her mug on the table. "Oh my god, you haven't had pie before in your life?"

"Well no…"

"What about cake? Or ice cream? I live for ice cream. I've been in a serious long-term relationship with Ben and Jerry since I was twelve."

My mouth pulled down into a scowl. Never before had it bothered me that I hadn't tried these things, but it was one more brick in the wall between Emma and me. Also, I didn't know who Ben or Jerry were, but I automatically didn't care to ever meet either of them.

"What about pizza?"

I shook my head.

Then the smile ever so slowly slid off her face. "Did you even drink that wine you bought?"

I blinked.

She burst out in incredulous giggles. "Oh my god. You haven't ever drank alcohol, have you? Here I thought you were a funny guy buying all these different types of wine and that you were maybe on a mission to try them all to pin down what you really liked." She frowned then flattened her palms on the table. "Wait, you lied to me. For a guy who makes such a big deal out of lying to others, you lied to me about why you were there."

My back and shoulders tensed. "No, I did not lie to you. I was letting you lead the conversation."

She leaned in, setting an elbow on the counter to point at me as she gave me a glare. "It's called a double standard bucko, and you totally did lie." Then she threw both hands up in the air. "Finally, something about you that isn't perfect. I can take this and run with it until I don't think about attacking you every second of the day."

Emma's smile faltered when she saw the intensity on my face. I tried to relax and clear my features, but I knew bitterness and disappointment were evident. I hated being so transparent. "Good."

Travis slipped back in the booth next to Emma. "Pie time?'

Travis was slouched, moaning in his seat, two plates with vestiges of whipped cream pushed just out of his reach. Impatience prickled at my scalp. I didn't like lingering here for so long. We were putting the diners in danger the longer we stayed.

As Travis demolished the cherry and honey custard pie pieces, I took a few moments to tap into my inner flow. What I imagined to be a cool flowing waterfall now felt like a rushing river full of choppy, tumultuous waves. Part of me wondered if the soul eater had done something to me in the liquor store, some kind of curse or spell to block me from my own powers. After seeing it come to flesh, I couldn't rule out any possibility.

Just as I was about to announce we needed to leave, someone slipped into the seat next to me, dressed in all black. She turned to speak into my ear so only I could hear. "The back corner table. Come alone."

Then as quickly as the woman appeared she was gone and heading for a table back by the restroom. She joined a man wearing all black as well. Both looked down into their mugs, but their lips were moving.

Travis and Emma blinked at me, expectantly.

"Who was that?" Emma asked.

I shook my head and got out of the booth. "Stay here."

CHAPTER TWELVE

I took slow measured steps across the
diner, taking my time examining the
eatery for impending danger as well as the
couple sitting at the table in back. Both were
fit with the builds of long-distance runners.
Lines of age gathered at the corners of their
eyes. Deep-set lines framed the woman's
mouth. The untrained eye might place them in
their early forties, but I'd put them
somewhere in their fifties. Her dark brown
hair was pulled back into a braid that dropped
just past her shoulders. The man's black hair
softly curled over his forehead. Gray crept up
his sideburns streaking into his hair. I

recognized the utilitarian, tactical cuts of their black, form-fitting clothes.

To everyone else, the couple might have seemed perfectly normal, but immediately I recognized them as panthers sitting amongst unsuspecting, grazing antelope. They'd done well to keep out of my sight until they'd chosen to reveal themselves.

When I reached their table, I stood for several long moments.

"Please sit," the man gestured toward the chair in front of me when he saw I wasn't going to make the first move. The woman's eyes were sharp and overly familiar with my face, like I was a long-lost friend she was pleased to see.

"You are from the Order of Veritas," I said, still not moving.

"How did you know?" The woman asked, pride in her voice, like I had pleased her.

"The stitching on your sleeve." A small white circle with a cross in it was stitched at the wrist of their left sleeves. Anyone else would have thought it was a clothes brand insignia. But my Master had educated me on the five Orders. This was the first time I'd met anyone from outside my own Order.

"Very good." the man smiled, revealing perfect white teeth in a way that would disarm most people. He was no doubt aware of this effect.

"And you are from the Order of Luxis," the woman supplied. "Please sit. We wish to speak with you. I am Regina and this is Phillip."

I glanced over my shoulder, still unsure.

"Your friends will be fine," Phillip reassured. "We mean them no harm."

Friends. What a strange concept, but I guessed that was what Travis and Emma were becoming. Perhaps the more fitting word was companions. Either way, I'd never spent this much time with civilians. All the same, I didn't care to have my back to them or the door, so I pulled out the chair and placed it at an awkward angle so I could keep them in my peripheral sight.

We sat for several long minutes, not speaking or moving. It would appear we were waiting, but it was a meeting of predators. We assessed and observed each other as if able to read the weaknesses and strengths of the opposing party.

Regina broke the silence first. "We've been following your trail since you defeated the Crib."

It took all my will to not visibly react. My Masters warned me against the deceit of the other Orders. I needed to stay calm, alert, and detached from whatever they tried to infect me with.

She continued in a hushed voice. "It was all over the news. The media is trying to rationalize the scene as escaped zoo animals who ravaged each other to death, but we all know at this table that those were demons who should have never made it to this plane."

I hadn't bothered to look at the few television sets since we arrived at the diner. My job was to protect, not to clean up. Most of the spirits disappeared leaving only their victims as evidence. Demons were a rarity and usually appeared one at a time, not in a pack. The Crib were only the third demonic entity I'd encountered on earth, though I was schooled in demonology enough to identify what they were. In the other two incidents, I had left the carcasses to the elements to erode with time.

"What do you want?" I asked, wanting to cut to their point.

Phillip reached over to cover Regina's hand. They were wearing matching silver wedding bands. Celtic-like knots encircled each ring; low-level power humming off them. They must be sigils from their Order, fueled by belief and observance.

Phillip said, "We couldn't know for sure before, but now we are. We know you are the one we have been searching for all these years."

Regina said, "You see, twenty-four-years ago, our baby was stolen from our Temple."

Phillip's distinguished jaw line flexed as he clenched his teeth. "We suspected the Order of Luxis. We even stormed their Temple to search for our missing child, but we never found him."

My stomach churned as I continued to grow more uneasy.

"Then one of our Elder prophets had a vision. He told us the fall of the dark children would herald our son's return and that is when we would find our child again."

Regina's hand flipped over to squeeze Phillip's, and her smile was full of hope and excitement. "Well?" Regina asked after several long minutes passed and I did not respond.

I leaned in, and they mirrored my movement to hear my quiet, steady words. "I am very sorry disappoint you, but I am not your son."

Regina's smile faltered while Phillip continued to study me with those intense green eyes. He looked at me as though he were reading a book, but I knew he wasn't reading me correctly at all. Not the way Emma did. He was only seeing what he wanted. Phillip said, "The Order of Luxis stole you from us. They were in such violent disagreement with our Order, they sought to punish us."

Their sincerity made them all the more treacherous. Perhaps they'd been fed these lies from a higher power at Veritas and believed it themselves.

I shook my head but kept my tone polite. "My Order would never do any such thing as steal a child out of revenge. Besides, I could not possibly be your child as I am a Chevalier."

Regina released Phillip's hand and straightened. Her blue eyes cooled to a frosty temperature. "They made you a Knight of the Light?"

Again, I shook my head, "They did not make me what I am, only showed me. So you see, I could not be from another Order."

Phillip's dark eyebrows slanted down over his eyes in a menacing glower. "Those bastards."

"Phillip," Regina chided then turned to me. "You don't know what the Luxis is capable of."

I had wasted enough time with these people, and I didn't know yet what they truly wanted from me. Standing, the chair screeched back behind me. "I am a Chevalier. And that's who I am." Though other Orders didn't have Knights of the Light, Regina and Phillip knew full-well what I was. It was impossible for me to be born in another Order. Surely, they sought to usurp the great power of the Luxis, the most formidable of all the Orders.

As I walked away, Regina reached out and grabbed my hand, stopping me. Her palm was warm and dry, and half the size of mine. "Please, you must listen to me. You belong with us at the Order of Veritas. Your Masters have been lying to you. They have been controlling you through lies. You belong with your true family, serving the truth. Not the Light."

Looking into her pained eyes, I felt sorry for the woman. Gently extracting her hand from mine, I said, "I am very sorry for the loss of your child, but I am not him. I wish light to you and your Order."

They didn't try to follow as I collected Emma and Travis, threw some money on the table, then left the diner to the disconcerting, cheery chime of the doorbell.

Emma skipped to match my pace. "You okay? You got one big ol' case of the frownies on your face because of whatever those people said."

I immediately cleared my face and my mind. "I am fine. We must get to the safe house, but I'm afraid our route has been compromised. It will take us additional time to take the safer path."

As if knowing it was best not to fight me right now, Emma simply said, "Okay."

Whether that couple truly thought I was their long-lost son or not, their contact greatly unsettled me. A pin prick of ice stuck at the center of my chest. I fell back onto the chants my Masters had taught me to hone my faith, silently repeating them in my head to clear all other thoughts.

When I informed Travis of our delay in the car, he was less accommodating. As he complained about the additional stretch, I pinched the bridge of my nose, feeling the hot coils of a headache form.

"Travis," Emma said, a quiet warning in her voice as she looked at me with concern. "Shut up."

For once, he listened to her and I was grateful.

CHAPTER THIRTEEN

Once again, Travis was slumped in the back, snoring noisily, after his driving shift. Emma's delicate fingers gripped the wheel and I was mesmerized by how they flexed and relaxed as she sat deep in thought. Though I'd observed her for only a short time, I'd learned the lower her brows dipped, the deeper her thoughts were.

We'd been driving most of the day in silence, everyone too exhausted to talk. Soon darkness would descend and take my view of Emma's beautiful face.

Emma broke the silence. "So, if you can't drive, how do you get around? I mean if you have a safe house so far away from where we were, I'm guessing you aren't walking back and forth."

"Sometimes."

Emma shot me a look of horror. "Sometimes?"

"I also hitch rides with people. Mainly truck drivers."

"You're an intrepid soul, aren't you?" Then she added to herself, "Well, I guess if you've been slaying demons and ghosts, strangers probably don't worry you."

I smiled.

Emma spoke softly, "Are you worried they're following us?" She was talking about the people at the diner.

I sighed. "Yes."

"Who were they?"

I struggled to explain. "They are from a different Order than me."

"Order? Like the Order of the Temple we are going to?"

"Yes, ours is called the Order of Luxis. Those people at the diner are from the Order of Veritas."

She snorted in disbelief. "How many orders are there?"

"Five."

Emma's eyes darted to me for a moment as if nervous. "What did they want?"

I didn't answer right away. "They wanted to deceive me. Convince me to turn away from my Masters, away from the light."

"So they're bad guys." Her fingers tapped along the steering wheel.

"No." I shook my head, unable to look away from her tapping fingers. "They are not bad. Misguided. They are led by a different doctrine. My Masters warned me that one day representatives from the other Orders would perhaps approach me in attempts to make me deny my Order. They would use falsehoods and tricks to turn me against the Light for what they believe to be the better good. The Order of Luxis is the most powerful of all the Orders and has been for the last two hundred years, which makes us a target. It was just as my Masters told it."

Emma laughed, weakly. "Guess that's the second time you've been lied to then?"

I turned to look at her. The sunlight streamed through the car as it made its slow descent behind the mountains. It lit up the gold strands of her hair and turned her eyes a deep honey color that reminded me of the light of my powers, except warmer. She shot me a smile. I wished the moment would never end. That it could just be her and me riding through the red rocky expanse of Wyoming headed to wherever we wanted. For several long minutes, I allowed myself the luxury of thinking just that.

Emma and Travis begged for respite for three hours before I agreed to stop.

Because of the agents of Veritas, we would have to endure a longer route and I needed to be sure the agents weren't still tracking us. At least this way, I could make sure we had truly lost them. Both Travis and Emma were weary beyond measure from the stress of the past two days. They took turns driving but both were unfocused, and I could tell they were nearing total exhaustion. Even I knew the value of a solid bed, a hot meal, and a couple hours of uninterrupted rest. As we drove up to the small motel I told Travis he could pull into, I knew rest would be a distant memory for me until we reached my safe house. I would have to remain on constant guard.

After paying for the room in cash, I took a turn about the premises for a threat assessment while Emma and Travis waited in the car with the engine on. Part of me worried Travis would use the opportunity to flee but he seemed to slowly but surely conclude I was his best bet at staying alive. I hoped after the brief respite, he would finally be mollified.

Once we got in the room, Travis flopped on one of the beds, heaving a sigh of relief.

"Sweet, sweet bed. You understand me."

The wallpaper was of dark green foliage, making the room appear small and dark. The quilts on the two queen beds matched the wallpaper, giving the place a pseudo-jungle look. Every piece of furniture had signs of heavy wear and age, and a few stains remained in the thin Berber carpet despite someone's best efforts to get them out. It smelled like mothballs and generic hotel soap.

Despite it being far nicer than my normal accommodations, claustrophobia fell over me like an invisible blanket bound by ropes. I fought it by taking measured breathes. Too many unknowns in one day. I had to stay focused and relaxed. I had to believe we were going to be fine staying here. If the agents of Veritas wanted to keep eyes on us here, I would be able to put eyes right back on them. I would not conclude our journey to the safe house until I knew they'd given up their pursuit.

Anxiety swelled up in me. If Order of Veritas discovered I had the Propheros under my protection, they would stop at nothing to obtain him. The Veritas also had interpretations of the prophecy and I couldn't let them control the savior of the Light. Today's deceitful attempt confirmed they couldn't be trusted.

Emma rolled her eyes but couldn't help smiling as Travis flailed his arms and legs open and close on the bed like he was swimming. Then she looked me out of the corner of her eye. "There are two beds."

"Yes."

Travis understood immediately. "As the guy who has to fight the coming darkness, I get my own bed. You two can share."

Oh. Two beds. Three of us.

The image of sharing a bed with Emma flashed through my mind and sent heat shooting through my body. Her cheeks flushed in kind as if she knew what images had flashed through my mind in vivid color.

I cleared my throat. "The bed is for you." I walked over to the mustard yellow chair with the threadbare arms next to the unoccupied bed and set my sword against it. "I will keep watch while you both rest."

Emma set her hands on her hips. "You have to rest at some point, too. You're not a machine."

"Terminator," Travis said from the bed with his arms still splayed out, eyes closed.

Emma cast a glance over her shoulder but didn't elaborate on what he was talking about. Instead, she said to me, "Can I keep watch for a while, so you can get some sleep?"

A smile softened my face. No one had ever tried to take care of me before. "I'll keep first watch. I'll wake you when I need it."

She nodded with a satisfied smile.

I didn't further explain I wouldn't need it. I would let her sleep through the night. It was more important she was rejuvenated. I was used to few hours of sleep when hunting, but I knew her urge to care for me was stronger than my reasoning. A pang went through my heart.

If only I were a normal man. I'd offer her my soul in a moment.

A gurgle emanated from Travis's stomach with alarming volume. He clutched at his belly.

"Yeah," Emma nodded at Travis, "I'm starving, too. How about we introduce our very own Terminator to the joys of pizza?"

Travis popped up onto his elbows and grinned.

Scratching my eyebrow, I finally asked, "What is this terminator you keep speaking of?"

CHAPTER FOURTEEN

Travis had disappeared into the bathroom with a large pizza box, saying not to wait on him. He preferred to eat in the tub. The water ran behind the closed door leaving Emma and me alone with the other large pizza.

"I did ask if they had salad," she said, apologetically.

We had both already taken the chance to quickly shower. My shirt was covered in ichor from the Crib and I'd sweated through it multiple times, so I washed it in the sink. It was hanging on a rack in the bathroom to dry, which meant I went bare-chested. I did my best to ignore the hot looks Emma gave me when she thought I wasn't looking. For that reason, I'd kept my pants on even though they could use a good cleaning, too. I'd wash them later when she was asleep. I felt exposed and out of control as it was.

Emma sat cross legged on the bed in black leggings that clung to her bottom half and a shirt resembling what I recognized to be the style that sports players wore. It had stripes and a number on the back, except hers was white and pink, form fitting, and smaller than the sports shirts I saw on men. Her damp hair was once again pulled back in a ponytail and her glasses were back on. I found her irresistibly adorable. Even after a week of watching her, I wasn't sure which was more appealing, looking into her naked eyes, or being able to gauge if she was thoughtful or nervous as she pushed her frames up her nose.

Emma opened the pizza box and patted the empty space next to it on the bed. Admittedly the scents wafting off the pizza were tantalizing, but the sight of grease and processed cheeses made my stomach roil. I'd left my pack of provisions back at the abandoned building next to those bottles of unopened wine.

There it was again.

My fantasy interrupted my thoughts as I remembered those wine bottles. The image swam in front of my eyes. It was just Emma and I, a blanket laid out under us, except this time I knew the taste of her lips and we'd do more than dine on food….

No. I ordered myself to stop. Burying the fantasy, I sternly reminded myself I could never have any such thing and it was no use entertaining impossibilities that would distract me from what was real.

Refocusing on my current food plight, I knew the vegetables in my abandoned pack were no doubt wilted by now, but I wished I had some of the canned goods and jerky.

When I realized Emma was waiting on me, I picked up the large, floppy slice of pizza. Strings of cheese dripped off it mercilessly, attempting to cling to the rest of the pie.

I gave her a helpless look and she laughed. "Come on, don't look at me like that. You're going to love it. Or I think you will. And plus," she said with excitement, pointing at the slice in my hand. "I put every veggie they had available on it. So, it's kind of healthy." She smiled hopefully at me.

I now realized how she must have felt when she was giving me false accolades for my dumpster fire.

Unable to escape now, I caught the tip of the slice between my teeth. It was hot but didn't scald my tongue. To show my commitment I took a healthy bite and gave her a wry smile through my mouthful.

Then something extraordinary happened. The bite of pizza melted into my mouth in a rush accompanied by a flavor explosion. The textures of the cheese and crust slid pleasantly against each other in my mouth and struck a perfect balance of salt and tang. My whole mouth sang in exultation. I shivered.

Emma leaned in toward me. Her eyes shone with lust, reminding me of the way she looked at me right before kissing me in her bedroom. Lips parted, her breathing became labored as she watched me.

"You like it," she said, her voice breathy.

Swallowing, I replied, "Yes, I do."

She shook her head, her voice rougher than it was a moment ago. "It wasn't a question. I know you do." She took her glasses off, putting them down on the bedside table.

Too tempted to stop my new exploration of 'pizza', I took another bite but looked at her with question in my eyes.

"I *feel* you," she said, and shuddered. Her eyes closed as if experiencing extreme pleasure, and suddenly my pants tightened against my lap as blood rushed down my body at her wanton expression.

I returned the slice of pizza to the box.

"Emma?" I asked.

When her eyes opened, they were nearly black, her pupils dilated, threatening to swallow the soft brown of her irises. "I thought it was just me but it's not. When you look at me, I feel this heat and need surge up within me. It's so intense I think..." she swallowed hard. "I think I'm going to drown in it." She was whispering now though Travis couldn't possibly hear her over the running water in the bathroom. "I want to throw myself at you and rip your clothes off and touch every part of you."

Gods. If I wasn't hard before, I was now. It was almost painful but I kept deadly still, afraid of what I'd do if I moved.

"Then just now, when you took that bite. Your enjoyment was so intense that I felt it too. Don't you see?" Her eyes begged me to understand and for more than I could give. "I can feel what you're feeling."

I didn't know what to say. I wanted to tell her that was impossible, but I remembered every shudder that rippled through her body. Every time she licked her lips with hungry desire. Every time her eyes had glazed over with lust because they all had mirrored my own intense desire to claim her.

My rational mind still attempted to chastise my indulgence in her fantasy.

"Emma," I started, but she put her hand on my bare chest and my breath came to an abrupt halt.

"You can't pretend you don't feel it, because I'm inside you now. Somehow," she said in a disbelieving tone coupled with a light laugh. She looked at her hand. The electric blue polish was mostly chipped off her nails now.

It didn't detract from her appeal in the least. There was something so spontaneous about the fervor with which she lived that she made perfection look like a two-dimensional bore. She was straight-forward, unafraid, hot-blooded, so... so *alive,* and about to make a mess of my whole existence.

"I know what this is doing to you," she said, her whisper breaking as if she were being tormented.

I was trapped between the torment and the most intense pleasure. Only the gods could have designed it.

"Then why are you doing it?" I asked, pain tightening my words.

"Because..." her words drifted off, eyes searching mine as if she could find the answer there. Her gaze seemed to rip the flesh and bone from me until there was nothing hidden. This was too much. I shouldn't be seen, especially not like this.

She went on, "I want you more than I've ever wanted anything in my life, Calan."

With those words, my name sliding off her tongue so deliciously, my last vestige of control snapped like a brittle twig. I grabbed her by the back of her neck and my mouth crashed down on hers with all the crazed hunger I'd felt for seven days, ten hours and some odd minutes.

CHAPTER FIFTEEN

Emma pushed the pizza box aside and lunged forward to sit on my lap, her legs wrapping around my waist. The contact of her sex against my mine, even through our clothing, evoked a hiss of shock from me. Heat radiated from her pelvis into my straining manhood which begged to be freed.

She threw her head back, exposing the expanse of her neck to me. Elegant. It was the only word to describe that stretch of skin.

"Oh god, Calan," her words were drawn out in intense pleasure. "I can feel what this does to you. I feel how badly you want me. It's turning me inside out."

I claimed her mouth again, forcing my tongue past her teeth, fully tasting her.

My hands burrowed up into her hair, snapping her tie away so the wet locks fell into my grasp. I tugged it lightly at the base of her skull. She gasped, then her sharp breath dissolved into a moan that struck me so hard, I worried I would embarrass myself.

Just because I'd never been with a woman didn't mean I wasn't aware of what couples did behind closed doors. My Masters warned against the evils of giving into lust, instructing I do everything in my power to please the gods with chastity.

My hands moved down to Emma's hips where I rocked them against my own and a guttural growl ripped its way out of my throat. It was so feral, I barely recognized myself. The warmth covering my lap soon moistened, and my eyes rolled back into my head with the effort it took to stop myself from coming right then.

Too much was out of my control. A part of me panicked at the thought. Grabbing her hips, I threw Emma off me and back onto the bed. Before she could finish her mewl of disappointment I covered her body with mine, kissing, sucking, licking, and nibbling at the flesh of her neck as she writhed against me, meeting my pace. The taste of her skin was intoxicating. Despite the generic hotel soap she'd used, I still tasted the vanilla of her skin under it.

It reminded me of the vanilla beans I'd once had to scrape the innards out of for Master Violetta's sacred tea. The beans smelled strong, sharp, and sweet, and begged to be tasted but I'd refrained then. Now, it felt like I was finally indulging in a sweetness long denied me, and it made me dizzy with desire.

My hips ground rhythmically down on hers. Emma bit my neck to suppress her sensual sounds. Slowly, my hand slipped under her shirt and traveled up each rib, carefully approaching the naked flesh of her sensitive breast.

The water turned off in the bathroom with a screech. I stopped cold, my fingers brushing the rising swell of her breast. Emma kept rubbing her body up against me, but I dismounted her in an instant.

Propping herself up on her elbows, Emma looked up at me in confusion. Still panting, her hair tousled, her swollen lips beckoned me back. For the second time, I saw her nipples tight, straining against her shirt.

My shoulders rose and fell in exaggerated movements as I tried to gain control over my breath and my body. I had to shut my eyes against the sight of her to do so.

"Calan?" she started, but I held up a hand to stop her.

As soon as the pleasure started, it froze and shattered inside me. What had I become?

I was succumbing to greed, lust, and coveting Emma for myself.

I owned nothing. Not even myself. I was turning away from the Light. How could I protect the Propheros, or Emma for that matter, if I couldn't control my basic urges? No wonder I couldn't wield my own magic. I was out of control.

Opening my eyes, I saw the loss in Emma's eyes and a new wave of guilt sliced through the first. She deserved better than me. I wasn't whole. After this, I wondered if the gods would ever return my soul after causing pain to such an angel.

"Calan, stop it." Emma said clearly, after licking her lips. She sat up. "I know what you're thinking and stop it right now."

Could she read my mind? No, she was just intuitive.

"It can't always be all about duty," she said. "Stop beating yourself up."

"Emma, please." My hands grasped at my head trying to control the barrage of conflicting thoughts and feelings. They crowded in around each other, shouting me down with demands and accusations.

"I have to – I have to do a perimeter check." Before she could say a word, I'd grabbed my coat and boots and was out the door, locking it behind me.

The bite of cold air calmed my bare flesh, lowering my body temperature. I clutched the door frame, resting my forehead against the chilled wood, but it couldn't erase what I knew was on the other side. My toes shifted against the sharp gravel. Every temptation the universe could conjure up was rolled into one beautiful girl who I could never have but could never forget the taste of now.

I pushed off the door, threw my coat on over my bare back, pulled on my boots, then stalked away to secure the perimeter and remind myself of my duties.

When I returned an hour later, Travis was passed out on top of the sheets, snoring like an elephant. Emma had succumbed to sleep, curled in a tight ball as if she needed to protect herself from the world even in slumber.

She certainly needs protection against you.

I swallowed hard and pushed the guilt down. Grabbing the mustard-colored chair by Emma's bed, I noiselessly moved it across the room so I could easily watch both while keeping close to the door, should trouble come knocking.

After taking off my boots, I planted my bare feet on the floor, squeezing the rough carpet under my toes to bring myself fully into the present. I held the broadsword between my legs, holding it at its hilt and straightened my back. Closing my eyes, I breathed deeply, deliberately.

I didn't dare sleep but I could use the time to rejuvenate myself with meditation.

Here. Here.

I silently acknowledged being here, in the present. I objectively observed my physical being. My calf still throbbed from where the piece of glass speared it yesterday. It was raw but clean since I'd showered. Tension squeezed between my shoulders and down my back. Simply observing the sensations caused my shoulders to drop several inches and the knots to unfurl a fraction.

Thoughts interrupted each other with hows and whats and whens. How do I protect Emma and Travis? What will my Masters do with them? When will my magic return so that I could transport us to the Temple?

A nasty thought slithered in like black tar, encircling the rest of them. *What if my magic doesn't return?*

"No," I whispered, stopping the vile thought in its tracks. "You are Chevalier. You are granted magic so that you may defend the Light. It will return to you as easy as breath." After that, I stepped out of the stream of my own thoughts, then watched them flow by like a river.

Emma's face, Emma's touch, Emma's taste whizzed by in the stream, each memory and thought beckoning me back into the rush, to swim in them. In tandem, the stream carried Emma's screams, fear, and visions of her death at the hands of the soul eater, the

Crib, or other dark forces. Each horror a result of my letting her down by giving in to my desire. I sat down by the river and watched it flow by, never reaching a finger out to touch the thoughts, so they continued rushing by.

When I blinked my eyes open, resurfacing from my meditative state, the garish green numbers on the bedside clock flashed 4:06 a.m. Though I had not fallen asleep or fallen out of tune with every twitch and shift Travis and Emma made in their sleep, I arose refreshed. It was time for another walk about the perimeter, and soundlessly I slipped outside.

CHAPTER SIXTEEN

The clouds had rolled in, a blanket of darkness blocking all light from the waxing moon. The only sounds were of the swirling wind on the plains.

The gravel of the motel parking lot crunched under my feet until I adjusted my stride to

silence my steps. All the doors were shut and curtains drawn in the U-shaped block of accommodations. The only light emanated from the small office where the surly-faced owner watched a small television set with dull eyes awaiting any unlikely night-time tenants. I widened the loop around the motel into the tall brown grass. The snow had melted some during the day and frozen over again into crispy ice patches that crunched under my steps. The terrain was flat, allowing for greater field of vision. Even so, clouds darkened the land. My false parents could be hiding nearby, so I would cover every inch until I knew we were safe.

The quiet soothed me. The cold earth smelled crisp and wild. The raging beast that pounded from the inside of my ribcage, begging for Emma, had reduced its fervor to dull thuds in my chest. I could fight this. I had returned to my center. Though I had never known such temptation before, I realized the gods were testing me. If I failed, Emma would surely be punished. I was already damned and knew I must keep her from me at all costs. The sooner I got her and Travis to my Masters, the better.

Then maybe my Masters could better explain how a soul eater could have become flesh? How the Crib could have come to our plane? Why now?

The Propheros.

Master Ylang's voice sprung to mind. *As Chevalier, you must never assume. Any knowledge of consequence must be relayed to your Masters so that we may interpret and guide.*

Then I realized I had been mistaken in trying to interpret the circumstances, when it did not change my duties. I fought the darkness in whatever form it presented itself.

That is what Chevalier did. I was not to question the whys, I was only to act as a tool for the Light.

Surprise leapt upon my heart as a flash of light warmed the palms of my hands. Instantly, I fell to my knees in observance of the miracle. My powers had returned. I could take us home. I closed my eyes, reveling in my return to grace. There was a sense of coming home as my powers wrapped themselves around my being once more.

With a lighter heart now buoyed with hope, I finished my reconnaissance. Finding no sign of the agents from Temple Veritas, I began my descent from the slight rise in the land back toward the motel.

The sky had lightened considerably, hailing the coming of dawn. As I walked to the parking lot, I spotted a family sluggishly lugging their bags to a silver mini-van. A sleepy girl about four years old rocked on her feet, eyelids drooping, as she clutched a stuffed bunny with only one button eye and a frayed ear. One of her ash-blonde pigtails was crooked. Her brother looked to be only a couple years older, with a bright green coat and limp blond hair falling into his eyes. His thumbs flew across a handheld device with a lit screen, while he leaned against the van. Their mother and father went about packing the vehicle. While I could not hear the words, their strained tones told me they were quarreling.

My head snapped to the right as a red light drew my attention. A middle-aged, bald man leaned on the wall just outside his open motel door as he sucked on a cigarette, which lit up again before he exhaled generous smoke plumes. The dot of red light flared at the end of his cigarette. His abnormally bony limbs poked through his faded boxer shorts and tattered t-shirt. His eyes were glued to the little girl in a way that made my insides bristle with warning. Somebody called from inside the room causing his head to turn but he chose to ignore whoever it was.

Faint smoke tendrils from the cigarette reached my sensitive nostrils with notes of tobacco and the heavy cling of intentional death. The world moved slowly for me now that I had retouched my inner powers and no detail went unnoticed. The chirp of the birds heralding dawn, the slamming of car doors, and the heavy smell of rotten eggs now hanging in the air.

"Oh gods," I breathed, breaking out into a run.

The mother turned from the open trunk of the van to see me racing at her with wild eyes and my broadsword drawn. She let loose a piercing scream. It was so shrill I almost couldn't hear the twin shriek that was not of this earth.

"Emma, Travis," I bellowed, knowing my shouts would resonate through the paper-thin motel walls. "Get up, get to the vehicle,"

The four year old's eyes had lost their heavy droop and now blinked up in awe at the cloud forming before her very eyes.

"Run," I yelled at her, but her little legs didn't move.

"Hank," The mother cried out to her husband.

Concern for the child narrowed my focus to only her until the door opened behind her. Emma came to stand in the doorway of our room. Her hair was disheveled from sleep but her shoes were on and her pack was slung over her shoulder. An ounce of relief swept through me.

Smart girl.

The dual points of focus distracted me from the third. Something hit me from the side with tremendous force. I went sliding several feet through the sharp gravel of the parking lot. The hand holding my sword was trapped at my side on the ground now. The fetid pants of morning breath puffed onto my face. The little girl's father had tackled me to the ground.

"Jeannie, call the police. Now," He demanded, his bloodshot eyes fiercely fastened onto me.

Looking back at his daughter, a strangled cry escaped my throat. The cloud's swirling had increased with fervor.

"Get off him," Emma screamed.

I tried to cry out to Emma, "The girl." But she was running toward me.

"Sophie?" I heard the little boy asked in a watery voice. His sister's arms had stiffened at her sides, her eyes bugged from her head, and her mouth was open in a silent scream. The soul eater had locked onto her.

I pushed against her father, but he slammed me back down. I was significantly stronger than this man, but he had me at a disadvantage of angle.

"Stay down, you psychopath," he said, spit spraying the side of my face.

"Your daughter. I have to save her," I insisted, wiggling my arm out from under my body.

"Get off him," Emma said. She grabbed the man's hair, yanking him back. He yelped. It gave me just enough space to slide out from under him. He threw an arm out, smacking Emma back. Emma skittered back a few steps and fell back hard onto her rear with an *oof.*

Before I could fully get to my feet, I knew I wouldn't reach the girl in time. The soul eater would digest her soul, masticating it into shreds of what the victim felt to be lifetimes of endless torment until it was wholly destroyed. The agony and helplessness I felt at not being able to reach her in time nearly split me in half.

She was going to die.

CHAPTER SEVENTEEN

S ophie was plucked from where she stood. Travis had torn out of the motel room when he'd seen the little girl entranced, grabbed her and hauled her away. He now raced in the opposite direction of her family to get her out of harm's way.

I heard Travis mutter a litany of emphatic, "No, no, no, no's," as he ran with Sophie.

"Kid, get away from it," I yelled to her brother. His head whipped up toward me, his green eyes wide under his limp bangs. Then he tore off, running back to his mother. She held a phone to her ear with a shaky hand. I finally allowed myself a sigh of relief when he'd gotten a good distance away.

This time, I sensed the man before he tackled me again. I sidestepped him, sending him careening head over heels into the gravel. I couldn't use my magic if he broke my concentration by attacking me.

"Please, get in your vehicle and drive away with your family," I begged.

Several people had emerged from their rooms to see what the fuss was about. Panic welled up past my chest and into my throat.

Hank stumbled as he tried to get up. The sharp rocks had torn the skin along the side of his face and blood now splotched the front of his plaid shirt, but it was all surface cuts. His burliness looked like it was built off fast food, but I remembered his weight had kept me down.

With a guttural growl, Hank charged me again. His fatherly instincts to protect his daughter were all directed at me. He didn't notice Emma sidle up, sticking her leg out tripping up his legs. Hank pitched forward, his face in the gravel once more. Emma skittered backward, her hand over her mouth.

Grateful for a moment of concentration, I took the opportunity to whip around and fall to my knee. The sword dropped to the ground. It would do me no good against an incorporeal foe, but I knew how to fight it like this. My hands formed a triangle and I chanted quickly. Light generated between my hands.

The soul eater fed on the attention of the growing crowd, drawing more people out into the open. Time was running out and there were too many distractions.

The man who had been smoking the cigarette had stomped it out before striding into the parking lot where I was chanting. My palms warmed but I needed more time. Without a moonstone, I had no quick, easy way to amplify my powers and would have to draw it all from scratch. I needed to generate more power than I'd ever attempted before, and I still wasn't sure it was going to be enough to hurt this abomination before it became solid again.

"You want a fight, buddy?" The smoker grinned, his bald head giving him the appearance of a bare, grimacing skull. Though he was human, he seemed nearly demonic as he threw his fist down at me. I had to release my holy triangle, the heat of my energy immediately dissipating, to throw up a protective arm against the punch he aimed at my face.

"Please," I begged through gritted teeth. Sweat poured down my temples. Sulphur polluted the crisp morning air until it sizzled with violence. Distantly I heard the little girl sobbing and more people clomping down the stairs to help, unaware of the true danger.

That was how the dark worked on earth. Possession and bodily entering this plane took a great amount of power which is rarely accomplished, so the Stygian primarily worked in influence and right now, it was amplifying and directing everyone's fears at me.

I got to my feet, punched the man in the jaw. He flopped to the ground like a rag doll. Another man rushed me, but I crouched down and let his momentum lead him straight onto my back. I bucked him off, flipping him over and slamming his body to the ground. Two more men came, and I threw punches to stave them off, putting both down.

The bald smoker was clearly used to a hit and got back to his feet quicker than I anticipated. He came at me with a war cry. I landed another punch on his cheek, snapping his face to the side. Rather than falling, he spat out a tooth and kicked me in the gut.

"What's going on here?" The owner of the motel emerged, wearing a dull yellow shirt with brown slacks. He'd pulled what little hair he had around his temples back into a sparse ponytail. His face was stormy as he took in the scene around him.

Only a few people nervously eyed the mysterious cloud hovering in the parking lot, the rest had their eyes fastened on me, mistaking me for the threat.

"Yes," the mother cried as she spoke into her phone. "He has a sword. A large one."

"You all must leave. Leave or die," I yelled out in desperate warning. Instead of scattering, people shifted in their spots, uneasy.

I grabbed the smoker before he could land his fist in my gut. I had to stop taking it easy on him or everyone would die because of the distraction he posed. I was afraid of hurting the civilians, but there was no more time. Spinning him around I brought his arm up behind him and with a resounding crack, I broke his arm and pulled it out of his socket in one move. It only took one kick behind his knee to get him to fall. Paralyzed by the pain, he could only groan and curse from where his face was nestled in the gravel.

"Teddy," A disheveled blonde woman emerged from Teddy's room in a skimpy camisole and shorts. With slurred shouts she charged out of the room, barefoot and smeared makeup, intent to join in the violence against me.

"Calan." Emma's quiet warning sailed through the air, caressing my ears. She was watching the cloud and it began to metamorphose as it had the day before.

Dawn had come, and with it, death.

CHAPTER EIGHTEEN

Two gruesome legs connected with the ground, shaking the earth with their arrival. The soul eater solidified up over that blurry face again. Like lightning it struck, moving as fast as I knew it to when it was in fog form. With an unnatural crack of thunder, it streaked over to the barely-covered woman crying out for Teddy. She stumbled on the gravel, as the soul eater blocked her path to me.

The soul eater bore down on her, its mouth yawning far past what any human mouth was capable of. A sickening crackle emanated from the woman's spine as her body suddenly bent at the hips, backward at a ninety-degree angle in the wrong direction. Time slowed in a horrific slow-motion sequence as the sight of her broken body ingrained itself in my mind to fuel nightmares for all eternity. The soul eater's jaw extended to its full length, well over a foot long, then it began to feast.

Most people gaped, some screamed, as the bright energy of her soul funneled out of her nose, mouth, and eyes into the soul eater's gaping maw. The feeding sounded like a wind tunnel sucking into itself as the malevolent spirit ripped the soul from her body.

Goose pimples stiffened painfully all over my body as if in response to someone scratching long, thick dirty fingernails down a blackboard. The sulfur thickened in the air until the soul eater's putrid stench became visible, pumping a toxic mustard yellow mist into the air. I'd seen a low-level demon rip the limbs from its victims, and still I could better stomach the sight than this. Watching the demonic spirit feed, I felt hundreds of imaginary maggots crawling all over my skull, and it became hard to breathe as every instinct screamed at me to run. But I had long learned to suppress my fear response.

While everyone stood watching in terror, I grabbed my broadsword and ran straight at it. If I didn't destroy the soul eater now, more people would die. No, more than die. It was worse than death. Its victims would never know the after-life or their next incarnation. They would be lost for all eternity.

Just as I came up behind it, lunging with a thrust of my broad sword, the soul eater whipped around and smacked me away with a massive arm. It released its hold on the woman. Her body collapsed to the ground, the vessel now empty, flesh already rotting.

I scrambled to my feet. Fortunately, I still grasped the sword in my hand. The soul eater now feasted on an aged woman standing outside her room in a thick terry-cloth robe. Bags hung under her eyes and everything about her body drooped to match those bags; her stomach, the extra skin on her arms and thighs. The bagginess hung the wrong way now as the soul eater bent her backward with a succession of snaps. Soon her skin peeled and rotted away as the monster sucked her soul away. The soul eater didn't notice me until I plunged the sword through its back, the blade slicing out through the front of it. It cried out in pain and the second woman's body dropped.

I pulled the sword out from its grayed flesh with great effort and began to hack away at its body. A long arm dropped to the ground and I cut away a leg. Except with every hack, the limbs grew back with expediency because it had fed. No blood or ichor spurted from its wounds. It was solid through and through. It was like stabbing through a tree softened with rot.

My sword pierced through its head. Taking a couple steps back, I panted. That would surely be the end of it. It let out a groan of pain but then its strange blurry face brought a mouth into enough focus so that I could see it smile as my sword still stuck from its head like a horn. It summoned dark energy with a hot sizzle. Before I could move, it threw the weight of its dark powers at me. It smashed into my body, sending me flying through the air over rows of cars until I crashed into the windshield of one. The dark energy lingered to caress me like a night terror causing sweat to break out on my flesh and fear to grip my heart. I had to focus to steady my breath and come back to the present before fear and despair swallowed my senses.

The windshield glass cut through the armor of my coat and pants, piercing me. Wiggling with a groan, I discovered my body was stuck in the windshield. All I could do was helplessly watch the carnage.

By now the bystanders had broken into a panic. They rushed to grab their things, ran to their cars, some of them peeling out of the lot, gravel spraying out behind their tires, but the soul eater still had plenty at its disposal. It streaked from person to person, sucking them dry. It snatched the bald smoker, contorted him and drained him, tossing the body next to the woman who had been inside his room. It darted into rooms, draining whoever was inside. It was growing too powerful.

I continued to wiggle, trying to leverage myself out of the glass. My vision blurred as tears filled my eyes. I was helpless while so many souls were destroyed. How could I have failed so many? This was all my fault.

The silver van drove by and I met the watery eyes of the young boy as his parents sped away. His sister was missing from the seat beside him. I wondered if her body now lay rotting somewhere around here.

"Calan," someone softly said my name. Emma was at the side of the car. She had stayed out of harm's way, for which I was grateful.

"Where's Travis?" I asked in a panic. As soon as the soul eater had become strong enough, it would go after the Propheros and I'd have no way of stopping it.

"He's safe, for now," she said, keeping a calm, low voice. The screams of agony echoed throughout the u-shape of the motel block. Over her shoulder, I watched the owner perish under the soul eater's hunger.

I grabbed Emma's arms and together we pulled me out from the windshield with another loud crunch of glass. The shards rained down, tinkling as they hit the paved parking lot. Instead of rushing back into the fray, I paused. Yet again, I was failing to protect. We should drive away and pray it wouldn't catch up.

"It's too strong." My words struggled to get past the lump in my throat. "Too fast, and too powerful now. Nothing can stop it. We must run." My heart broke into pieces at the prospect of retreat. I had never run before, especially when so many could be harmed, but I had to protect the Propheros. These people were lost and there was nothing I could do.

As I watched the scene in abject horror, paralyzed by fear, Emma's hand curled around my bicep and she lifted up onto her toes to whisper into my ear. My eyes shut of their own accord and I leaned into her.

"Calan, you can do this. Use your magic again." Emma then laid a sweet kiss on my cheek that warmed my face. The warmth traveled down to warm my body with a comfort I was unaccustomed to. "I believe in you."

Power erupted inside me like a geyser, so unexpectedly that I lost my breath. What felt like liquid sun raced through my veins, renewing my energy. Could her very words be magic? I didn't know what it was, but the effect was power unlike any I'd known.

Time slowed once more. Striding forward, I walked over the bodies until I was ten feet away from the feeding soul eater. I dropped to a knee and held my hands in a triangle. The pads of my fingers met each other in familiar greeting and my palms sang with comforting heat. The soul eater turned, its heavy step vibrating the ground. The words my Masters taught me fell from my mouth like a rushing waterfall.

The soul eater let out a sound resembling a laugh except it was grated like a manhole cover scraping against asphalt as it was removed.

Sure of myself, I built the power between my hands until I felt I held the sun itself. The pressure was so intense I thought my very heart would burst from joy. Despite my eyes focusing on the soul eater, all I saw in my mind's eye was Emma.

A cheer whooped out behind me. "Get him, Calan."

My mouth quirked in a smile and I remembered the words Emma had whispered to me, her breath caressing my ear. The soul eater advanced on me but it had barely crossed half the distance to me before I felt the crest of the wave and let it land. My magic thundered from my hands in a blast of blinding light like nothing I'd ever unleashed before. My body shivered violently with the waves the rushed off me, but it was rooted in pleasure. Pleasure like pizza. Pleasure like kissing Emma.

The soul eater screamed, the light surrounding its form, enveloping it. Then with a last cresting wave, my light grandly exploded once more and the soul eater did so along with it.

I blinked to keep the tiny, gray dust particles of what remained of the soul eater from getting in my eyes.

"Whoo, suck on that soul eater."

I turned around to see Emma dancing in victory bringing a smile to my lips, but it soon faltered as I took in all the decaying bodies surrounding me.

Gods. How could I have failed so many?

Emma ran out into the street and began jumping up and down in a strange dance. A car pulled into the lot, distracting me from my grief. It was Emma's jeep. I hadn't even noticed its absence. As it neared, I saw Travis was at the wheel. He gave me a salute with a shaky hand, his mouth set in a tight line.

Emma bounded up to me. "We got the girl in the back." Her eyes took in the sight of the bodies and her face sobered. Eight were visible, but who knew how many were putrefying in their rooms? "Should we go?" she asked, forcing her eyes back on me.

Swallowing hard, I nodded. "Thank you."

She smiled again, though it wasn't as bright as before. "You were the one who did it. After all, you are Chevalier."

My heart sank. I was. She had given me the gift of power I'd never known, but it changed nothing.

I followed Emma to the passenger side of the car, where she quickly hopped into the back. I caught a glimpse of the little girl, white-faced, and clutching her stuffed bunny like a life line. I felt some solace from the opportunity to return the girl to her family. It wouldn't be hard to track them if we left now.

My fingers closed around the door handle at the same time something stung me on the side of my neck. I looked in at Travis's face through the window, my mouth opened but no words came out. He met my look with a confused expression, then his eyes fell over my shoulder and I watched recognition dawn on his features.

"Go," I said. It was barely audible, but Travis saw my lips move around the word.

From the back of the car, I heard Emma's muffled voice. "Calan?"

The car handle ripped out of my hand as Travis slammed his foot on the gas and the jeep jumped forward and away from my already falling body.

Darkness swallowed me into oblivion.

CHAPTER NINETEEN

A click then the relentless light from a bare bulb hanging from the ceiling brought me back to consciousness. Even after I managed to open my eyes, I had to blink them to try and bring the swinging light into focus. Fog enveloped my brain and my mouth felt like I'd been sucking on cotton for a day. My limbs were stiff and cramped where I sat. Cold had crept into my naked torso, and rope bit into my wrists.

Where am I? Where is Emma? Did they get away?

Instead of allowing panic to engulf my senses, I focused on taking note of every little detail around me. After some shifting, I discovered I couldn't move my legs either. The strong smell of mildew and concrete reminded me of the liquor store, except it lacked the scent of yeast.

Emma. Where are you?

I wanted to call out for her, but I kept my mouth sealed as I tried to orient myself. The light switch cord clanged against the bulb softly and I detected the sound of dripping nearby.

When I could finally see clearly, I realized I wasn't alone. Two people dressed in black had been waiting for me to return to my senses. One stood, arms crossed, in a relaxed waiting stance. The other figure was perched on a cabinet counter in a sizable, yet empty, basement. The wood stairs behind the standing man ascended to what I assumed to be a suburban household. The agents of Veritas had caught up to me once again.

"How are you feeling?" Regina asked from her spot on the counter. I might have believed the concern in her voice if they hadn't tied me up.

I leveled my gaze at her. "Like I've been drugged." I vaguely recalled the sting of the needle in my neck.

"I apologize for our methods," Phillip said, his hands folded behind his back, "But it was doubtful you would have voluntarily granted us a second interview."

I narrowed my eyes at him. He was right.

I consciously relaxed my shoulders. "Well now that you have me as a captive audience," I said the words with pointed disdain, "what is it you want to tell me?"

Phillip said, "You must know the balance has been interrupted."

"The soul eater," Regina said, disbelief and fear colored her voice. "It became flesh."

"So you saw the whole show?" I asked drily. I couldn't expect help from anyone when it had attacked, especially not someone from a different Order, yet the stinking seed of bitterness shivered in my heart when I thought of the lives that could have been saved if these agents of Veritas had intervened. "From a safe distance, naturally." I subtly worked my wrists behind the chair, trying to find any give in the ropes. I spotted my brown armored coat lying across the stair railing.

Regina's expression became distressed. "You can't think that would have helped anything. We were not trained to engage with such entities."

"But you *are* trained," I accused, trying to confirm what I suspected.

"Well, yes," Phillip said this time. "It takes a great number of us and many sacred artifacts, but we have managed to send dark beings back to the Stygian before. When we detected the Soul Eater nearing you, we planned to intervene but once it became solid, we thought it best to hold back."

"So you just watched innocent people die." My teeth ground against the words. I'd never known hate before, but it was the only word I could think of to describe the bag of hot snakes roiling around my chest, making it difficult to breathe.

Phillip's forehead and eyes wrinkled in distress. "You don't understand. We are not even qualified to banish a normal soul eater. We would have been completely out of our realm attempting to aid you. We couldn't possibly be of help to you once it became flesh."

Seeing the look on my face, Regina straightened her shoulders and said to Phillip. "He isn't going to be reasonable, dear. They made him Chevalier. They don't think past what they are told." The word "Chevalier" dripped with derision and the tension in my chest intensified until I thought I would explode.

I wanted to correct her. The Luxis didn't make me into anything. I was what I was. But these people were beyond reason.

Phillip held up a hand and continued to study me. "We are as sorry for the casualties as you are, but you also must know we could not risk our lives for them. It is more important we report the imbalance to our Order."

"Then why do you need me?" I asked, my voice gravelly with repressed hate. "Go tell your people of the imbalance and leave me be."

He continued to stare at me in an unerring fashion. After a long moment, he responded. "Because we suspect you are either the cause of the imbalance or know what is."

My eyes fell away from his and I shrugged. "Why should I know anything? I merely tried to save those civilians."

Regina spoke this time. "Because first it was the Crib coming to this plane and now a Soul Eater has been made flesh. And they both appeared at your location. What have you gotten yourself into, dear son?" Her words were cold, but her eyes betrayed a warmth toward me that let me know they truly believed this preposterous lie of me being their kin.

"I'm not your son," I spat. My wrists continued to move, feeling out any give. My fingers toyed with the edges of rope.

"What has the Order of Luxis gotten you into?" Phillip asked, though it sounded more like he was asking himself.

"The only thing the Luxis has granted me is illumination. Illumination of everything, which is where I ground my power. Which is how I saved at least some of those civilians you deemed expendable. And it is also why I see past your lies meant to manipulate me. You have no power over me."

"Who are those people you were with?" Phillip took a step closer. "They do not seem to be aligned with any Order. Why travel with them?"

He was coming too close to the truth and I felt like a bucking horse trying to shy away from it. "People who I have been able to garner a ride from."

Regina clucked her tongue. "My dear son, the Order of Luxis may have taught you many a thing, but not how to lie."

It was a partial truth, but even I heard the weak delivery I made of it.

She cocked her head to the side. "Are they the cause of the imbalance? If the darkness is crossing over, it must mean one of them is…" her mouth slackened as her eyes widened with realization.

No. NO. I cried internally, willing her to bypass the realization she had stumbled upon.

"Phillip," she jumped off the counter to stand next to her husband, coming at least a foot shy of him. Her voice hurried. "The Prophecy. *The darkness shall cross the threshold to harken the Propheros is near. And with it, the dawning of a new age,*" she quoted a text I had heard my Masters speak of. She turned to me next, anxiety written over her features. "You must tell us where the Propheros is."

My lips tightened in an obvious rebellion of silence.

"You don't understand," she pleaded, coming closer. "The Order of Luxis is not what you think. If you deliver the Propheros to them, evil will befall us all from their terrible deeds."

I stuck my chin up. "The Order of Luxis's sole purpose is to protect the Light."

Phillip crossed his arms. "Which they do so by wielding deceit and subterfuge. As Chevalier, you could not possibly know what they are capable of. They are more interested in helping themselves, than they are concerned with the fate of this world."

Regina came to kneel by my side, her cerulean eyes earnestly searching mine. I tried to ignore their likeness to my own. "They have brainwashed you, my son. They will order you to assist in the greatest trespass of all. You cannot trust them. They are using you."

The greatest trespass of all? What could she mean?

I stared at her coldly. "And I should believe your lies?" I wished I was with Emma. Their words made me uneasy. Though I was clear and true to my Masters, I did not like having my beliefs challenged. It was an insult.

A sad smile pulled at her lips. "We are the Order of Veritas." Her fingers softly touched my leg. "The Order of Truth. We interpret differently than your Order, as we do not use deceit in our methods. For that, they think us weak and despise our agency."

I sighed. "Then I suppose I should tell you the truth."

Regina's shoulders straightened but stayed kneeling before me. Behind her, Phillip uncrossed his arms.

My freed hands came up to either side of me. "Your ropes could not hold me."

Before they could properly react, I head-butted Regina, sending her careening backward to the floor. Phillip lunged at me, which I anticipated. Instead of fighting his advance, my hand slipped to his belt, pulling out a small switch blade he'd thought was well hidden against his person. With a glint, the blade released and cut through the restraints at my ankles. I used my forward motion to smash into his gut with my shoulder in one fluid movement causing him to let out a *hrmph* as he was knocked backward. As I slammed Phillip to the ground, I kicked off the ropes and pushed the chair away from my legs. When he was down, I threw a punch that cracked Phillip's head soundly to the side.

I didn't wait for them to recover. I scrambled over Phillip's body and up the stairs, grabbing my jacket along the way. My hand quickly found the knob unlocked, but footsteps clattered behind me. I threw open the door then turned to see both Regina and Phillip racing up the stairs after me. I slammed the door closed and found a sturdy lock on my side. I turned the deadbolt over with a resounding click just as the door handle shook and pounding emanated from the other side. The door would hold.

It all happened so fast, I barely had breath in me, and hadn't yet observed if I'd walked into a bigger trap. But as I glanced around at a modest kitchen attached to a living room covered in family photos and various household items and toys, I knew I was alone, and this was neither Phillip nor Regina's house. A note on the kitchen counter instructing someone named Todd on how to water the houseplants told me the resident family was away on vacation. I stepped out the front door into the cold night air on a suburban cul-de-sac. It smelled like rain but slushy snow gathered in the corners of people's lawns and along the street gutters. I didn't know where I was, but I knew I had to find Travis and Emma. Now that the Order of Veritas knew the Propheros had arrived and that he was traveling with me, it was more important than ever I get Travis to the Temple. I had to get to them fast, so using the stars for guidance I started walking northeast, in the direction we'd been traveling to the safe house.

For almost an hour, I trudged north along the darkened streets, slick with sleet. My head throbbed dully with aftereffects from the drug which made my mind foggy. I had left one suburban neighborhood behind only to enter another. I wished to stop at a fueling station for directions, but they were all closed this time of night. The nearly identical houses were dark and quiet through and through, save the occasional blue light from a TV left on. Ice cold rain dripped from the sky onto my neck. I crossed my arms over my chest in attempts to warm myself. Even with my coat, it was difficult to keep my core temperature up.

As I considered the real possibility I would need to seek some kind of warm shelter, I heard the wet slaps of fast approaching footsteps.

I would have thought it was Regina and Phillip in pursuit, but these footsteps came from up the road. Maybe it was a late-night runner? Before I could further speculate or duck out of sight, I heard a familiar voice call out, "Calan."

CHAPTER TWENTY

"Emma?" I called back as I saw her form come into view in the middle of the road. The street lights cast their glow over her like they were throwing a halo on an angel. I picked up my speed to meet her. "How did you find me?"

Anxiety had tightened her face. Worry filled her large eyes and she was biting her lip as she ran at me. When she got to me, Emma threw her arms around me and held on for dear life. "Oh thank god, I was so scared."

I held her tightly, burying my face in her neck. I breathed in the ambrosial scent I'd come to associate with her. "What are you doing here?"

Emma pulled back to look me in the eye, morning frost clinging to the ends of her eyelashes. She wasn't wearing a warm enough jacket to be out here either. Her muscles quaked underneath my hold in attempts to generate warmth.

She gave me a wry, lopsided smile. "I was coming to save you?" she offered, uncertainly.

The laugh originated from deep in my belly and vibrated throughout my body.

Emma's expression warred with displeasure and confusion. "Is it really so funny that I could be the one to save you?"

I tried to control myself but the deep sonorous laughter hadn't subsided. "No, no, you don't understand."

Openly irritated, Emma tried to pull away, but I wouldn't let her.

"You so wholly surprise me and it's the most wonderful thing I have ever known."

She relaxed her struggle to escape my grip, but her expression remained skeptical. "I surprise you?"

My laughter had finally settled, and I felt both exhausted and supremely delighted. Perhaps it was a side effect of the drug Phillip and Regina had given me. "Emma, if someone had told me a week ago that you would come to my rescue, I would have dismissed such an idea without a second thought." My voice became more serious and raspier from exposure to the cold damp air. "Chevalier are to protect the innocents," my voice thickened further, with emotion, "but no one protects…"

"You," she said, simply. Her amber eyes, luminous under the street lamps, shone with compassion.

For the first time in my existence, I felt sorry for myself. So intensely did I want Emma that I did the only thing I could to block out such a horrible indulgence as self-pity. I kissed her.

When I covered her mouth with my own, my cold body warmed as I molded her against me. She eagerly kissed me back, trying to slide her tongue past my lips though I didn't grant her access. Clutching my shoulders, her short nails dug into my skin exciting my appetite for more, still I didn't deepen the kiss. When I pulled back, I looked down at her trying to find the words I knew I had to say.

"Yeah, yeah, yeah," Emma said, her bottom lip jutting out. "I know. You're Chevalier, and this can never happen again." There was a lack of sincerity in her voice.

I struggled to cover a smile. She knew exactly what I had been going to say, but obviously didn't believe this would be the last time I touched her. Part of me didn't believe me anymore either.

Bringing myself back to more important matters, I asked, "Where is Travis? Do you still have the girl?"

She nodded. "Travis is fine. I knew if I brought him in on the rescue mission to get you, you'd pitch a fit." She turned and began to walk us back the way she came. "Sophie was asleep when I left. We would have tried to return her to her family, but I had to come find you. I know you're Travis's only hope, so big picture, right?" She turned and led me back the way she came.

My chest swelled with pride. "You could be a Chevalier."

Emma's face wrinkled in distaste as we walked. "Nah, there are too many rules. Plus, don't you have to be a guy to be Chevalier?"

Though I hadn't told her as much, she once again used her intuition to find the truth. "This is true, but you still have the heart of a protector and know how to serve the mission."

She blushed as she looked away.

"How did you find me?" I asked for the second time.

With a sidelong glance, she said, "I don't know, I just kind of felt you. Like that game, hot or cold? I knew traveling in a certain direction that I was getting warmer, so I went with my instinct."

This bothered me more than I could say, but it was undeniable there was some kind of bond, perhaps psychic in nature, between us. I wondered if I hadn't been drugged recently, if my senses would have been sharp enough to feel the same thing.

"It's similar to when we were... touching...." she trailed off. Heat curled in my belly then sunk lower as I remembered the motel. The memory of diving into her hot supple skin, kissing and sucking every inch I could find caused me to harden despite the cold.

After we'd walked two blocks, Emma took a left turn.

"What did they do to you?" she asked.

I stiffened, remembering the full extent of the danger we were now in. "Nothing, but the agents of Veritas know the Propheros is here."

Then I remembered Emma wasn't in danger at all anymore. I blamed my sluggish thoughts on being drugged, though her intoxicating kiss could have been cause for the lapse in thought.

"Emma, you no longer need to stay with us. With the soul eater destroyed, you can return home. You are safe to live out your life." I hated myself for saying this out loud. I didn't want to let her go. I wanted her by my side, though I knew it would put her in greater danger.

She didn't speak for seventeen long steps.

"You're wrong."

"Wrong?"

"I can't go home. The coming darkness you keep talking about? That's gonna affect everyone. I can't just go back to my life and not do anything." Her words tripped over each other as they streamed out. "I can't stand behind the counter at Smoky Badger Liquor's, or some other dead-end job, and worry. Worry about the end of the world. About you trying to fix everything. Besides, I won't really be safe until this plays out. Nothing is the same. *I'm* not the same." She reached over and threaded her fingers through mine. I let her. Then she said more cheerfully, "I'm like your partner now, *Lethal Weapon* style, though I'm not sure if you're Riggs or Murtoch."

I could have asked her to explain what she was talking about, but something else pulled at my thoughts. Greasy tendrils of guilt and sadness entwined in my gut. "I'm sorry about Travis."

"Sorry about what? That he is a ginormous pain in the ass? Because I've known that a hell of a lot longer than you."

"Emma, you must understand, the Propheros, he must be sacrificed to save the world from darkness. That is the destiny of the Propheros."

Emma stopped walking to look at me. Her expression was unreadable, but it seemed like she was trying to decide something. I instantly regretted telling her, terrified she would march off and I would never see her again. I was going to aide in the death of her friend. Civilians did not always understand the measures it took to protect our plane of existence, but I had bet on the odds that she would. Or maybe I was being selfish in not wanting to be burdened alone with this knowledge. Another failing on my part. Now, there were more than I could count.

Finally, she said before marching on with purpose, "He's not dead yet. Maybe if we work together it won't come to that."

I didn't reply. What could I say? Prophecy was the powerful river dragging all of us to the inevitable. The Propheros was destined to sacrifice his life to protect this world. There was absolutely no other way. I wished to spare Emma the pain of this knowledge, which was why I didn't say anything to disagree with her after explaining Travis's fate. If I examined my avoidance, I might have found I was really trying to spare myself the pain because I so very much wanted to believe her.

Another block and Emma brought us to the parked jeep. She knocked on the window and Travis jerked up from the reclined driver's seat like a flailing puppet who'd been woken by a blasting cannon. I got into the back of the car. Now that the soul eater was no more, I did not need to keep vigilant in the front seat. Sophie was dozing in the back of the car under a pile of coats. The stuffed bunny had fallen from her grasp and onto the floor. I picked it up and tucked it into her arms once more.

Her dreams would never be the same now that'd she known a real monster. I couldn't protect her from the knowledge there was true darkness lurking at the edges of her world.

And I was finding I couldn't protect Emma from myself, though I claimed I would. If she knew I was the real monster, she wouldn't look at me with such adoration or reach to touch me so easily.

Between the drugs still lingering in my system, and my walk in the cold, I was too tired to think about what this meant.

From the passenger seat, Emma said, "Gang's back together, now let's get Sophie to her family and meet Calan's Masters."

Grateful for Emma's strength, my eyes slammed shut of their own accord and I fell into a deep sleep next to Sophie.

CHAPTER TWENTY-ONE

W e were parked a distance from the firehouse but could plainly see Sophie walk up the steps to the front door. We watched her open the front door, cast a last look at us over her shoulder, then she disappeared inside. Through a lit window, we watched two firemen cross the room to greet her.

"She'll be alright," I said, more for myself.

Emma nodded. "They'll get her home. I'm sure her family is frantically looking for her."

Travis snorted behind the wheel. "If they aren't locked up in a mental ward by now." His words were bitter and dark.

I swallowed hard.

Emma's body was twisted to better watch the firehouse. She caught the look on my face. "Hey, they are alive. If it weren't for you, everyone would have died."

"We never should have gone there. We could have avoided unnecessary loss of life if we hadn't stopped driving."

Travis's shoulders sagged in the driver's seat and Emma turned her head away but not before I saw her face. I realized too late that I'd made it sound as though it were their fault. They were the reason we had to stop, and why we stayed in a motel.

"I didn't mean—"

Emma interrupted brusquely. "Where are we going?"

Travis turned the key over and the engine thrummed to life cutting off any insufficient apologies I had. I closed my eyes, silently cursing myself. Around Emma and Travis, I was clumsy and foolish.

It struck me hard that I shouldn't be indulging in self-conscious feelings. My guiding light was the mission, and I realized in that moment how much I had let my judgment be swayed by these two people. It unsettled me. I had been gone from the Temple for too long, but now my powers were restored and everything was going to return to its natural order.

I quietly said to myself, "Home."

A half hour later, bundled in heavy clothes, we tromped through the woods far away from the spying eyes of the modern world. We were still many hours from the safe house, but it wasn't necessary anymore. We just needed a safe, remote place. Neither Travis nor Emma said anything since I misspoke in the car, which created a leaden weight on my heart, but had also given me time to think. The scent of pine was heavy in the cold air. The dark sky began to lighten, and birds chirped excitedly. Travis had pulled off the road, parking Emma's car out of sight from the road behind a large boulder where tree limbs hung low, adding to the coverage.

The longer the silence stretched out, the more I recognized how much I'd let them compromise my mission. What would my Masters say when they heard of the troubles I'd encountered? I could claim it was the fault of Emma and Travis for influencing me, but I was the one who decided to listen, and I shouldn't have. I shifted my shoulders back, owning up to my grave mistakes. I should not have been so malleable to these civilians. It was time I stop considering Travis and Emma's wants and desires and focus solely on the mission.

Suddenly, I was excited to go home. I could return to life free from complications. It wasn't my place to think, or compromise. It was to simply follow the guidance of my

Masters, in service of the mission. Protect the Light.

Leading the way, I made sure to keep my eyes off Emma. I was going to have to tell her she couldn't come. Where I had first wanted her to stay with me, I knew now it was impossible. My Masters would never condone it and they would see how weak she had made me in my belief. It was better for her too. She wouldn't be in direct danger anymore. It was a Chevalier's job to protect this world. I gave her a sidelong look. If I'd learned anything about Emma, it was that she didn't give up without a fight once she'd made up her mind. I would tell her at the last possible moment to give her little time to react.

Or to give yourself a precious few more moments with her and avoid letting her talk you out of it.

I batted away the thought, but the truth of it lingered.

We came to a small clearing and I nodded to myself, satisfied with the location. It was time to return things to normal.

Kneeling, I formed a box with my hands. "Illiminae homonae recurso meito." The dark visage of trees in front of us ripped open, causing Travis and Emma to stumble back and gasp. The doorway-sized view in front of us now looked down on a large stone parlor. The backs of two leather tufted chairs were visible, set in front of a blazing fireplace. Books lined the walls on either side of the fireplace. I could already hear the crackle and smell the comforting smoky scent of burning wood.

Home. I'm going home. My Masters will know what to do.

Grateful to wield my powers once again, I turned to Travis and held out my hand. "It's time."

His cheeks looked drawn and ruddy from the cold as he eyed the portal. "And I'll be safe there?"

"Absolutely."

"Come on, Trav." Emma nudged his shoulder. "I bet they treat you like royalty. Besides, how many from our graduating class have been to a secret Temple?"

When her eyes met mine, her smile faltered. She knew my thoughts before I'd said a word. "I'm coming with you," she said, her voice tight, an unnaturally high pitch to it.

My features hardened, and I shook my head.

"But you said..." Her words faltered before anger flashed in her eyes. "You lied to me."

"No, I changed my mind. It is for the best."

Sensing a scene coming on, Travis grimaced and took a couple steps away from us. He shoved his hands into the deep pockets of his puffy camouflage trench coat and looked at the ground.

Emma shook her head vehemently, her eyes now glassy. "Don't do that. Don't talk like some kind of brainwashed soldier. I can't go back now that I know so much." Then in a quieter voice, "You need me...."

I kept my mask of indifference on. I needed her to believe there was no chance of her going with us, in order for her to give up. Any chink in my armor and she would dig in and rip it all away. It's what she did. It's who she was.

"No, Emma. I need to take Travis to my Masters. You need to go home. You'll go on with your life. You can't help." I clenched my right hand into a fist to keep from reaching out and dragging her into the portal with me.

"*Help us*." The words seemed to come on the wind in a quiet, childlike warble.

Emma hadn't heard it. "This is bullshit. I've helped save your ass multiple times. You say it's the fate of humanity against the darkness. You'll need all the help you can get."

"Quiet," I ordered.

"No." She stomped her foot. "You can't order me around. You don't always know best. Hell, you don't even know what's good for you. You refuse to allow yourself to think outside your stupid orders."

I thought I heard the childlike warble again, but Emma was on a tirade. I swiftly crossed the distance between us and clapped a hand over her mouth, which stunned her into momentary silence. The warmth of her startled me, too. It always did. Touching her was divine. Being able to smell her was intoxicating and so tempting, but that wasn't what had me to distraction now.

"Help us."

Emma ripped my hand away and was about to give me what for, but this time she heard it too and stilled.

Travis looked around, searching for the owner of the voice. "Who was that?" The sun was high in the sky lighting the forest and vestiges of snow in a white, cold light. There was no one around.

I said quietly, "The birds."

A few minutes ago they had been happily chattering with one another but they'd gone silent. Emma and I searched for the speaker as well.

"Help me?"

This time the words came clearly and close by. Travis and Emma whipped around to look behind them. Though I had already been facing that direction, the girl seemed to appear from thin air. It was a child with long, straggly dark hair standing twenty feet away. The sheet of her hair obscured most of her face, and her gray dress was covered in a print of small flowers, and what looked to be grease and dirt stains.

"Oh, hi there," Travis responded, obviously startled. "Are you alone?" He looked around as if an adult would appear next.

"Help me."

"Are you hurt?" Emma asked, taking a step toward the girl, but I grabbed Emma's arm and yanked her against my chest.

I said in a calm, even voice. "Travis, walk slowly toward me and the portal."

He looked back and forth between me and the little girl but did as I said. He was learning to trust me.

"Help me," the girl cried out as soon as Travis began to retreat. She threw out her hands as if in anguish but didn't move from her spot. Her nails were broken, black dirt caked under them.

Emma flinched against my chest, still watching the little girl. "What is it?"

"It's a *She*," I said, quietly. "Shes were once little girls who brutally murdered someone close to them, like childhood friends, or their families."

The She pulled out a gray balloon from her back, like a magic trick. It had a smiley face drawn on it, one eye bigger than the other, giving it a manic look.

"Occasionally one will cross over from the Stygian. They lure people by asking for help before ripping their entrails out and feasting on them."

Travis's voice shook as he finally reached my side, still watching the girl. "What is it about this Stygian place and babies and children?" He shivered.

The She moved the balloon to and fro, giggling as it glided through the air.

"The Stygian loves to subvert the innocent. Now we must go. She doesn't look it, but the She are incredibly fast. On the count of three, we jump into the portal. I'll go last."

"Are you going to leave me behind to have my entrails ripped out?" Emma asked in a bitter tone.

"Of course not." I gripped her shoulders more firmly. "I would never let anything happen to you. Now, on the count of three. One, two, three."

We turned around but stopped short, when we faced another She standing just to the side of the portal. Her fingers dipped into the portal, as if she were testing the temperature of a pool. Panic seized me. A black eye peeked out from beneath the sheath of hair, darting back and forth between each of us. I sensed more than saw her smile.

"Help us."

"Help us."

"Help us."

I turned my head and suddenly found there weren't just two Shes. Thirty of them stepped out from behind the trees.

CHAPTER TWENTY-TWO

"Gods," I whispered, before throwing up the holy triangle, "Luminatos treahgo eearhovotas." I said it quickly, so the energy burst was short and weaker than if I had taken my time, but it blasted the She in the face enough that it stumbled back and away from the portal. The rest leapt into action. Some had dropped into a distorted crabwalk and scurried across the pine needle covered ground. Others ran straight for us. I grabbed Travis by the lapel and threw him into the portal. He yelped as he disappeared.

Just as I turned to throw another power blast at a She, I saw out of the corner of my eye the She I had just blasted recovered and was climbing into the portal. "No," I dove for the portal.

"Calan," Emma screamed and I stopped in my tracks. Three She had dug their dirty long fingernails into her legs, tearing away at fabric, pulling her away. I whipped out my broadsword and swung. One head rolled away. With another few chops, two hands dropped to the ground. The She reared back, but I couldn't stop them for long. I grabbed Emma and threw her into the portal, following behind.

I hit the ground on my feet, but Emma coughed hard, having fallen flat onto her chest on the antique tile floor. Looking up at the portal, I watched two more She scramble in.

"What is this?" A familiar voice boomed. Master Ylang had been sitting in one of the red tufted chairs facing the massive fireplace, and for a moment I wondered if I could maneuver the She into the fire. I didn't want a bunch of She enveloped in flames running around, so I reconsidered the idea.

"Stay back, Master." I cried out while looking for Travis. I knew I should close the portal but I had to protect the Propheros. I found him on the ground, wrestling a She who screeched and clawed over him. But he had her by the wrists, keeping her at bay.

"Little help," he managed to get out. Sweat dripped down his Temples as he tried to hold the She back. She giggled wildly, like she was about to tickle him. More like tickle his liver after tearing him apart.

I ran forward. With a lunge, I sliced the She's head off, then pivoted, assumed my holy position, and closed the portal. Yet five of the She scurried about on the walls like spiders, two of them bleating for help while the other three laughed their heads off. Feeding my faith, I chanted and directed my light to two of them in a powerful wave. They squirmed, their laughter reaching the pitch of hyenas. They were rooted in this world more firmly than was right. As I continued to wear them away, I sensed movement from the corner of my eye.

"Help him," Emma cried to Master Ylang who remained unmoved by her pleas. She didn't understand that it was my place to protect my Masters and she was doing me a disservice by begging him to intervene.

The two Shes finally melted away under my powers into black muck. Before I could refocus my attention, another She was upon me. Her long nails pierced through my shirt and into my stomach as she let loose a delighted shriek. The She rocked back and forth as if in unhinged ecstasy as she clawed through my flesh. I grabbed her wrists to keep her from digging in, but I didn't have the leverage to throw her off.

That's when I saw Travis come up behind the She with my broadsword and I knew I was saved. My relief dissolved instantly when I watched how he wound up his blow. His swing had too much momentum. It would cut through the She then straight through my own jugular.

I watched his eyes widen as he realized his mistake, unable to slow down his swing. The blade cut into the She's neck, slicing through and continuing its path down toward me. I closed my eyes and thought only of Emma's sweet kiss.

The blade sliced the skin of my throat. Then it stopped. The blade was pulled back and away from my flesh. Opening my eyes, I watched Travis stumble backward as he had jerked back to retrain the aim of the blow. I swallowed and licked my lips. Rivulets of blood seeped down my neck, but other than the disconcerting sting of a cut on my throat, I was fine. Throwing the dead She off me, I leapt up and grabbed the sword from Travis's hand, plunging it into the two remaining She who thought they were sneaking up behind him. With two quick swipes, that was the end of the She.

Still panting, I touched my neck. My fingers came away wet with red.

"Oh god, Calan," Emma rushed to me. "Are you okay? Your- your throat."

"I'm fine."

Then seeing my Master behind her, I dropped to my knee and bowed deeply. "Master Ylang."

Master Ylang was four inches shorter than me but carried a presence that demanded respect. He wore a long blue robe with ornate gold trimming. Master Ylang seemed to glide forward. My Master waved me up to my feet with slim yet knotted fingers. His bald head was almost as knotty as his knuckles but long hairs fell, like waterfall whiskers, from beneath his nostrils. Waterfall whiskers were what I always thought of them as. His eyes were wide but clouded over. Anyone might mistake him to be a blind man, but I knew better. He'd swat your hands before you even thought to steal an apple.

"Chevalier," he addressed me with formal authority, "Why have you brought these people here?"

"Master, a soul eater came to physical form before my very eyes. And you saw the She. They have amassed in unprecedented numbers."

The skin over his eyes rose where there should have been eyebrows. "That is impossible, my son."

I shook my head. "It is not for me to speculate on what it is possible, but I have witnessed it all the same." My shirt was soaked. I held a hand against my stomach where the She had tried to disembowel me. I would need medical attention, but it could wait. I glanced down at Emma's legs, her pants were torn and stained dark with her blood.

The sight of Emma bleeding sent a trill of fear through me I'd not known before. I'd seen her in danger, but seeing her flesh marred hurt more than my own wounds. My insides went cold.

Emma boldly stepped up. "I saw it too." As if sensing my distress, she came over and put a hand on my shoulder.

My Master rose another non-existent eyebrow at her. "And who is this?"

Before I could say anything, Emma continued. "My name is Emma, and that's Travis." She waved to Travis who turned and gave a slight nod of acknowledgement. He had migrated to the lit fire place that was as tall as he. Travis hugged himself near the flames, probably cold from shock, but he seemed to be keeping it together.

Emma went on. "We were attacked by a soul eater, but Calan saved us."

My Master looked into my eyes. I closed my thoughts and feelings until there was nothing on the surface but the need to fulfill the mission and obey my Order. From the outside, I could appear to be the same faithful servant of the Light. He folded his hands into either sleeve of his robes. I knew he was displeased I had named myself to these civilians and I expected due discipline.

"Travis there is the Propheros. We've been trying to get him to you for days." Emma added, putting everything out on the table. My Master looked displeased with her forward nature, which made me want to squirm, but I remained still.

My Master's head snapped to Travis. "Is this true, Chevalier?"

Travis was warm enough to turn around so he could give his backside some attention from the fire.

I nodded carefully, "The creature indeed named the virgin."

Travis's hands flew up. "Whoa now, what did you just say? Did you call me a virgin? I'm not gonna stand by and let you accuse me of being a virgin. What's wrong with you, man?" Betrayal shone in his eyes, though I didn't understand why he was so upset.

Emma crossed her arms. "For heaven's sake, what is it with guys and their manhood? It's perfectly alright to be a virgin. It's nothing to be ashamed of."

Travis scowled. "Hey, I didn't say anything about there being something wrong with people who are virgins. I just don't happen to be one of them."

I chanced a look at my Master who was now staring at Emma. A cold stone dropped in the pit of my stomach.

The two went on bickering as if we weren't there.

"Oh yeah?" Emma said. "And who exactly have you slept with, big roller?" she glanced over her shoulder at Master Ylang. "We went to high school together."

"Jeanine Stalwart for one," Travis said, hands on his hips now. "Peggy Lipton, and oh yeah, Tawny Johnson."

Emma's lips twisted but she seemed to believe him. She turned around to face my Master and me. "Well, your Propheros has been sullied by some of the loosest women in Smoky Badger, but you win some you lose some. Why are you both looking at me like that?"

CHAPTER TWENTY-THREE

No.
My heart thundered in my ears.

My Master waved a hand to her. "Where were you, my child, when the soul eater named the Propheros?"

No. No. No.

My hands balled into fists.

"Travis was trying to pull me off the ground when…" her mouth turned into that small 'o' again. She understood the importance of her proximity.

Travis guffawed. "No, seriously? You're still a virgin, Em?"

First she blanched, then she went red in the face.

"It's not her." My denial came out in a low rumble.

She blinked at me as if she didn't recognize me for a few seconds. "Destined to stop the coming darkness, huh?" she said in small voice.

"It's not me?" Travis asked. He had unzipped his coat and clutched the front of his shirt. "For real, I'm not the Propheros?" Tears of relief welled in his eyes and his shoulder sagged. "Does this mean I can go home?"

I wouldn't believe it. I refused to believe it. Travis was the Propheros and he was destined to die to protect us from the Stygian. I would continue to act as Chevalier after his sacrifice, and Emma would return to her life and live to an old age. I'd never see her again, but she would be safe.

She should have never come. It was confusing the truth of the situation.

"Are you well, Chevalier?" Master Ylang asked. To Travis or Emma's ears he no doubt sounded sympathetic, but I knew better. It was a warning. I straightened my stance.

"Of course, Master."

He waved a hand spotted with pigment of age. "Regardless of who you have brought to us, you have successfully brought the Propheros." He walked over to Emma, examining her with cloudy eyes. The urge to grab her and run was almost overpowering. Then Master Ylang's attention swept toward me.

"It took you days to deliver the Propheros to us?"

Looking straight ahead, I answered, "Yes, Master."

Slowly, he made his way toward me. "And what could have delayed your journey for so long?"

My lips tightened, but I forced myself to speak. "I met with a complication."

"What complication?"

"I temporarily lost my ability to use my magic."

Master Ylang stood in front of me, nearly nose to nose, yet I maintained my blank stare. He didn't speak or move for a long time.

"Well," he finally broke the silence and moved away from me. "We must make our guests comfortable so I may gather our House to hear of all we have missed. Days can provide an eternity of information."

I bowed my head. Master Ylang clapped. It wasn't loud, but less than a minute later a servant of the House appeared in a brown robe. He was instructed to take Emma and Travis to guest quarters.

Emma tried to catch my eye, but I kept my head bowed, aware that my Master was closely watching. It still felt like a building was falling from the sky, crashing onto my head. Thousands of tiny invisible needles pricked at my forehead causing it to break out in a sweat. As Emma passed by, my feelings of shock intensified ten-fold. I knew in that moment I was experiencing her feelings as well, like I had when I felt the heat of her desire. She knew the Propheros was a sacrifice for the greater good.

As soon as the doors shut, my Master held his hands behind his back.

"How many days, Calan?"

"Three."

He allowed the alarm to show on his face this time. "You lost your abilities for three whole days?"

I shook my head. "Less than two days, but we met further complications."

I proceeded to tell him about the soul eater, the Crib, and the agents from Veritas up until we reached the She and our dramatic entrance into the Temple.

He nodded but kept staring at me in an unnerving fashion. I told myself it was a paranoid thought of the guilty. I hadn't told him about my familiarity with Emma, but it felt like he was looking right through me and into my transgressions.

"I sense a shift in you," he finally said. "You have been gone too long, I think. I wonder, do you still seek to serve the mission?" His voice softened. "To protect this world from the terrors of the Stygian?"

"Of course I do." I was almost offended he had to ask, but I had strayed from the path. My Master had every right to question me.

He spoke slowly. "I feel you already know how she looks at you."

I didn't respond, unsure of what he wanted me to say.

"Does she know what you have done?"

My gaze fell to the floor. He circled around me.

"Ah, I didn't think so. You have trespassed against so many, Calan. You have caused destruction, violence, and evil. Do not let her be one of your evils in this life. Or you will doom us all, and her to an eternal hell."

"Are you sure?" My words came out strangled, as half of me begged not to ask the question.

"Of what?" he asked once he came to stand before me again. He released his hands from behind his back.

"Are you sure nothing can be done to save the Propheros? There isn't another way to prevent the coming darkness?"

Master Ylang's mouth twisted, distressed with my question. "Calan, it is not your place to question such things."

If it were any other Master, I would have been whipped ten ways from Sunday. Master Ylang seemed to favor me and granted me more patience than I deserved.

His tone hardened. "Your mission is ours to give, and the mission is to protect the Propheros at all cost until the time comes for her to be sacrificed. If you cannot fulfill this duty, we will call on another Chevalier who can."

I nodded, afraid to speak. I wanted to cry out that no one could protect Emma as well as me. I didn't trust anyone else. But I kept my lips sealed and face as impassive as I could manage.

"We'll discuss this at length with the Order." Master Ylang moved past me. "Get some rest, Chevalier. There will be much to do."

As soon as the grand wooden doors shut behind him, I fell to my knees and shoved a knuckle into my mouth to muffle my scream of despair.

CHAPTER TWENTY-FOUR

I wound my way through the large stone halls, sunlight streaming in through the tall, narrow windows. We had traveled a long ways from the dawn where the She attacked us. Looming ficus trees surrounded the Temple like an army. I'd missed their lush foliage in my travels. The heavy scent of moist earth and flowers infused the humid air. Yet, I did not feel the usual comfort in returning home.

Reaching my modest quarters, I saw the stone tub had been filled with hot water for me. I took my time cleaning and treating the wounds on my abdomen. The scratches on my face from the Crib were almost completely healed. I cleaned the cut on my neck but left it un-bandaged.

When the door to my quarters creaked open, I did not flinch. Though I was completely undressed and still wet from my bath, I did not move to cover myself. I hid nothing from my Order. During many training sessions, I was required to complete tasks in the nude to shed modesty for the sake of being wholly present in my missions. It also toughened my skin to feel the scrape of rough of bark, brush underfoot, and harsh sunlight or the cold of night.

When I looked up though, Emma's back was to me as she peeked out the door to make sure no one saw her enter my quarters. She had changed into a long, sheer white dress, no doubt provided for her. Bandages peeked out from the bottom of her dress. Someone had tended to the scratch wounds on her legs from the She. When Emma turned around, her mouth dropped open and she fell back against the door as if her legs suddenly couldn't keep her up.

Paralyzed, I didn't know what to do. I hid nothing from my Order because my body and person were not considered to be of consequence. I wanted to abide by my teachings, but the way Emma's eyes hotly soaked in my exposed flesh, I felt the urge to cover myself. It was like when she looked straight into my eyes, reading my every emotion, but this was a million times more intimate. Dark heat flared in her eyes, and I somehow sensed her mouth was watering.

"Hello," I said stiffly, unable to act natural. I cursed myself for another unnecessary dalliance with the ego.

Emma swallowed, but let her eyes slowly travel up my body starting with my feet and traveling up my calves, thighs, then her gaze lingered on my groin. Her eyes were puffy and red, as if she'd been crying but they were dry now. The necklace she'd forced us to stop for still hung on her neck, the pendant disappearing under the dress between her breasts. I looked away from her as I realized my manhood was rising to the attention, but I didn't move. To cover up, would be admittance I thought myself special and separate. Chevalier were neither of those things.

"Jesus," she breathed. "You're like a goddamn Greek statue brought to life."

Desire ignited in me like gasoline set aflame. My sex stiffened so hard, I gasped. It ached with desperate desire to press against and then into the woman before me. My length took on a will of its own the way it demanded its needs be acknowledged. My inner voice swore that I would die if I did not make this woman mine this very instant.

Finding her feet, Emma slowly crossed the room as if worried she'd startle me. I briefly wondered what she thought of my barren quarters. Where hers had been full of colors, pictures, and books, mine was gray and devoid of life. There was a narrow bed and a simple table with one chair tucked under it. She wasn't looking at my room though.

Through her dress, I could see the slight darkening of her areolas. It wouldn't take much to remove that slip of a garment. She hadn't yet washed her hair and it wildly framed her face in a way that reminded me how it looked after I ran my hands through it when I kissed her senseless.

Emma reached out a shaking hand and touched the side of my abs that weren't bandaged. I felt it then. Underlying the electric heat was pure unadulterated fear.

She knows she's going to die.

Looking up into my face, my normally powerful and confident Emma was without hope. As she spoke, her words broke. "Calan, I need you." With that, she reached down and closed her hand around my hardness.

My eyes slammed shut and my head fell back as my body surrendered to her touch and begged to claim her. I too was ready to give in to oblivion, to forget everything that threatened to tear my heart out from my chest.

I pushed the straps of her dress over her shoulders and tugged them down until she was forced to release me. The fabric of her dress slipped down and over the peak of her hard nipples and at once I knew the scratch of the material against them sent a wave of moisture to her sex. I felt the feminine sensation like an echo, resonating through my body.

The sight of her bare breasts overwhelmed me. They were the perfect size for me to palm and a blush crept along her pale flesh. Each time we had given in to lust, we had been clothed. This exposure took my feelings for her to a new depth when I thought I could not delve any deeper. My desire now felt utterly raw in the wake of her naked breasts. Having trapped her arms at her sides with the straps, I leaned over and worshipped her tight nipples, laving them with my tongue. They were tangy and sweet, and my straining length begged to bury itself in her hand again but I refused and kept her arms pinned at her sides.

Moving up, I lavished her neck with slow, hot kisses then dipped back down to flick the tips of her nipples with my tongue. She gasped with each tap of my tongue and I sensed through our strange connection pleasure jolting to her sex in time with my tongue. I pushed the dress further down her body and over her delicate hips until it puddled on the ground leaving her clad in nothing but her necklace. She whispered my name in a husky voice, and her need went from hot to molten. Again, I *knew* wetness was rapidly pooling between her thighs.

She took my breath away. Her limbs were so delicate in comparison to mine and lacked muscle definition because she had lived a softer life than I. Her skin reminded me of the baby lambs after they'd been shorn, but it was pulled taut over her slim, nubile limbs. My sex twitched in desperation.

I was so in awe of this angel, I wanted to fall to my knees before her. So I did. Tracing my hands down the sides of her stomach, my grip tightened at her hips for a moment before one hand slipped to the small patch of soft, tawny curls between her legs. My fingers explored the folds of impossibly soft flesh. I reveled in each gasp of pleasure, every moan. I felt the twist of her pleasure echo in my own body as the psychic biofeedback of her arousal fed my own. The amount of restraint it took to not throw her on the ground and enter her caused me physical pain.

Emma's face contorted as my thumb brushed over a small nub. I brushed it again and she gasped harder than before and begged for more. So I gave it to her. I brushed against it lightly, over and over again then dipped my mouth to those now dripping hot folds. I touched my tongue to it. The intoxicating taste mirrored the tanginess of her nipples but was a darker, deeper flavor. I craved more. I sucked on her lower lips and Emma's nails bit into my shoulder.

"Calan, I don't think I can stand for much longer." As she said it, I noticed her knees wobbled unsteadily.

I thought to move her to the bed, but it was so small. I decided to pull her down to the ground instead. As I laid her back, she brought her knees up. I crawled in between them and tested the wetness of her sex again with one finger. The sight of her exposed and laid out was the most erotic sight I'd ever know. The image burned itself into my memory right then, and I knew I would never be more fulfilled than this moment where I was allowed for a time to worship her body. Dark thoughts of Emma's impending sacrifice threatened to swallow my absolution. I fought them back, they would overcome me soon enough.

I dipped my finger in as deep as my second knuckle a couple of times before Emma gave a guttural growl. When I looked up, she was scowling down at me. I added a second finger and pushed them all the way into her body. Her body arched off the floor like she'd been struck by lightning. Her wrist flew to her mouth where she bit on it to suppress a scream. I pumped my fingers into her again and again, feeling the shooting bolts of her pleasure go through me.

Continuing to pump, I grabbed my length tightly with my other hand to keep myself from coming. My balls were drawn tight and the tip of my manhood was sticky and wet. Swallowing hard past the lump in my throat, I waited until I was sure I could control myself then bent over and sucked on the nub that had caused her so much pleasure before.

Her hips shot up again and I felt the orgasm rip through her body. Not just squeezing and pulsating around my fingers, I felt it from the inside. It was like a rubber band had been twisted almost past its breaking point, then when it broke, the bands wildly shuddered as they released at the speed of light. I had to reach back down immediately to grab ahold of myself to stop from orgasming. I grasped myself painfully tight.

Emma screamed my name into her wrist as she bit down on it again. When her body relaxed and her hand fell away, I saw she had drawn blood with her teeth. I slowly removed my fingers from her now gushing center. She jerked when they slid out.

Her hand moved to cover her eyes instead of her mouth this time, and the shudder rocking her body was no longer sexual. It was a sob.

I crawled up to lie next to her on the floor, propping my head up to better observe her. I wished I could see her eyes but what I saw were the tears rolling down from under her palm, dripping off her cheeks and onto my bicep.

"I don't want to die." Her voice was ragged, and a gang of razors tore through my heart. I reached over and pulled her into my body where she buried her face in my chest and broke fully into sobs. Tears formed in my eyes and soon wet trails led down my cheeks, too. We held each other, unable to pretend everything was going to be alright anymore.

Prophecy is the powerful river dragging us all toward the inevitable.

CHAPTER TWENTY-FIVE

There on the floor, crying with Emma, I closed my eyes, trying to block out the fear that threatened to engulf both of us. I thought I knew the hardness of a life of repentance, but this was almost more than I could bear. For a moment, I didn't care if the Stygian claimed this world, because the thought of losing Emma brought hell on earth to me. I held her tight, never wanting to let her go.

When she pulled back, Emma realized I was still hard and reached a hand down to touch me but I stopped her.

"I can't," I said softly.

"Do you want me to use my mouth?" She asked, wiping her eyes.

I shook my head, my heart tired and leaden now. "No, I mean I can't, Emma."

She looked at me with disbelief before extracting herself from my arms and trying to get to her feet, but her legs were unsteady and it took a moment. "So what, you are just doing me a favor? Servicing me before I go to my death? Preserving my virginity for the sacrifice?"

Getting to my feet as well, I watched Emma grab her dress and angrily tug it on. "Emma, we can never be together because I'm a Chevalier."

Officially boiling with rage, she yelled, "What does that even mean?"

Deep down I knew it was despair fueling her anger, but it still didn't dull the sting. I lowered my voice hoping she would bring down her volume, too. "I have no soul."

Whatever she had been about to say died on her lips. She stared at me, agape this time with shock so very different than when she had first walked in on me naked.

"You have no soul," she repeated slowly.

"I— I should have told you before. In my last life, I committed unspeakable atrocities. The gods took my soul but have afforded me a chance at redemption in this life. They made me a Chevalier. Chevaliers must serve the Light, the mission the Order of Luxis serves, until perhaps, one day the gods would deem to grant us our souls again. So you see, we cannot be together. You deserve a man, not a soulless monster."

One eyebrow arched higher than I'd ever seen before, and the corners of her mouth tugged down in displeasure. "Are you kidding me?" Then rolling her eyes she answered herself, "Of course not, you don't even know how." She repeated it again as if trying to absorb. "You have no soul."

I looked away from her, shame burning me up. "I know I should have told you. It's why I tried so hard to stay away from you. I don't know when, or if, the gods will ever return my soul."

"Bullshit."

I reared back. "What?"

Emma's expression had morphed from incredulity into a hard mask. "I said bullshit. You absolutely have a soul, Calan."

"I understand this is difficult for you to hear, Emma. To find out while I protected you from monsters, I was a monster all along."

Her eyes were dry now, and sharp with clarity as she stared up at me defiantly. "No Calan, you have a soul, I'm telling you. And I can prove it. The soul eater went after you every time we fought it. It wanted your soul, too."

I gave her a wry smile. "No, Emma. It recognized me as a threat and we fought because it knew I would prevent it from feeding, not because I have a soul."

She rolled her eyes but wouldn't let it go. "How did you know you were a Chevalier?"

"My Masters told me."

"And how do they know you don't have a soul?"

I struggled to answer her questions. These were simple facts I knew to be as true as the ground beneath my feet, but I lacked the knowledge-base and eloquence of my Masters.

"Magic, I think. They find Chevalier when they are babies and bring them back here to the Temple."

Her eyes widened. "You mean, those people from that other Order really could be your parents?"

I ran my hands through my hair, scarping my blunt nails along my buzzing scalp. "No, no that's not possible. Chevalier are not born into Orders. Those agents are liars. The Chevalier should not be reared in civilian circumstances. It is too dangerous for the general public."

"I thought you said to separate yourself from others was to turn away from the Light."

"Yes. Well no, this isn't the same."

Her eyebrow arched. "This doesn't count, because your Order... said so?"

Anxiety at not being able to explain churned agitation through all my limbs until I began to pace. "No, the way you are saying it, that's not right. It's *not* the same."

"Because the Order of Truth or Veritas, whatever it's called, serves the dark?"

"No," I said, my voice getting louder with frustration. "They don't serve the dark but turning against them isn't turning against the Light like it would be against anyone else. My Order, they know more than I do about why."

Emma stood in front of me, stopping my pacing. Her hand cupped my cheek in a gesture to soothe my obvious distress. "Calan. Look at me. I know to my very core that you have a soul. You are the most loving, compassionate, strong, *soulful* person I have ever encountered." Her voice hardened. "I think your Masters have been lying to you." Hope suffused her voice next as her hands slipped to my shoulders. "Which means they might be lying about me. Maybe I'm not the Propheros. Well, I guess the bad guys kind of outed me and why would that soul eater thing lie? Unless your Order actually controls the bad guys, but that's a bit far-fetched. Maybe your Order is just lying about the sacrifice. Maybe I don't need to die." Her words squished together as they came out in a torrent.

I gently pushed Emma's hands away from me. "Emma, stop it. My Masters would never lie. They protect this world from the darkness and they know best."

My head throbbed from Emma's chattering. The things she was saying were blasphemous. I had been afraid of her seeing for the monster I was. I hadn't anticipated this.

She tried to grab my face again to make me look at her but I jerked away. "Calan, you have to believe me. You have a soul."

"You can't... you can't say these things, Emma. You don't know what you are talking about. I'm scared too, okay? But it is clear what must be done."

"Because they told you what to do, Calan. You've got to use your own senses for once."

I turned my back on her. I couldn't look at her another minute. "You need to go, Emma. I won't hear this. I must make amends for my trespasses, and I won't add to them by listening to your wild accusations."

"So you'd rather kill me than trust me?" Her words came out in a ragged whisper.

I didn't respond. I didn't even turn around until I heard the door close behind her. Emma's words buzzed in my head like a cloud of angry hornets. She was trying to take away my faith, my belief, my family. It tore up my insides because I could not deny that I was completely, undeniably, irrevocably in love with Emma. Yet it did not change that she would have to be shown the Light. That she was destined to die to save the world, just as my destiny was to hold her hand to that end.

CHAPTER TWENTY-SIX

I stood before the four Masters of Luxis in the main hall, their high backed, wood-carved chairs arranged in a semi-circle around me. They all donned the same indigo-colored, velvet robes with intricate gold stitching. Patchouli and sandalwood incense burned aggressively from the corners of the room.

My Masters' faces shifted between disbelief and concern as I related the events of the last three days. Yet again, I left out details of my relationship with Emma. I wanted to disclose everything, yet something held me back. At the end of my report, I bowed my head as they conversed, leaving me to struggle with my inner contradictions.

Master Violetta spoke first. "The actions by the Order of Veritas are outrageous." Her white and gray streaked hair was pulled back into a tight bun, making her face severe. "Now that they know we have the Propheros in our possession, they will do anything to intervene."

Master Wu pressed his fingertips together. "There is no telling the war that could break out if the other three Orders find out." His eyes always reminded me of two small black pebbles struck by harsh sunlight.

Master Ilsa thoughtfully propped her knuckles under her pointed chin. "The war could be brief or drawn out for decades. The Propheros has been named, but the matter of when her role shall be played is yet to be determined."

Master Violetta waved her hand, and closed her eyes, calling upon the memorized text she carried with her. "When the night sky becomes ill, we shall know the time has come. Where the earth breaks, the Dark Lord shall journey in a fortnight's time to set his deathly foot upon the soil of the earth."

"That is not of importance yet, we cannot anticipate the event," Master Ylang interrupted. "What is of importance is that we have the Propheros. Our only concern now is how to best protect her."

"We should keep her here, of course," Master Ilsa, the youngest of my Masters, though I'd never known her without deep age lines in her face. Her ice-blond hair was plaited into two long braids and her eyebrows arched dramatically even when she made no expression at all.

Master Wu sat up. "No, we cannot. The other Orders will surely come to take what they wrongly believe is theirs. It is only a matter of time before the agents of Veritas come, since the Chevalier did not slit their throats as he should have to silence them on this issue."

A ripple of unease shot through me. It was my job to protect the innocent. While the agents spouted lies of my heritage, it surely did not warrant their deaths.

Never before had I questioned my Masters. I kept my head bowed and attempted to clear my mind until they deemed appropriate action for me fulfill.

I felt Master Wu's eyes on me. "We must also choose the appropriate Chevalier to assign to the Propheros. Someone who knows what is necessary to best serve the Light."

"The text says the Chevalier will be chosen by the Propheros," Master Violetta said in her slow drawl, conjuring the text from memory again.

Four sets of eyes fell on me. I resisted the urge to lift my head, waiting for instructions.

"My ward," Master Ylang called, beckoning me to join the conversation.

"Yes, Master?" I gave a short bow.

He stroked his long, stringy mustache for a moment, then straightened in his chair. "We are about to share the sacred text with you."

I bowed deeply this time and replied, "Blessed be the word of the Light."

Everyone turned to Master Violetta who closed her eyes. "And the Propheros shall choose Chevalier. Where truth meets power, a bond to bind, where the wind meets the mind, the Propheros shall instill its being to Chevalier."

When she was done, Master Ylang asked, "What say you, Calan?"

He had never asked me to interpret text before. The words crowded and cluttered each other up in my head. Normally I would release them as easily as they came but for once I tried to sort and sift through the words until they made sense. But I knew better than to admit such a thing out loud. "I am not one to translate the Light, only to do its bidding."

Master Ylang nodded as if he was pleased I had confirmed something. "We believe the texts refers to a bond that the Propheros will make. Perhaps psychic in nature. Maybe some kind of alarm to warn the Chevalier that the Propheros in danger so that he may better protect her."

I stifled my reaction, maintaining a blank face.

Master Wu leaned in with a thin black eyebrow raised. "Have you experienced such a bond with the Propheros while she has been under your protection?"

I paused. "I believe I have."

Surprised mumbles were exchanged.

"Explain," Master Violetta said simply.

"In times of extreme emotion, I have felt a shared fear that has allowed me to better aid the Propheros when she has been in danger."

"And when you first felt this bond," Master Wu said, "what did you think it was? My understanding was that you thought the long haired mook you brought with you was the Propheros. Did you also form a bond with him?"

"No, Master. It has only been formed with the true Propheros. I cannot say what I interpreted it to mean."

"You are withholding something from us," Master Ilsa said sharply. "I won't stand for this insubordination. Speak it immediately, Chevalier."

This is what I had feared most. She was right. I was lying by omission and it was a transgression that would further prevent me from regaining my soul. "I have felt the bond to the Propheros through many extreme emotions."

"Such as?" Master Violetta asked patiently.

"Fear. Fear and lust," I said it before I could think about it too much.

Master Ylang closed his eyes, disappointment radiating from him. I pressed my hands into the sides of my legs.

"Lust?" Master Ilsa repeated. "Lust for others, or lust for something in particular?"

My heart beat so hard it felt like it would break my chest into a million splinters. "Lust for me." I couldn't help the heat that no doubt stained my cheeks with flush.

The collective gasp confirmed my fears. Master Ylang looked at me with pity in his eyes, which was worse than if he'd taken the staff to my palms. I should have told him at our first interview, yet I withheld it.

"Did you redirect the child on how preposterous these feelings were?" Master Ylang asked.

I kept my stare focused on the knot of wood in the chair, just above Master Ylang's head. "Yes, Master. I have made many attempts to illuminate her on the natural order of the Light, and how I am far from it."

"There you see," Master Ylang said, turning back to my other Masters with satisfaction.

Yet I could feel the burn of one of their stares boring a hole into me. My stomach felt like there was a hill brimming with skittering ants in it.

It was Master Violetta who spoke. "And you, Chevalier, ward of Ylang, do you return such... lust to the Propheros?"

My tongue felt heavy. My heart pounded erratically. The words felt thick but they had to be said. "To lie would be to turn away from the Light. Yes, I also share in this feeling of... lust." The word came out husky where I meant it to ring clear as a bell. Lust was such an underwhelming word for what I truly felt. Emma was so much more than an object of lust. She bore confidence and strength, tempered by compassion and heart.

"This won't be borne," Master Wu insisted. His voice reached a near-screech when he addressed me. "We must assign a different Chevalier at once. Have you soiled our Propheros?"

I shook my head and the words came out in a stutter. "I cannot deny there was opportunity to turn away from the Light and give in to the temptation she presented, but the Propheros remains a virgin."

Thoughts of my tongue lapping between her thighs as she orgasmed on my fingers sprang to my mind and the instant arousal was weighed by guilt and sin.

I should have kept silent but suddenly I couldn't help myself. "I would never compromise the Propheros. My feelings for her only ensures my dedication to her protection."

"Oh gods," Master Violetta sighed with a frown.

Master Wu's mouth tightened as he glared at me.

Master Ilsa seemed uncomfortable with this progression, and looked away from me as if I could taint her simply by laying her eyes on me.

"Master Ylang tells us you lost your powers temporarily," Master Wu accused, a bony finger shaking in my direction.

"This is true. For almost two days I could not call on the Light to bring us to the Temple." My brows furrowed. "I cannot say why, but it did return."

Master Violetta said quietly, "You broke your faith."

My heart skipped a beat. "No. That cannot be so. I am faithful to the Light, to the mission. It is all I am."

Master Violetta continued, "Your power is fueled by your belief, your faith. The only reason you may lose it is to subverted faith." She looked at me curiously.

Master Wu addressed Ylang this time. "He broke the faith. He is not fit to serve our Temple anymore. I told you this would happen. You coddled your precious golden boy." The last words were said in a sneer.

Master Ylang's voice cracked through the room. "My ward has gone through the trials as every Chevalier has and at each turn excelled past expectation."

Hope sprung inside me. Master Ylang could make them see how dedicated I was. My life was theirs. I did not break the faith. I'd make them see that.

My Master's cloudy eyes froze over. "Yet my ward has turned his back on his Order and against the Light. Chevalier, you are to stay confined to your quarters. Until further notice, you are to no longer have any contact with the Propheros. Do you understand?"

My jaw tightened but I bowed deeply then turned on my heel and left. Before the door shut behind me, I heard Master Violetta call in a servant to the Order and say, "Call for my ward. Bond or no bond, Ylang's ward is no longer fit to protect the Propheros."

CHAPTER TWENTY-SEVEN

I t didn't sit right.

In my quarters, I tried to push away the blasphemies Emma had spoken and focused on my faith in my Order. Counting out thirty pushups, I moved to doing them one-handed in an attempt to expel the harmful thoughts from my mind.

It just wouldn't sit right though. My thoughts and feelings couldn't be tamed. There was so much I didn't know. Before I could give my actions too much thought, I pulled on my usual mission clothes and slipped from my room and made my way to the sacred reading room. Silently, I closed the door behind me, knowing if I was caught, my

Masters would flay the skin from my body. Which would be ridiculous as I'm unable to read and thus, as helpless as a babe in here.

The circular room was small but at least four stories high, packed with books. The mustiness, tinged by the vanilla of aged papers, was cloying in the small space. Many books were pulled regularly, but most were buried in blankets of dust, especially those several rows above my head. The ladders were impossibly tall and looked precarious at best. Of course, my Masters had bird-like frames, so their weight wouldn't jeopardize the stick-thin ladders crawling up the walls.

In the center of the room sat a podium displaying a large, leather bound book. The skylight twenty feet up filtered rays of late-afternoon sun down onto it. The sacred text of the Light. Casting my eyes upon it sent a shiver of fear through me for my irreverence. What was I doing? Even with the scant few words I'd learned for navigation purposes, I didn't stand a chance at reading what the book said about Emma. I could sneak Emma in here to read the book, but I didn't want her to see me break my faith. If I were to bring her in here, the betrayal would be sealed. It would be confirming to her that I no longer trusted the people who made me what I am.

"I do trust them," I insisted to myself, my words swallowed up by the stacks of books. I just... also needed to prove it for myself. My face dropped into my hands and I let out a frustrated sigh.

Then an idea struck me. I slipped back out of the reading room as quietly as I came in. It didn't take long to find Travis and bring him back with me.

"Are you going to tell me what this is about?" he protested as I shoved him inside and shut the heavy door behind us. He had bathed and been provided with light linen pants and matching shirt, but earlier I had heard his voice carry down the halls demanding to know where his Metallica shirt had gone. It appeared as though they got it washed and returned because he wore the billowy pants but with the freshly washed, still-damp Metallica shirt. I wondered briefly whether it was a family heirloom like Emma's necklace.

"Shh," I cautioned, speaking in a low voice, hoping he would follow suit. "I need your help."

He crossed his arms. "Why should I help you? Since I met you, it's been nothing but a crazy train, man."

"Because if I hadn't been there at the liquor store, your soul would have been consumed by that malevolent spirit."

His arms dropped as did his mouth as he tried to formulate a fitting retort.

"Please, Travis." I begged.

With a sigh and slump of his shoulders, I knew he would help. I turned for him to follow me to the book. "I need you to tell me what the book says."

"What makes you think I can read some archaic word of your gods?" he groused but followed me.

"I believe it is in text you can understand."

"Then why don't you read it?" he asked, still petulant.

"Because no one ever taught me to read."

That seemed to shut him up and take some of the sulk out of him too. "Oh."

I opened the book up to where I remember Master Ylang reading to me about the Propheros. I remembered about how many more pages were weighted to the left side from my vantage point.

"Read this, please," I added. "If you can."

With a shrug, Travis looked at the script and muttered, "Fancy writing but you're right, it's English."

"What does it say about the Propheros?" I urged him on.

He flipped through some pages until he found it. "*The darkness shall cross the threshold to harken the Propheros is near. And with it, the dawning of a new age.* Well, that's heavy."

It was the same thing the agents of Veritas had said.

"The soul eater, when he became solid and stepped onto our plane," I said, then urged him to continue, not sure how much time would pass before he was missed. The

Order did not trust having strangers in their midst and would keep a close eye on him.

He spoke slowly as he made out the words. "The Propheros shall be a tide against the coming darkness. When the dark lord of Stygian passes through the gate and sets foot on the earthly realm, the Propheros shall make the greatest sacrifice to destroy the dark lord and save the fertile lands of the living."

Looking over his shoulder, though I could not read what it said, I asked, "Does it say anything more about the sacrifice?"

But Travis had stopped. After a moment, he asked in a quiet voice, "Does this mean Emma is going to die?"

I ignored his question. "Does it say anything else, Travis?"

"Yes, Travis, does it say anything else?" Another voice joined us from the shadows.

I jumped forward to put myself between Travis and whoever else had snuck into the reading room but the intruder was invisible to my eye. The room was so small, we would have noticed if they had come through the front door. How did they get in?

"Gatsby," I said, recognizing the voice though I could not see him.

"Did you miss me?" Gatsby asked drolly. My gaze moved upward as I realized he was shrouded in the shadows, several ledges above us.

"Yes," I replied automatically.

He let out a dry laugh. "That's Calan for you. Polite to the end. Don't worry, I'm not happy to see you either, brother. I was called back and I see why now." He leapt from the ledge, landing silently on his feet before straightening.

He looked the same as when I had seen him five years ago. The same sharp eyes, the dark blonde hair pulled back in a low, short ponytail. There was still the long, jagged scar running through his left eyebrow and the same sneer pulling the side of his mouth. Gatsby reminded me of an animal who never got used to being caged, always impatient and on edge. The only difference was his face and body had become more angular, as if he'd been deprived sufficient nutrition at some point. He was athletically thin compared the amount of bulk I had on my body and I knew from fighting him that he was the fastest of all the Chevaliers.

"You've been a bad boy, Calan," he tsked, and the sound bristled up my back. "They called me because they don't think you can do your job. Something about how you plan to sully the purity of the Propheros?"

He was always jealous of the freedom the Order had given me. Gatsby questioned their authority enough times that they kept him on a short leash. The last time was five years ago, when he had tried to run away. I briefly wondered if his more honed, malnourished features were a result of their correctional actions.

"I thought Tomas was their first choice?" I asked innocently enough, but I saw my mark land and Gatsby's mouth twist.

"Yes, well I'm usually not their first choice, but very occasionally I'm the only one who is around to get the job done." Gatsby was also Master Wu's ward, and I did not envy him that. Gatsby looked over my shoulder at Travis who managed to stay silent behind me. "Though I must say, I'm surprised by what gets your gears going, Calan."

"I'm not a virgin," Travis said too quickly from behind me. "So, I'm definitely not the Propheros."

Gatsby smiled, though only the barest hint of humor reached his eyes. "Ah, I see. So you brought a complete stranger into the reading room. What do you think our Masters will think of their golden boy, now?"

I didn't know what to say. Every part of me demanded I come up with a lie as to why we were there but it wasn't in my nature. Lying demanded a creativity I didn't possess.

"Gatsby," I pleaded. "I am just trying to figure out how to save the Propheros. I believe there could be a different way to defeat the Stygian. A way where she won't have to die."

Gatsby nodded his head solemnly as if he were listening to me.

I continued. "Travis is only trying to help me find that way. If we could read the book, perhaps we could do more."

"You are an unexpected fool, Calan." Gatsby sneered through a smile. "You know there is only one way, and the Order tells us what that way is. If the past five years have taught me anything, it's that they know what is best for us." Though his words were bold, something flickered behind his eyes as he said them. "What you choose to do about your soul is your choice, but I'm getting mine back."

With that, Gatsby leapt to the other side of the shelves like a spider monkey and slipped his body through a small opening as quietly and vanished as quickly as he appeared. I ran to the door but heard the dead bolt lock from the outside just as my hand curved around the handle.

"No," I slammed my fists against the door causing books along the upper shelves to rattle, some plummeting to the ground. Travis yelped as one smacked his head, but he quickly dodged the next two.

"What a charmer," Travis said, rubbing his head, though there was a nervous twinge to his voice, too. He knew he was here uninvited. "Guess there are worse guys than you out there. Though why you all look like ridiculously good-looking fitness models... the hell do they feed you guys?"

I turned around, my back pressed against the door. "I'm sorry, Travis, I didn't mean to implicate you into this. I was just trying to save Emma."

Looking up, I calculated the distance to the secret opening Gatsby had used. I quickly scaled a ladder, two of the rungs breaking under my weight. When I got to the opening, I saw a small, metal door had been shut behind Gatsby. I shook its hinges but apart from its loud screeching protest, it did not budge. Gingerly stepping back down the ladder, I had to leap the last several feet where three more rungs broke, effectively destroying the ladder for further use.

Travis's long fingers drummed against the book as he waited for me to find a way out. "Were you going to let me die?"

I didn't answer right away. I had to obey my Order in deliver the Propheros to the dark, but a part of me was ashamed I felt Travis would have been easier to sacrifice. "It isn't up to me. I am merely a foot solider for the Light."

Travis gave me a strange look. He knew I wouldn't have fought as hard if it were him. Tension rolled out into the room, a thick blanket of unsaid accusation. Discomfort stiffened the muscles between my shoulders but there was nothing to say. There may be nothing I could do for Emma, either. I could feel sorry, but guilt was a useless ruse that changed nothing. I couldn't indulge, I could only correct what was before me.

Finally, Travis put his nose back into the book while I waited by the door, listening for approaching footsteps.

CHAPTER TWENTY-EIGHT

"Whoa," Travis said after five minutes of reading from the book. "What?" I snapped, impatient and on edge at the door, waiting for them to come for us. Best case scenario, the Luxis would send me back to purgatory, life between lives, and I would stand no chance of regaining my soul. Worse case, they would deem me a Dark one. They would torture me before banishing me into the Stygian using a portal. It was a punishment reserved for the most wicked. As my agitation grew, my fingers ached to pull my broadsword from its sheath on my back.

"Your upbringing is super intense. Like child-star messed up. I didn't know...." said Travis.

"Oh," I said, my shoulders sagging a bit. He must have read the part about me trying to regain my soul.

"I mean, being snatched from your crib and trained into a thoughtless soldier of the Light would screw anyone up."

I perked up at that. "What? What do you mean?"

Travis held his hands out as if they could do the talking where his mouth struggled. "I don't know. Like it's pretty messed up how they snatch babies and force you to obey their every whim."

"It is for my own good. It is so I can redeem myself and regain my soul."

Travis's face scrunched in confusion. "What are you talking about?"

"It must mention in there how I had committed untold atrocities in a past life and must serve the Light until I can regain my soul. They used magic to find me and offered me a chance at redemption. It is what the Chevalier are, creatures of darkness, serving the Light."

Travis's eyes turned back down to the sacred text. "No," he said slowly, "it only says that whenever the Chevalier ranks have been whittled down, they go out into the world and snatch some babies. Doesn't say anything about how they choose. It doesn't say anything about Chevalier missing their souls, it just says," he leaned into the book and read off the page, "Chevalier must be trained to facilitate complete and utter obedience, no matter the means. It is done so that they will unerringly follow the Light."

My body went numb as he read. They lied to me? Emma was right, they lied to me so I would obey their every command. I wasn't missing a soul. There was no reason why I could not love, or read, or enjoy the earthly pleasures like anyone else. I had nothing to prove.

"I'm sorry, man," I distantly heard Travis say. "I've heard of brainwashing cults and all, but dayum."

"They lied to me." I said the words out loud as if it would make the idea easier to swallow, but it went down like razor blades soaked in lemon juice.

Footsteps approached the door, and I knew they'd arrived. I pulled the broadsword from my back and squeezed the handle with a rage never known before. Unable to digest the lie of my entire existence, my vision turned red.

When the door creaked open, I swung my sword high, ready to bring it down on whoever was on the other side.

"Calan, no," Travis cried out just as my sword swung down. His cries met my ears just as I recognized the liquid brown eyes of

Emma widen in fear as she watched my steel slice through the air toward her face.

It was too late to pull back on the momentum I'd created but I moved the axis of my swing and it swiped down past Emma's face and away from her body. A few of her hairs floated to the ground from where they had been cleanly sliced away from her head.

I forced out a breath. I had almost killed her. I fell to one knee and held myself against the storm of emotions erupting from the close call.

What was wrong with me? I wasn't a killer. I'd never slayed anything other than demons and malevolent spirits. I couldn't let the Luxis further manipulate me away from what I was. They'd made me soulless enough already.

Emma molded her body over my hunched over one. "It's okay, you didn't hurt me. It's okay now, Calan."

I never wanted her to move away. Feeling like a raw, pulsating nerve, she acted as a skin, protecting and soothing me.

"I think I peed a little," Travis squeaked.

When I turned to look at him, his pants appeared dry but his face was drawn and pale. I gathered my senses and stood up, allowing Emma to wrap her body around mine for a moment, enjoying the warmth and comfort of her embrace. I laid my head atop of hers. Emma was the only one I could trust anymore.

"How did you know to come find us?" Travis asked, after a couple of uncomfortable throat clearings.

Emma pulled her head back and looked up into my eyes to respond. "Some guy came to me. His name was Gatsby." Her lips pulled into a frown. "He said he was a Chevalier and he had to come see what all the fuss was about." Her eyes flattened as if recalling something distasteful or annoying. "He looked me up and down, then said he 'got it.' Then he mentioned something about how funny it was Calan's end would come from a girl who was only five foot five." Then she said matter of fact. "So I slugged him."

I sputtered, pulling away from her. "You did what?"

She shrugged and cocked her head. "What? I knocked him right to the ground just like I did Travis."

"Great," Travis said grimly, rubbing the part of his face she had connected a fist to not all that long ago.

I looked down to see Emma rubbing at her now bright red knuckles. I couldn't help the grin from forming on my face. Gatsby had a tenuous position as it was. When word spread he was bested in one shot, he would never hear the end of it.

It was then I noticed Emma had somehow found a change of clothing from the thin white dress the order had supplied. She now wore a forest green tank top, dark brown cargo pants, and combat boots that fit just a little too big on her. She had probably stolen them from Vico's quarters. He was the shortest and most compact of the Chevalier. With her short, messy hair, and look of defiance recounting her meeting with Gatsby, she looked fierce and dangerous.

Something primal flared in me, urging me to test this side of her. There was still a softness about her cheeks and in her eyes, but something more daring seemed to emerge from her with every trial we encountered.

She was changing. With each hardship, she was evolving, hardening into something different in order to survive. Part of me crowed with pride in her ability to adapt, but the larger part of me wanted her to remain the carefree girl I met, with her nose stuck in a book.

"He didn't see it coming." Emma continued to explain her run-in with Gatsby. "And I didn't like the way he was talking about you, so I figured you'd gotten into trouble somehow and came looking for you."

Travis moved from around the podium, tucking the grand volume of sacred text awkwardly under his arm. "Yeah, well if you thought that, it won't take long for someone else to think of it."

"Yes," I agreed, also realizing we were wasting precious time. "We must go."

Pressing Emma out in front of me, I followed her with Travis trailing behind.

Before I could turn to tell him, Travis's arm holding the book smacked into some kind of invisible force so hard it knocked Travis flat on his back.

When his mouth opened, a dry raspy sound emerged. Reaching over I grabbed the book and threw it on the ground and yanked Travis to his feet like the day I first met him. "You can't take the book from the room. It's bound here."

Still unable to catch his breath, Travis settled for glaring at me as we hurried down the halls.

"Are you going to portal us out of here?" Emma asked.

I tried to summon energy to my hands and was met with what I expected. Nothing.

"No. My powers have failed me again." The words came out fiercely as I thought of Master Violetta informing me I had broken the faith.

"I don't get it, man." Travis said, "Do we need to like get you to some kind of magical gas station to fuel you up or what?"

"My powers are rooted in faith. I have no faith left in me."

My head bowed in grief as I lead them down a back passage. Emma and Travis's footsteps echoed down the stone hall, while mine were silent. How could I believe we would be able to escape? Travis was right, the only way out of this was a portal and I couldn't even manage a spark.

"So what do you believe now?" Emma asked, trying to study my face even as I hurried us along.

After a beat, I told her the truth. The words strangled my throat. "Nothing. I don't know what there is to believe in, anymore."

I led us down a flight of stairs that opened to the dining hall. The long oak tables were empty, and no sounds emanated from the attached kitchen. It was empty, as most members of the Order would be paying their devotions across the Temple in the prayer room at this time. I paused, needing to think.

Emma eyed the considerable length of the tables. "Wow for as many card-carrying members your Order has, I sure haven't seen many running around."

When Travis caught his breath, he asked, "Wait a minute, should we be running, here? I mean, I know they lied to you, man, and I'm sorry for you but this coming darkness thing is a big deal." His eyes drifted over to Emma.

She looked at me uncertainly. "He knows?"

I nodded.

"Wait," Travis blinked then held his hands up. "You knew?" He asked Emma.

She licked her lips nervously but didn't respond.

He spoke louder this time, demanding an answer. "You knew I was going to have to die to save the freakin' world and you didn't tell me? Answer me, Emma."

She swallowed and nodded her head. "I knew."

Betrayal strained his features. "And you didn't tell me? You helped him bring me here? I get why the brainwashed Terminator had to drag me here, he can't even wipe his ass without his Masters' permission."

Anger flashed in my chest like a whip, quick and hot. Never had I been so quick to enmity. I wanted to march over and punch him out like Emma had done, but instead I clenched my fists and kept them at my sides.

Perhaps I was so quick to anger because some of his vile observations contained seeds of truth. I was just a tool, a means to an end, and obedient dog begging for his whipping.

"But you, Emma?" Travis asked. "You helped him get me here and you knew it was to kill me? That is sick, man." His mouth curled in disgust.

Going on the defensive, Emma shot back, "Well, what the hell does it matter, Travis? Turns out, you aren't the doomed virgin. It's me, okay? I'm the doomed virgin. Are you happy now?"

Their fighting caused pain to lance through my head, but I knew it wasn't wise to jump in to try and stop a dog fight. You'd get your hand ripped off if you tried.

"No Emma, I'm not freakin' happy. You were willing to throw me into the volcano to save the world, but now that we've learned it's actually you, you're going to run?"

Emma sighed, her shoulders slumping. "Now that we're here, it doesn't feel right.

I don't want to throw my life away on the word of some mysterious, shady Order. I can honestly say I would do the same for you."

"We need to go now." I urged. There truly wasn't time for this. Gatsby would be up and about soon, motioning the entire Temple to track us down. There were two hundred people in this Temple, willing to die if it meant they could bring us to the Light.

Travis took a step back from us. "No."

CHAPTER TWENTY-NINE

"No?" I asked, not comprehending his rebell-iousness.

Travis took another step away from us. His eyes became glassy, and his shoulders shook as if under extreme stress. Red seeped up his neck then his face, making it look puffy. "No. I wouldn't even be here if it weren't for you. You dragged me all the way here and I have nothing to do with your creepy underground war. I wish I'd never met you." He ran a hand over his face then squared his shoulders as if getting a hold of himself. "But you know what? You shouldn't leave either," he said to Emma this time. "Sure, they lied to Calan about his soul…"

"I knew it," Emma shouted. Her head whipped around to grin at me in victory.

But I couldn't share her mirth. Later, I would untangle the lies and find out what was left of me. The smile on her face died when she saw my expression.

Travis went on, "But their book didn't. And the book also said the dark lord, whatever that is, is coming. It says if you don't make the sacrifice, the dark that comes will stay."

Emma held out her in hands, pleading. "Travis, we can't be sure they're right. These people have already shown corruption."

Travis yelled over her, causing Emma to snap her jaw shut. "And what if they are right?"

For the first time, I was tempted to respect him. All belief had fled me, but Travis stood with conviction and in that moment, I envied him the ability to clearly see to what was right and wrong, what must be done. But all I knew in that moment was I had to keep Emma safe and that Travis wasn't coming with us.

"We have to go," I said quietly to Emma, encircling her arm with my hand.

"Travis." she said, her face contorted in pain as though he had punched her in the gut. She didn't fight when I pulled her along, but could only slowly shuffle alongside me. I took us out the side door that led to the west wing.

As soon as we were out of sight, Travis screamed his head off. "They're here. This way. Help, they're getting away."

Emma finally broke into a full out run with me. Part of me understood Travis doing what he thought he had to do. The other part of me wanted to shake him until his face turned purple then his head fell off.

I led us to a parlor and went to the far wall. I splayed my hand on a particular spot then pushed. Stone scraped against stone as a secret door opened. I pulled Emma into the pitch black as the door closed behind us on its own.

Emma sniffled behind me, but I didn't have time to stop and dry her tears. Instead, I gently cautioned, "We are going down a stairwell. Watch your step. We have to be very careful. It curves down and around in a spiral." I kept my voice low, but my words still bounced around the stone walls.

She didn't answer. Distantly, a gong began to ring. They were raising the alarm to all the members of the Order to find us.

"Are you with me?" I asked, reaching in the black, trying to find her hand. When I found it, her fingers wrapped around mine.

"Yes, sorry. I nodded. Forgot you can't see me." Her voice sounded thick, like she had something caught in her throat.

I led her down the steps, quickly but quietly. As we neared the bottom, I prayed they hadn't anticipated my escape route. If they were waiting for us, I would have to fight our way out. It wasn't likely I'd survive the fight. There were too many members of the Order who would overwhelm me, especially if I would not kill them. If Gatsby anticipated us, it would be worse. He might force me to kill him. He had already tested such limits in training, putting me in kill or be killed situations until our Masters called him off.

Finally reaching the bottom, I pushed open the secret door leading to the back courtyard. No one was training or praying, so the well-manicured courtyard was empty right up to the oppressive, wild tree line of the jungle.

There was only one option. "We must flee into the jungle."

Emma's hand curled around my arm. "You don't seem sure of this."

Yelling arose inside the Temple, and I knew it wouldn't be long now.

"The jungle offers many dangers. But we will have a chance at survival in there. If we stay here, we forfeit that chance."

The memory of my trials always wrapped a tight cord around my chest. We were ten years old when the Chevalier were sent into the jungle for a fortnight, pitting us against the elements, wild animals, and our will to live. Knowing now the trials were meant to manipulate me, the cord squeezed with unrelenting fervor. I turned to Emma, her face giving me the scrap of strength I needed from the depths of her enquiring brown eyes.

"Then what are we waiting for?" She asked before running toward the thick tree line.

Our pursuers were gaining on us. Soaked in sweat and heavy humidity, the only sounds I could hear were the berserk chirps of birds and insects. They too seemed to know we were giving chase. There was also Emma's uneven, labored breathing as she tried to keep up without tripping into sink holes or over fallen branches. The humid air was heavy and sickening sweet with flowers and rotting dead plants, smothering me as I desperately tried to suck air into my burning lungs. I knew it must have been even harder for Emma, who was used to the cool, crisp, clean air of the mountains.

We were repeatedly slowed by having to climb over fallen ficus trees or navigate around the behemoth trunks of the trees still standing. There wasn't time to go back and cover our tracks. No time to mislead them in another direction, our only choice was to move as quickly as possible and pray we would find a spot to hide.

The logical part of my mind knew there was nowhere to hide. My Masters need only cast the spell of last light to find us. Granted they could only conjure the spell just as the sun hit the mountains on its descent from the

day to illuminate the missing, whether it was
an item or person they were trying to locate.
Judging from the slant of sunlight barely
breaking through the treetops, it wouldn't be
long before they could siphon that power into
a powerful spherical artifact. It was the same
spell they'd use to find the bodies of those
who did not survive the trials. Rather than let
the jungle swallow the failures, my Masters
would display them to the whole Order,
claiming they were never true to the Light.

I remember standing in line outside the
Temple with the four other remaining boys.
No longer were we just soulless heathen boys,
we were now Chevalier, Knights of the Light.
We'd been allowed to bathe, our wounds
tended, and we were given white linen
pajamas. So very different from the gray and
brown rags we had worn up until that point. I
had survived with three broken ribs, an
infected leg wound, and severe dehydration
which had me continually licking my lips with
a sandpaper tongue even as I stood in line. My
hair was slicked back, still wet from the bath,
just like others. I had chanced a glance at
Gatsby at the other end of the line. His blonde
hair was pulled back in a tight clean ponytail
but his face had a greenish tint to it. He was
covered in a sheen of sweat. He leaned against
a stick meant to prop him up but seemed
likely to plummet face-first into the ground
any minute. Gatsby suffered a snake bite,
which poisoned his blood, then he contracted

the jungle sickness. He had emerged from the trees raving mad, vomiting blood, but he made it the two weeks and they treated him for his illnesses. Standing in line at the ceremony, his face was screwed up in intense concentration, as if he was willing himself to keep conscious.

Our Masters had cast the spell of last light and members of the Order went directly to retrieve the bodies. As the sun disappeared behind the mountains, the sky lit up in brilliant red and orange streaks that seemed to mimic the slash wounds on the chewed-up bodies of our soulless brothers lying on the ground before us. Eight bodies. I was proud to have survived and knew the divine had been at work in the trials, but my chest hurt when I looked at the fallen so I kept my eyes slightly averted from looking directly at them.

"They did not believe." Master Ilsa's voice boomed from where she stood, on the small podium behind the line of corpses. The rest of our Masters were lined up to the side of the courtyard with grim, yet fiercely proud expressions on their faces. That year, there had been more survivors than any of the preceding trials. The rest of the members of the Order stood in rows behind us, the hoods of their robes pulled over their faces. They did not speak to the soulless ones.

The second time I chanced a glance at Gatsby, it was after the bodies had been brought out. His cheeks were covered in tears. They corrected him for that later.

"They did not believe in the Light," Master Ilsa was still speaking though it was hard to focus on her words. "And the hellfires of the Stygian came and claimed the nonbelievers. You remaining, may be soiled, soulless, and unworthy, but the gods have offered you the opportunity to prove yourselves. To serve the Light with your whole being and in turn, bestowed with that which you have lost."

Master Ylang's voice rumbled from just over my shoulder. I had been declared his ward, and was secretly grateful I had not been bound to Master Wu. "Look at them, Calan," he said, his voice both stern and soft in a way that confused me. "Do not shy away from the fate you escaped. You are not a man. Men have souls, but you are now a knight. You are a fighter, and you mustn't squander your opportunity to serve and redeem, where the fallen will now never know rest. Just do as you are told, and you'll know eternal glory once more." His touch on my shoulder was so light and brief, I wondered if it happened at all.

It was after that we were honed to siphon our devout belief of the Light into magic which would allow us to fight forces of the Stygian.

Running through the woods with Emma, it felt like I'd swallowed a rotten plum and it wouldn't go down past my throat. My eyes watered as I swallowed the acidity of my Order's lies. They had been just regular children. *I* was just a regular child. It had nothing to do with what we believed. I once heard a saying, 'thrown to the wolves.' That is what they did to us quite literally, except the beasts in these jungles were far more dangerous than a pack of mutts.

I glanced over at Emma. They wouldn't get her. I wouldn't let them. Not now, not ever.

Emma's face looked thin and haggard as she fought for breath and to keep up with me. She wasn't a trained warrior. From what I knew of civilians, few voluntarily pursued physical conditioning.

I wanted to tuck her into a safe place until her health and mind could be restored. Something in her broke when Travis accused her of abandoning her duty to save the world. A spike of heat shot through me as I thought of how Travis's opinion had affected her so. Perhaps she cared more for him than I could admit to myself.

I shook off the disturbing image of them locked in an embrace. Emma and I had shared multiple moments of intimacy, bound by a fated psychic connection. I knew where her desires lay. Still, a small part of me was scared to stop running because I didn't know if I could put Emma back together again. I didn't have the answers. She'd been following me around, as I promised answers and guidance, but now I had none left to give. If only I had my magic, I could open a portal for us to step through, leaving all this behind forever. But I couldn't. I wasn't even sure we'd last another ten minutes.

Leaves rustled overhead. Something was following us. Something not human.

Maybe less than ten minutes.

"Faster," I urged turning to grab Emma's hand, ready to drag her if need be.

"Calan." Her voice wavered.

She had already been pushed past her limits. Her soaked hair stuck to her forehead and neck, and her skin had paled to a sickly pallor under a sheen of sweat. The green tank top was darkened entirely from moisture. Her red-rimmed eyes met mine, she bit her lip, silently asking me to forgive her for her weakness.

The leaves overhead rustled louder this time.

"No, we cannot stop. I will not lose you." Before Emma could respond, I picked her up and threw her over my shoulder and broke into a run. Hampered by the obstacles of the forest, I was still too slow.

A growl emanated from the trees above, reminding me of a gravel grinder I once heard in the city. Instinctively, I dropped Emma and pulled my sword just as a creature crashed through the limbs above. Landing in front of us, was a jungle cat as large as a bear, with long powerful legs and cat ears covered in thick, dirty gray fur. Leaves rained down on its feral head. Its jaw unhinged with voracious hunger, allowing us a preview of a hundred needle-thin teeth, dripping with bloody saliva. It stank of freshly killed meat.

Emma yelped and backed away, only to hit a ficus tree. If we tried to get away, we'd have to have to get around the tree trunk which was almost fifty feet wide. The beast had cornered us. It rose onto its hind legs, the only thing between it and Emma was me, and I had already calculated the odds weren't in our favor in such close quarters.

The crack of a gun went off. The beast jerked with a roar. Frothy saliva flung every which way from its mouth, some smacking against my cheek. Another crack, then another, and another. The creature brayed in pain, turning to the nearest tree and climbed up and away, large splatters of blood plopping into the floor of dead leaves.

As it retreated, it opened my view to the gunman, or rather, gunwoman. Regina stood in the open door of a modified car, a rifle propped against her hip. It was a small, round car, with rusted, eggshell-blue paint. There were no windows and long mechanical legs protruded from underneath the cab, like that of a spider. Phillip sat in the driver's seat. They were both in their usual garb of black cat suits.

"Need a lift?" Regina asked, with a small knowing smile.

Phillip leaned over the passenger seat to catch my eye. "We have an outpost not far from here. It's hidden and protected against any casting."

I wiped the stinking goo off my cheek. That meant my Masters wouldn't be able to use a spell to find us. If we were walking into a trap, we could deal with that later, but right now we had to get away from the Luxis before last light. Before I could think too much, I turned around and grabbed Emma's hand and rushed us forward into their vehicle.

CHAPTER THIRTY

Emma sat quietly. Her face was still white and her hand lay limp in mine. I wished she were still wearing her thick pink glasses. I wanted a glimpse of the girl with a secret smile as she read. But the glasses, and her ease had long been left behind. We'd have to muddle on without either.

As if sensing her shock, Regina turned around as Phillip easily navigated the vehicle through the dense jungle. "The Luxis have their own designer monsters trolling the jungle."

Emma stuttered around her words then cleared her throat to speak more clearly. "You mean the Luxis made that *thing*?"

Phillip threw over his shoulder, "It keeps out unwanted visitors."

Regina and Phillip shared a secret smile, as if no place could truly keep them out.

It was then I remembered the last time I saw them, I had dead bolted them in a basement. I wondered if the family of the house came home and received a shock, finding a couple of strangers holed up in their basement, or if the agents of Veritas had found a different means of escape.

I looked out the window as we crawled through the jungle. Another stab of betrayal cut through me at Phillip's explanation. I didn't know the creatures had been designed. I had thought them indigenous to the area.

"They also used the creatures to hunt my brothers and me during the trials." I said out loud. "If we lived, we were proclaimed Chevalier. If we died, supposedly we were sent back to hell. I was aware the creatures in these jungles are both abnormally intelligent and blood thirsty. Knowing this now, I suppose you could say their presence also ensures the right people stay in."

Emma's hand tightened around mine finally. When I looked up, her gaze was full of such compassion, it hurt me in a whole new way. Pity. I was something to be pitied. I swallowed and tried to give her a reassuring look. Now that I'd left the fold, they couldn't hurt me anymore.

That's what I told myself.

Last light came just as we arrived at the tree house. I felt certain between the sigils painted all over the inside walls and the height of our position, over fifty feet up into the air, that we would not be found. The agents had also climbed the car up into the limbs of a nearby tree, leaving it under a cover of many branches.

Regina sat on a stool near the small stone fireplace which cast dancing light onto the whole interior of the shack. They assured me they cast a concealment spell to hide any evidence of smoke. I was still doubtful. Phillip laughed, a deep, rich sound that sounded strangely familiar to me. I wasn't sure if that was because I knew it from a lifetime ago, or if it resembled my own. I had only experienced maybe two or so belly laughs like that in my lifetime.

The only time I could recall was when Master Ylang slipped on a plantain peel in the courtyard. Master Violetta had been walking by and I was outside training. At first, Master Violetta's laugh emerged as a sharp snort, and then another. Soon, she couldn't help but throw her head back, her hands emerging from her robes to brace herself against her knees and laugh at Master Ylang as he slowly got up, rubbing his backside. A similar snort emerged from my own nose, and it took me several moments to realize Violetta was imbuing me with humor. It was contagious. Master Ylang glared at her for a moment before he began to laugh, too. Soon the three of us were laughing so hard, Master Ylang had to lean against a small flowering tree to keep himself upright. When Master Violetta wiped away some moisture from her eyes, we all managed to cease our laughter. I remembered it feeling wonderful, and it empowered the remainder of my practice though we never spoke of the incident again.

A sharp feeling of loss cut deeply through me as the memory our laughter was violently interrupted by the rush of knowledge that they had been lying to me. Even though they raised me, made me strong, I was nothing more than a tool to them. An obedient dog, told my only choice was to serve them. I pushed down the dark confusing feelings of loss inside myself, hoping to never taste their bitterness again.

When Phillip's laughter died down, he said, "If you think you aren't keen on being caught by the Luxis, imagine the many brave souls of Veritas who came to this outpost so near their enemy. No one has been caught here yet."

"You mean brave spies?" I asked, lifting an eyebrow.

He shrugged with an easy smile then disappeared to do a sweep of the perimeter.

We had been offered clean water to drink and wash with. Emma passed out on the straw cot in the corner. The stress had taken its toll on her. I gently removed the now-empty tea mug dangling from her hand and set it on the crudely carved table in the middle of the tree house.

Meanwhile, Regina sat on the stool, sharpening her knife, doing so with an absentminded precision, indicating it was a task she did often. She kept her eyes on me though I did not start conversation. Fifteen minutes later, Phillip ducked back in through the doorway.

"They are miles away and off track."

I nodded then looked into the fire. After a long moment of wrestling with myself, I asked, "Why would they do it? Why would they take me from you?"

Regina sucked in a breath, and Phillip closed his eyes as if in prayer. They were relieved to find I'd finally arrived at the truth. Though I hadn't, not truly. To look upon the faces of these strangers and know they were my parents… it didn't set with me. They didn't feel like my parents. They were still just strangers.

"Of the five Orders," Regina said looking down at her glinting blade. "The Veritas and Luxis have battled each other most fervently the last two hundred years."

Phillip wryly chuckled. "Often we share the same goal, to serve the Light, but we use different means to achieve it."

"We seek the same resources." Regina said, now flipping her knife over her hand and catching it in her palm over and over again, in a practiced move. "The same texts, the same objects of power, and there is no compromise to be found on either side as to their use."

I finally allowing myself to sit down at the bench set against the table to absorb their story. My muscles and bones ached, not only from running -- they didn't feel like they were set right. I felt like a wooden marionette put together all wrong.

Though the jungle was cooling and the fire was small, I felt like I was suffocating. When the heat finally became too much, I fluidly pulled off my armored, long sleeved black shirt, stripping down to a white tank top.

"Twenty-four years and six months ago," Phillip said, "we fought over the Orb of Thesis. It was a powerful object that would fuel a powerful person with the sight."

"The sight?" I asked.

"The ability to see into the future," Phillip supplied. He stayed standing in the doorway, his body erect, actively guarding us.

Regina continued, "The order of Luxis discovered the object, but Phillip and I had followed them and stolen the orb in the dead of night." Regina stopped flipping her knife, her wrists going limp as her head bowed. "So they retaliated, coming under cover of the dead of night and stealing something of ours in turn."

"You," Phillip clarified.

When Regina looked up, fire burned in her blue eyes. "We walked right up to the Temple and banged down their doors until they let us in. I tore the place apart looking for you, but they continued to claim they did no such thing. I never found you." Her eyes suddenly showed their age. Her life had been hard, and where she looked healthy and young for her age, it was her eyes that betrayed all she had endured.

My understanding was losing a child was one of the most difficult travesties a person could undergo. It was strange to realize I was the object of such pain. It became too much to look at such naked emotion, so I turned my focus back to the fire.

"Did it work?" Emma asked behind me. I turned around and saw she was awake and had been listening. On one side of her head, the hair was smashed flat against it from where she had been resting. For whatever reason, emotion swelled inside of me.

"Did what work?" Phillip asked Emma.

"The Orb of Thesis," Emma said. "Did it help you see into the future?"

Philip looked off in the distance, as if recalling the events of what happened. "One of our most powerful Elders used it. Since Regina and I had been the ones to retrieve the Orb, and it came at such a great cost to us, he used it to find out what happened to our child."

Regina's voice was rough as she continued to stare at me in an unerring fashion. "Though we were certain the child had been slain by the Luxis."

Phillip said, "The light of the Orb engulfed our Elder and as he was infused with the power of sight, he turned to us and declared we would one day find our child, a grown man. When the barrier was thin, our son would be at the center of the chaos."

Regina's eyes closed. "The fall of the dark children would herald our son's return and that is when we would discover our child again."

The Crib. The dark children were the Crib, which is why they had doggedly followed us.

Regina looked over at Phillip, "But then the Elder burned from the inside out."

"The Orb was a one-time shot," Phillip shrugged, "but we didn't know that. I'm sure our Order wouldn't have been so generous with granting us the first sight if they had known."

"But he was right," Regina straightened in her chair. "As soon as creatures from the Stygian crossed over, we found you, my son. At the center of it all." Her eyes shifted over to Emma, and I felt uncomfortable letting this woman look at Emma. "And we found the Propheros with you. It can't be coincidence."

Regina stared at Emma like she coveted her, like Emma was a thing, but she wasn't a thing. Emma was dynamic, fragile but so incredibly strong. She was the most alive person I'd ever known. In all the darkness, she *was* the Light. My Light. I had to keep her safe at all cost.

Emma sat up all the way on the cot, swinging her legs over the side. Her brown eyes were no longer red-rimmed, though there was slight bruising under her eyes from lack of rest. Even under great stress, she was the most beautiful thing I had ever beheld. It pained me to see her slowly unraveling the further we traveled together. If I could stop everything for her, I would do so instantly.

"Then you both know the sacred book or whatever it is, says I have to die to save the world," her voice was hard and bitter.

Regina reared back as if she had been slapped. "Die? Our job is to make sure that exact thing does not happen." She sheathed her knife then shoved it in her belt.

"But Calan read it in the book," Emma said.

Regina raised an eyebrow at me, pinning me with a look. It took everything not to squirm under her gaze. "They let you read?"

"No. I solicited the help of someone else."

I caught the look on Emma's face. She looked shell shocked. "You can't read?"

CHAPTER THIRTY-ONE

I shook my head. "No, it was not my place."

Emma sat up straighter, her elbows locked as her hands gripped the side of the straw cot. "But I saw you read." Her eyes moved away from mine, searching the tree house wall as if trying to call up a specific memory. When she grabbed the information she needed, she looked back at me. "You read at the diner, when you ordered food."

I slowly shook my head. "I learned quickly in my travels that most establishments carry vegetables and proteins, so I know what to ask for depending on the region."

Emma stared at me, her jaw slack in horrified awe over the fact I was illiterate. Shame buzzed uncomfortably in my forehead and made my chest tight with anxiety.

Regina explained to Emma. "The order of Luxis is the only Order that created its own army. It's better if they don't teach their soldiers to think for themselves."

The corners of my mouth tightened. The way she described me with such little regard angered me, but I couldn't disagree with her assessment now that I knew the truth.

Emma reared back. "How many Chevalier are there?"

My parents looked to me for the answers. I struggled to respond. It felt like a betrayal to number the Chevalier in case the agents of Veritas sought to destroy us. I firmly reminded myself the Luxis were not worth protecting, and I was no longer of their ilk. They lied to my brothers, as well as me. We were innocents. The concept I was an innocent, not a soulless monster, was still almost impossible to reconcile. "Last I connected with my brothers there were still five of us. Though I would not be informed if one of them had perished in battle, unless we were all gathered at the Temple."

"Army, huh?" Emma rose her eyebrows at my parents. They too seemed surprised by the answer.

"Do not underestimate them," Phillip cautioned. "There may only be five, but their belief and their will is molded to be single-minded. They believe more devoutly in the mission than any member of the Order, even more than their Masters." The word Masters rolled off his tongue as if the word were made of poison.

"Single-minded fanatics," Regina said. Then she looked at me, guilt pulling on her face in an awkward way. "No offense, my son."

I tried to brush off her continued objective description of myself and my brothers, but it still crawled under my skin. That's what I was to everyone else. A mindless fanatic.

Phillip rubbed his chin thoughtfully and said to Emma, "I suppose you could consider them to be like one of your military's special forces, but a force unto themselves. It is their unerring belief in their Order that gives them the power of fifty times what we access." He gestured to Regina and himself. "It is why Luxis has maintained its position as the most powerful Order."

I brought the conversation back to relevance, no longer wanting the talk about myself as if I weren't present to continue. "I had Travis read for the book me, and indeed he confirmed the Propheros must sacrifice herself to save us from the coming darkness. When the night sky becomes ill, we shall know the time has come. Where the earth breaks, the Dark Lord shall journey in a fortnight's time to set foot upon the dirt of the earth."

Phillip walked over to his wife and put a hand on her shoulder. "What you read, I mean, what your friend read, is not the sacred text."

"Yes, it was. I can verify…"

Regina cut me off, "No, he means that it couldn't have been the sacred text because the great sacred text was destroyed centuries ago. Ages ago, there were five men who studied and interpreted the great text but when a fire swallowed the original book up, the men separated with their interpretations, unable to agree on anything with the original text gone. They formed the five Orders. I wouldn't be surprised if the version you read isn't even a more recent iteration of that interpretation, especially if your friend was able to read it."

"So I don't have to die?" Emma asked, hope lighting her voice.

I couldn't help but revel in the warm bristle of hope in my chest, as well.

Phillip's grip tightened on Regina's shoulder. "On the contrary, it is with your life that the darkness shall be defeated. Not your death."

Emma nodded to herself, thinking it over. "Okay sure, still a lot of pressure, saving the entire freaking world and all that jazz, but it can't be so bad if I get to live." She gave me a crooked smile.

I tried to return it, but it felt false and unnatural on my lips. Something didn't feel right. Maybe it was having my faith torn from my body, though my soul, or at least the idea of my soul, had been returned to me. All I wanted to do was whisk Emma far and away out of harm, where the two of us could sit and dine on a blanket like in my fantasy. I could kiss and explore her beautiful body, disappearing into her while becoming alive.

"Son," Phillip said, ripping me from my fantasy. "You shall work with us. You shall return to the fold of the Veritas and work against those who deceived you for so long." As he spoke of the Luxis, his eyes darkened.

I was distrustful after all I'd learned, and it compelled me to turn down Phillip's proposition. But I reminded myself that I should not separate myself from others with judgment, that is how I separated from the Light.

Cold realization sliced through my conditioned response.

I didn't know the Light. I would never know the Light. It was all a lie, and what did it matter what I thought or believed? I was already whole, I had a soul. Though I couldn't have felt further from it. I felt as though I'd broken into pieces and I'd never find a way to put myself back together again.

I looked at Regina and Phillip. They seemed to want me. They seemed to care for me. They wanted me to go with them into their Order. Something inside me awoke. A deep yearning to belong to a family. A real one, not one I was indentured in servitude to. My new family could make the world make sense again. A relief swept through me, turning my bones into softened butter at the prospect of having someone tell me what was right once more, so I could know what must be done.

Emma stood up and crossed the distance between us so she could lay her hands on my shoulders. I further melted into her comfort, feeling like things were going to be okay again.

"So your Order is going to take him in, just like that?" Emma asked, snapping her fingers, skepticism heavy in her voice.

Something hardened in Regina's eyes as if Emma had challenged her. "Well obviously, he must prove himself to be worthy to our Order. We can say he's on our side all we want, but some members may believe him to be a spy."

"How does he prove himself?" Emma asked for me.

Regina continued to stare at Emma as if seeing her for the first time. Phillip spoke to me, pausing to carefully pick his words. "He must kill his Masters."

Emma gasped. "All of them?" Emma had been interviewed by the council of Masters, as I had. Though she couldn't know what they were truly made of, she must have sensed their power. They were not powerful like the Chevalier, but together they cast strong magic. It was only used in great times of need.

Phillip shook his head. "Only his siring Master."

Emma looked down at me for an answer.

I cleared my throat, realizing I hadn't spoken in a while. "We are each assigned a sire, who is primarily in charge of our orders, or corrections."

She lifted an eyebrow and the corners of her sweet, pink lips pulled down at the corners. "You mean whippings."

She didn't miss much. Though whippings were not the only means of correction. If I were to go back, there was an entire room dedicated to extracting information from spies or to correct the most wayward member of the Order. It was rarely used, but I knew they would use every single device in that room on me if we went back now.

"You require me to kill Master Ylang?" I clarified, unsure of how I felt about their demand.

Regina's teeth ground audibly. "No doubt, it is your Master Ylang who is responsible for ordering your kidnapping. For he was the one we robbed of the Orb of Thesis. That he assumed the place of your keeper sickens me to the core. It should you too. He has stolen your life and for that, death would be a blessing compared to what he deserves."

I remembered the sickening lurch in my stomach when my blade came close to ending Emma.

"I don't want to kill anyone." To my own ears, I sounded like a lost child. I stood up, quicker than I intended, as if I could shake off the weakness I felt. Emma's hand slid away from my shoulders and I regretted the loss, but I couldn't think straight sitting down.

"Son," Phillip countered, "It is the only way for you to join the true Order. Don't you want to come home with us? Don't you want to belong with us?"

That yearning that already pulled at my guts, yanked at me ten-fold. *Yes, yes,* my inner self cried. *You can tell me what to do and you will be so very pleased with me.*

Regina's eyes pled with me. They seemed full of hope for our future. "You can come home, son. It is such a small thing that is required." Her words slithered around me like a snake's. But she was my mother. Why should I distrust her?

"He's not a killer," Emma said flatly.

Regina stood up in a challenging posture. Though she was considerably shorter than Emma, she was lithe and deadly. "How do you know what he is or isn't? From my understanding, you have barely known him longer than we have." Her chin was set regally, but her eyes leaked danger.

"You're right," Emma said, taking a step back from the compact predator that was my mother. "But I'm the only one who doesn't want to use him to destroy my enemies or do my evil bidding." Her eyes fastened on me, and everyone else followed suit.

Would they be using me? Did I care as long as I knew what to do? What did I want?

I wanted to belong again, to know what was right, but something cautioned me to not to speak that out loud, so I remained silent.

Emma turned to Phillip. "I'm betting he gets that strong silent vibe from scary mama bear over here," she jerked her head toward Regina. The barest ghost of a smile appeared on Phillip's face before Regina's sharp glare chased it away.

"Fine," Emma said, sitting down on the small bench and leaning in to the table. "While blue eyes over there works out what he wants, I have some questions. If there are five interpretations, how do you know yours is the right one? Has stuff from your interpretation been the only stuff that comes true, or have events been right from the others? Do you have like a percentage of accuracy?"

Regina's lips tightened. "Of course, we are the truest of any of the interpretations."

Emma's eyes narrowed, to better study my mother's face. She was in full-on interrogation mode. "You didn't answer. Have events ever been right according to the other Orders and not to yours?"

"Don't you worry about that, my dear," Phillip said, casually propping his hands on his hips. "We know what must be done."

The questions Emma asked created a snake of unease that wriggled in my belly. I stood then walked over to the window behind us, looking out at the shadowed trees and below. The window cutouts were large and lacking panes of glass like the car with legs. The sigils painted on the treehouse not only repelled magic, it seemed to repel the violent creatures who might try to creep into the treehouse for a delicious meaty meal. I wished Emma would stop her questions, but she carried on.

"And what does your order plan to do with me?" she asked. "Since I'm supposed to live, what am I to do now?"

Regina and Phillip exchanged a look.

I only barely caught it. I turned around to face them. "Answer her question." When they did not, I said, strain tightening my jaw, my hand moving to the broadsword at my side, "If you do not tell the truth, I may start the killing with you." It was an empty threat but I was out of patience.

"We do not lie." Regina stood, offended. "We are the order of Veritas, the wheel house of truth. It is your precious house of light that seeks to bend the truth to whatever whim they see fit." She turned to Emma. Her birdcage-sized ribs puffed up with pride. "It is with your life that we destroy the coming darkness. You will be able to fight back the demons."

Emma looked over at me like Regina had gone insane before turning back to her. "I'm pretty sure if anyone is qualified to fight dark demons it's tall, soulful, and handsome over there." She jerked her thumb toward me.

I suppressed a smile. So much had been going on, I hadn't fully considered that my options with Emma were so very different now, since I had a soul. And if my parents were to protect her life, we would finally have a place to be together. Maybe we could all fight the Stygian together. Like a family. My mind moved awkwardly around the concept. I'd had an Order, but it wasn't the same as a family. My understanding was that families took care of each other before their own needs. *I could do that*, a small voice inside of me cried out.

But I would have to kill someone. I tried to brush off the idea that I would be killing my father, but it was difficult seeing as Master Ylang was the closest thing I had to one. He lied to me and used me, but I didn't know that I wanted to kill him. My temples throbbed from all the conflicting wants battling it out in my head. I pressed a finger to my temple hoping to relieve some of the pain.

Phillip took a step forward. "You would be conditioned for battle."

Emma wrinkled her nose, then stood, shifting her weight back and forth between either foot. "I'm not really the bootcamp type."

Something about the way Phillip said it didn't indicate to me Emma would be forced to do pushups. I dropped my fingers from my Temple. "What do you mean, conditioned?"

Regina walked over to the fire, setting a hand along the narrow ledge above it, she stared into the flames. "To fight darkness, you must know its truth. It is not enough to see the dark, you must *know* the dark." When she brought her head up, the light was behind her, casting shadows over face, making her expression indistinguishable. "When the time comes, you will become the dark to defeat it."

A chill scraped up my spine. Emma stepped closer to me as if she too had gotten inexplicably cold.

"Yeah, but what does that mean?" Her hand wrapped around my bicep as if steeling herself for the answer.

Phillip folded his hands together. "We shall call a reckoning."

"Okaaay." Emma drew the word out. "Still don't know what that means."

But I did.

"No." It came out just above a whisper, ripping its way out of my throat though I wanted to scream at them. It felt like I was falling into an abyss. My stomach clenched as if it could stop its invisible descent but I kept plummeting.

Emma's hand tightened on my bicep, frustrated to be left out of the conversation. "Tell me."

Even the thought of it tore my heart in two. "The reckoning is punishment for those who have turned away from the Light."

Regina's head snapped up. "It is not a punishment as they would have you believe." Her chin rose with haughty pride. "It is an honor bestowed upon the bravest warrior in the gravest of times. It gives the warrior strength to defeat the darkness by becoming it."

Emma said carefully, "Uh yeah, I don't think I want to become darkness."

I turned to Emma and held her gently by her shoulders, belying the tension wracking my body at the very idea of what they were suggesting.

"They will lock you in chains and call forth a malevolent spirit from the Stygian. It will pass through you over and over again, giving you a taste of its hell, infecting you, until you are driven mad by the darkness."

"It is not an infection." Phillip frowned. "It shares its energy, its powers with the chosen one."

Without turning away from Emma, I said, "It will strip her of her humanity. She will become a savage beast, an unholy weapon as you put it. Correct me if I am wrong."

Silence fell.

I licked my lips. They were suddenly so dry, it was hard to speak. My voice was as hard as a cold stone at the bottom of a river.

"I have seen it with my own eyes. A member of our Order had been found a traitor to the Light. Though I did not know his crimes, we were all made to watch his reckoning. For his crime of choosing the darkness, the Luxis proclaimed they would grant him passage straight into hell, since that was what he desired." I closed my eyes against the memory of his screams as the dark spirit passed through him over and over again until his eyes had turned wild and red. When he was no longer human, he snarled and hissed, lunging when they tried to move him, attempting to rip the guts out from anything and everything. They confined him in chains in a shack at the edge of the jungle. After three days, they found him dead, having chewed off his own arm to escape, he bled to death in the process.

A giggle broke through the silence. Then another louder one, until soon, Emma was doubled over laughing.

CHAPTER THIRTY-TWO

W hen Emma managed to get ahold of herself, wiping tears from her eyes, she managed to speak through the last few unhinged giggles.

"So let me get this straight. My options are to either die to save the world, or to stay alive and be tortured until my humanity is ripped from me." Her voice hit a hysterical pitch which made Travis's face flash through my mind. "All so I can keep the darkness from coming, whatever that means. Which, by the way, no one has ever said what it means." By the end, she was shouting. Two tears rolled from her eyes and raced each other down her cheeks. Her arms hugged at either elbow as if she was afraid she would blow away into pieces at any moment.

Phillip's eyes crinkled in wariness of her strange behavior. "Well, it certainly doesn't point to anything good, does it?"

Emma's voice had dropped, her words coming out hoarse now. "No, I suppose not. And you want Calan over here to become a murderer so he can get rid of your Order's problems?"

Regina's small hands balled into fists, blue veins along the tops of them protruding from her tight grip. "They have treated him abominably. The Luxis have turned him into a weapon against us."

Emma snorted with derision at Regina, as if she were lower than pond scum. "You're just pissed he wasn't your weapon. Hell, you want to make me into a weapon. Let's everybody be weapons," She waved her hands around, then dropped them to her sides. "You don't care about him as your son. You just want one more soldier for your ranks. You want to use him to make the Luxis suffer."

I took a step back, the words slapped me in the face, disorienting me. When I came to my senses, Regina and Phillip looked at me pleadingly. They could see Emma's words had affected me. They seemed to recognize it before I did, but following the shock, realization came like pile of bricks upon my head.

"No, no, son," Phillip implored. "We need you, we have missed you. You just have to do this small task, then we can take you back into the fold."

"To do what?" Emma growled at them, which was unnerving considering her slight frame. "To force him to continue to play spy against his old Order? How long before you send him back to kill another one of his Masters? How long before you send him into the Temple, only he knows so well, to steal things your Order needs? Your loyalty is entirely to your Order. It's not to your son. He's just an afterthought. Your Order is just as manipulative as the Luxis." Her face screwed up in disgust. "It is actually almost worse that you are so openly honest about it."

"Do not speak of the order of Veritas in such a way." Phillip's voice boomed through the small wooden house.

My heart sank into my stomach. Phillip looked at me, realizing his mistake. He showed where his one true devotion lie.

"She's right," I said, the words soft to my own ears. "I am just a tool to you. Just as I was to the Luxis. I'm something you can bring to your Order as an offering of service. Revenge for what was taken from you."

Regina rushed up to me, and Emma stepped back allowing it. My mother reached up, clutching at my shoulders, forcing me to look down into her perfectly matching blue eyes. How I could have ignored the familial resemblance before seemed preposterous to me now. "You can come home. You'll have a home. We can work together. We can be united in our hate for the Luxis. Don't you want revenge?"

"No." I gently removed her hands off me. "I know what I want now. I don't want to fight anymore." I looked up at Emma. She swallowed hard and set her chin, she knew my pain. She always seemed to know my pain.

Regina's eyes darted back and forth between mine, looking for a shred of give, but when she did not find it, her expression hardened, bringing out all the lines in her face. "You may not have a choice."

"She is wrong, my son," Phillip said, not done trying yet. "We do care about you." His voice was strained, and his eyes too hungry all of a sudden.

"Then what is his name?" Emma asked softly.

I turned to look at her, and saw she stared at my father with open disappointment.

"His name?" Phillip asked, perplexed.

"You haven't even asked what his name is."

"You want us to call him by the name *they* gave him?" Regina spit the words.

I worked to clear my face of any emotion and pulled my shoulders back. "I named myself. They do not give damned, soulless children names, we are merely wards to the Masters. So we gave them to ourselves after

our third mission in the world." Before
Regina could open her mouth again, I said, "I
will not fight this war anymore. I don't want
any part in your squabbles. I just want Emma
and me to be left in peace." I nodded to her, to
indicate we were leaving. Emma stepped in
closer to me. "Don't try to follow us, or I'll be
forced to show you the true nature of single-
minded fanaticism."

Regina's face cooled like a lake freezing
over, smoothing itself of any lines or emotion.
Phillip squared his shoulders and came to
stand next to Regina, only the crude table
between us. "I'm sorry my son, but surely you
realize we cannot let her leave. The Propheros
must undergo the reckoning. It is our only
hope."

I saw his hand move to his belt toward his
knife, while my mother reached into her pants
pocket. Her fist was closed around something,
but through the fingers I saw pale green,
glowing light. She had a sacred object with
her, just as I carried moonstones.

I looked down at Emma's face. It was
etched in defiance toward my parents and I
could have kissed her right then just to feel
how alive she was, and for courage, but I
resisted. Instead, I flicked my eyes behind us
toward the large window opening. Her lips
tightened and I knew she understood.

"Well then," I said slowly, turning to face
my parents again while taking a few steps
backward with Emma. They advanced in

kind, but they were too late. "You better figure out a plan B," I said, mimicking the informality in which Emma and Travis spoke. With that I grabbed Emma's arm and yanked her along with me as I dove backward out the open window.

CHAPTER THIRTY-THREE

I heard the sound of someone tripping over the table and watched as a green light zoomed just over my body as we fell away from the treehouse. It came so close, I felt a numbing tingle emanate from it. It was meant to paralyze me, but they were too late. I felt rather than heard Emma stifle a scream as we fell. I grasped her hand harder before letting go. I spun in the air until I was falling face down, then closed my eyes, and waited for the inevitable.

We hit the sticky net hard, but it was rigid enough that it dipped less than ten feet under our weight before springing us back up. By my estimate, there were still thirty feet between us and the ground. The web had only two corners, giving it the appearance of an oversized hammock. Having deliberately fallen toward one of the two taut corners of the web, the spring had been less giving and my body immediately bruised from the hard impact.

The web was wet, hairy, and sticky, which aggravatingly itched my bare arms. The powerful stench of formaldehyde burned my nose. If I pulled hard enough, I could get unstuck, but I wouldn't be able to move fast enough if my plan was to continually unstick myself while moving toward Emma to get us out of here.

"I can't move," Emma said, panic climbing in her voice but I could hear her fight it. Indeed, we could not, the net was fiercely viscid and my clothes, neck and face were adhered to it. The covering of the tree tops blocked out any light, so even when my eyes adjusted to the pitch black, I still couldn't see much.

"Don't worry," I said with a grunt. "We won't be here long." When I had turned around in the air, I brought my sheathed sword to the front of my body. With my hands wrapped around it, I was able to pop the hilt up with a sharp metal scraping sound and use the exposed bit of blade to cut at the gather of web that led to one of the trees it clung to.

"Your parents are coming down," Emma said.

They descended toward us, my mother's fist still emitting a pale green light, slightly illuminating the web as I worked on it. She would be moving slower, expending a great deal of energy to keep the power active.

The web was as thicker than a three-strand rope, but I kept sawing away with my sword.

"Yes, well, didn't think they would give us up so easily, did you? After all, if they go back, they will have to tell their elders the *truth,*" I mocked.

"Did you almost make a joke just then?"

I paused very briefly but went right back to cutting through the thick sticky strands. "Yes, I believe I was in danger of it."

"You know, for a second there, I thought maybe we were jumping out a window to… to jump out of a window. But then I told myself you would have a plan, if I just trusted you." She seemed to be talking to calm herself down. "And you did have a plan. Well one that didn't involve killing ourselves rather than be taken alive. Oh hey, I got my arm off…. aaand it's stuck back down."

The net moved underneath us. It was too soon for my parents to have reached it as it would require a careful climb down several trees to reach the net. When I'd caught sight of the web as I gazed out the window of the treehouse, I had also noticed they had cut away most limbs of the nearby trees to keep anyone or anything from climbing toward them.

I kept sawing, but lifted my gaze to see what had gotten on the net. "Yes, but I'm still not sure you're going to like my plan."

"What do you mean? Man, you must be cutting away at that thing. But hurry, your parents are halfway down."

"I have good news and bad news. Which would you prefer first?" I'd heard the expression used twice before and felt it fitting for the moment. Beads of sweat popped out on my forehead as I doubled my efforts.

"Good news. I could really use some good news after all this bullshit, right about now. Lay it on me, hot stuff." She was doing her best to sound bold, but she couldn't keep her voice from trembling.

"All right. The good news is I've almost cut through an essential corner of the net."

"Good, because they are really booking it our way. Damn, you got this thing shaking."

"You see, that is where the bad news comes in. The bad news is this is an oversized arachnid's net and he'll think we've come to be his dinner."

Emma swallowed audibly. "Then I guess we better get the hell out of here before it gets home."

"I should have mentioned the bad news has two parts. He is home. That is what's making the net shake so badly." I was able to just make out Emma's head tilt in the direction of the creature straining the net. I was sure in the dark she could still make out long, hairy legs about five feet long, and she may have been able to see some of the fat, purple body. But even if she didn't, she could definitely see the thirty, milky yellow eyes blink hungrily at her.

"Okay, time to go," she shouted. "Time to go, right now."

The creature shrieked back at her, making me wish I had use of my hands to cover my ears.

I was glad it wasn't light enough for Emma to see its gaping maw filled with tiny jagged teeth. I only knew what it looked like from when I had encountered its horde during my trials. However, I had spotted them first and knew to go around their den.

Two more bounces came from the opposite side of the net.

"Quickly, let us help you," Phillip said. "We'll get you out."

From the bounce of the net, I knew they were hurrying toward Emma, though the arachnid stood between them. I wasn't sure how they could walk on the net but my guess was they had attire equipped to use these webs as a means of travel when they were empty of their owners. The creature whipped around and screeched at the intruders interrupting its dinner.

"The point was to get you in," I said. With a final grunt, I cut the last thread of the net's corner. One whole side dropped, slamming the remaining net and us against a tree. My cheek slammed into the rough bark, knocking the wind from me. I heard Emma's *oof* somewhere above me on the net. Where Emma and I were still stuck to the net, my parents bellowed as they were dropped down and out of sight, the creature screaming as it fell after them.

"Oh god," Emma breathed after a few heartbeats. "Are they dead?"

"No," I said, managing to angle my head down. Glowing green light was being hurled at the creature below. "I just needed to give them something else to focus on other than you." If the creature was violent before, it was positively incensed now. It wouldn't go down without a hell of a fight.

Slowly and painstakingly, I pulled myself off the web and started my way toward Emma. "What do you say we get out of here?"

"I say if you get me out of here, I'll let you do anything you want to me, stud muffin." Her voice was shaky despite her half attempt at humor. I couldn't say her incentive didn't speed up my efforts.

CHAPTER THIRTY-FOUR

"There." I pointed for Emma to follow. A break in the trees aimed the full moon's glow directly onto a cave entrance. She weakly nodded next to me, likely to agree with anything I directed us to do at this point. "I'll go first," I murmured before holding her by the shoulders and dropping a kiss on her head.

Emma closed her eyes at the contact, her arms wrapping around each other as if it was all she could do to hold herself up. I crouched to crawl into the cave through its small entry, which I noted would also make it harder for predators to get through. It opened into a larger cavern that was just right for the two of us. It had long been abandoned by whatever had lived there. Probably eaten, no doubt. The cave would be safe for us tonight.

"Oh my." Emma breathed after she ducked in after me. Her eyes turned upward as she took in the unusual sight. The cave's interior was engulfed in soft blue glow. Countless blue slugs clung to the walls, emitting the soft light. Emma mused about their bioluminescence.

I would have asked her to explain what that was, but I was too tired, positive I was unable to absorb any more information for the day. Maybe for the rest of my life. The center of my bones ached, and my throat begged for cool water.

Emma sat against a side of the cave not covered in slugs, arms wrapping around her knees. The blue light on Emma's face enhanced her appearance of being closed off. Since we escaped the web, it was like she switched off the valve to her emotions. It disturbed me more than I could say. I feared she was hardening from the inside out.

I sat next to Emma and wrapped her up in my arms. Instantly she released her knees, leaned into me and closed her eyes. I sighed in relief when reached back for me.

"It's just too much. It's all too much," she murmured.

I ran my calloused fingers through her hair. Even the tangles from running through the jungle didn't detracted from how soft it was.

"What is?" I asked, not truly paying attention. My mind was in a fog, and all I wanted to focus on was the feel of Emma curled safely into my side. Inhale the faint vanilla of her hair, mixed in with sweat, and her unique, intoxicating scent that was imprinted on me for all of eternity.

"Everything is. Me being the Propheros, you losing your powers, being lied to by your Order your whole life, everyone hunting us down," her words slowed. "Travis choosing to side with the Luxis."

Again, I was confused as to the depth he had wounded her. "Are you so bothered by what he did because you have feelings for him?"

Emma's head reared back and off my chest to shoot me a look of disgust before swatting me on the chest. "Ew, no. Gross. Besides, I thought I made it very clear who I have feelings for." She blushed at the end.

I nodded and touched her soft cheek so she would look me in the eye. "Then explain to me why he has upset you so."

"Because what if he's right?" Her words were strangled, as if her body could barely bear to let the thought out into the real world. "What if the Luxis, or the Veritas, or whoever, is right about the darkness coming? Which, let's face it, sounds like the end of the world. Then it's my job to figure out who is right, and then do what needs to be done." Her arm wrapped around mine and her fingers tapped along my forearm in agitation.

I stiffened next to her, but my hand resting on her knee, tightened. "You mean die."

She shook her head. "I mean save the freakin' world. Whatever that means." Then she said quietly, accompanied with a small bark of laughter, "Like how all the heroes and heroines do the right thing in my books. Except it's not like it is in the books. We might not find a way out of this. We might not get our H.E.A." Any trace of a smile slid off her eyes and mouth. She looked hollow and haunted. As if the past week had clapped an anchor on her soul and it was slowly drowning her.

"H.E.A?" I asked.

"Happily ever after." Her hands tightened on my arm, clutching me closer to her.

"What is that?"

"What is happily ever after you mean?" At first her face was incredulous as it was when she'd discovered I was illiterate. Then it morphed into sadness. She reached up and brushed the hair away from where it dipped on my forehead. Her thin, chipped fingernails lightly scratched up further at my scalp. I never wanted her to stop. "It means that you've found a way to solve all your problems and you get to be with the person you love and stay in love forever."

I spoke slowly, trying to comprehend what she'd just told me. It was difficult with her ministrations. "Does that really happen?" Despite my deep voice, it came out as a timid whisper, as if I was afraid to hear the truth. It almost perfectly described how I imagined it would feel to have my soul returned to me, but I never had a term for it. But now that I had my soul after all, I couldn't have felt things were further from a happily ever after. I was with the one I loved but our problems hunted and plagued us.

Emma licked her lips and leaned her head back against the cave wall. Her arm wound back around mine again. "I don't know. I think so, in a way. My parents were in love their whole life together, but I guess there are still problems that can't be avoided. My mom died in a car crash, and well," she paused as if her words pained her. "I guess my dad is gone now, too. But for a while there, things were really great. And even after my mom died, my dad said it broke his heart, but he wouldn't do anything different."

She turned away. "Then he said some mushy stuff about how she gave him the greatest gift of all, which was me." Her fingers automatically reached up to touch the pendant that had fallen under her shirt.

For some reason it scared me to say the words out loud, but I couldn't keep them from her. "I would like that. An H.E.A. for us."

Emma managed to both smile at me and look miserable at the same time which urged me on.

"You said it. They are all liars." My voice dropped and I fought the urge to grind my teeth. "I am only something to be used." I grabbed her hand, threading my fingers into hers. "Just as they wish to use you too. If we go far away where they can't get us, we can have a happily ever after."

It all hadn't quite hit me. I understood the Luxis had lied to me, but I still couldn't believe I had a soul. I tried to search inward, as if by knowing it was there I could contact it within myself. But I came up feeling empty, broken, and tired. And not a trace of my former powers warmed me. I felt naked and exposed without them. As if any slight wind could bowl me over. But I could be strong for Emma. I would do anything for her.

"What they did to you makes sense," Emma mused.

I blinked.

Seeing my expression, she straightened, "I'm not saying it's good or even by any means okay, nosiree, I'm just saying I see why they did it to you. You said your power came from faith. Well the Luxis made sure you believed in 'the Light.'" She made finger quotations with her fingers, which gave me the impression she was somehow mocking it.

I was surprised that she responded to my silent thoughts about my powers. Though I shouldn't be surprised anymore. I just never knew if it was because of our unique connection, or if she somehow intuited what I was thinking. She seemed to see through everyone.

She continued, "You believed so wholly and unquestionably that you got power from that. I always kind of thought that kind of pure belief could create magic. I mean not the crazy evil zealot kind of belief, but the kind where you believe in yourself so much that it changes the world around you."

Again, I was surprised by her level of insight into how my power worked. I was still digesting the information. I was not used to interpreting, only acting. She seemed to be proficient at both.

"If I had my powers back, I could just open a portal and take us far away to our H.E.A., but..." I held up my hands and willed energy to flow through them. Nothing.

"Well obviously, that's not going to work," she said, frowning at my hands. "You can't believe in the Luxis and what they stand for anymore. Not after they lied to you and used you. Maybe you need to believe in yourself now?"

I continued to stare at my hands, silently saying that I believed in myself. Trying to access it as a truth. They continued to be nothing more than dirt covered, calloused hands of uselessness.

"They said I broke the faith," I said, finally voicing what had been bothering me. "After the soul eater, I broke my faith, but I don't know how." I turned to look at her, laying my burden at her feet. "Perhaps it was because I loved you the moment I saw you. Perhaps that was enough to make me turn on my duties as a Chevalier."

Emma snorted in laughter. "There is no way. You have been nothing but a good little soldier, okay? You always obeyed the rules of their game." Her face cleared, lines on her forehead smoothing as if hit by a realization. Emma seemed to be gazing into a place past the cavern wall. "That's it. You were given a set of rules. You knew the rules until that soul eater became a physical creature." Her eyes snapped up to mine. "That defied the rules of everything you had been told. My bet is you weren't taught how to adapt when the rules were broken."

I chewed on the thought, though it made my head hurt. When I stalked the perimeter of the motel before dawn, before the soul eater appeared again, I had regained my powers.

"Yes," I said slowly then got more excited. "Yes, I didn't know what to do with that. That morning before we were attacked at the motel, my powers returned to me because I consciously decided to stop interpreting and solely act on fighting evil in whatever form it appeared in."

Emma nodded. "You redefined the parameters of your belief and once you were in alignment, you were a freakin' powerhouse." She gave a low whistle. "Just think, if you could direct your own beliefs, you could completely control your power." She turned to me with a question in her eyes. "I saw Regina. She had green light in her hands. Why didn't she just use her powers to stop us from the beginning?"

I shook my head. "If their belief is strong, they have power. But they rely on artifacts infused with power, and what they can do are parlor tricks compared to the power of the Chevalier. She hoped to stun me, and she might have done so but for a very brief time and ineffectively. Thank goodness, she was unaware I was powerless then, otherwise she would have tried sooner and been successful."

"That makes sense. If they had your kind of powers, I think they would have been whipping that out long ago, smacking us with it until we said uncle." Emma laid her head on my shoulder. The excitement of our realization left me tired as well.

"Uncle?" I asked.

"Never mind," she said, sounding tired, but her hand smoothed down my arm repeatedly in a soothing gesture that compelled me to close my eyes.

"Stop it," Emma said, chastising me through a small smile.

"Stop what?"

"I can feel you getting aroused, and I'm trying to figure out how to save the world over here."

I smiled. "I can't help it. When you touch me, it moves me." I wrapped my hands around her delicate ones. Her hands were covered in mud and small scrapes. I brought them to my lips to kiss her fingers, more aware than ever I was at her mercy. "You can't imagine what it feels like to never be touched your whole life, then know the touch of an angel." Feelings overwhelmed me so suddenly, I had to close my eyes tight against them and press my lips against her hands for salvation.

Emma's lips fell on my head before she leaned back against the cave wall and sighed. I loosened my grip on her hands but didn't stop touching her. Her eyes moved up, seeming to search the glowing slugs for something. "Calan. You still didn't answer me. What if the orders are right and darkness is coming?"

"They are all liars."

"Technically, that was only your Order, and supposedly it was for the greater good. The Veritas are the ones who don't lie, but granted, they are major douche pickles," she was rambling.

I brought my hands to cup her face, pulling her attention away from the dilemma. I wanted all her attention on me. "You could go mad trying to solve all of this. I don't want any part in this anymore, Emma. I just want to be with you. I just want to keep you safe. I want... I want to...." the name for my fantasy was on the tip of my tongue again. What was it called? The blanket, the food, the kissing under the stars.

Emma's eyes were glassy with unshed tears as her hands came up to cover mine. "I don't know if we have a choice."

My hands fell away from her and I pushed off the ground and stood, running my agitated hands through my hair, thick with dirt and sweat. I had to crouch, as the cave wasn't tall enough to let me stand to my full height. "Of course we do. We can do whatever we want now. Don't you see? I have a soul, Emma."

A smirk pulled at her lips but her eyes remained glassy. "I always knew that, dum dum."

I walked back to her, falling to my knees. "It means I'm not a soulless creature, unworthy of you."

The way her face tightened looked as though I had wounded her. She brushed her hand through my hair. "Of course not. You were never unworthy of anything. You're the best man I know." She leaned forward, her lips a hair's breadth away from mine. I could taste her sweet breath. "You're a true hero, and crazier yet, I've gotten you as my own personal savior."

I grabbed her hand and brought it to my chest. "You saved *me*, Emma. You are the only one who has ever cared for me." I closed my eyes at the rush of pain that thought brought. It made me want to abandon everything I had ever known. The Orders claimed to work for the greater good, but I knew now they were only capable of causing pain. I didn't want that for Emma. I wanted her far away from their games, squabbles, and deceits.

Despite my soul and my words, I still felt unworthy of this strong woman who now carried the weight of the world on her shoulders. I had lost my desire to save the world and was retreating into this new world of selfish preservation I'd never been afforded. All I wanted was her, and damn the rest of the world. Even with her life at stake, Emma still wanted to do the right thing for the greater good. Somewhere between finding out I had a soul, and meeting my true parents, I lost my faith in the idea that a right course of action even existed.

As if sensing my distress, Emma's soft lips found mine. It was a slow, sensual kiss. She took her time tracing the lines of my mouth, learning every curve. Her lips were hot in contrast to the cool air of the cave. Her taste immediately acted as a drug to my system. It heated the blood in my veins and urged a sluggish desperation to both spend forever plundering her mouth and also push in for more. Emma's delicious tongue pushed past my lips and her hands grabbed at my hips, nails digging into me with fervor. All the tension, anger, fear, and desire I'd been holding onto exploded into an inferno. Everything in me screamed to devour her and this time, there was nothing stopping me.

CHAPTER THIRTY-FIVE

I grasped at her body, bringing her up onto her knees and smashing her against me. A groan of pleasure ripped from her throat, heightening the hum of anticipation already radiating throughout my body.

From the moment I met her, Emma had set me on fire, embodying temptation itself. So grateful to be released of my bonds, the only thing I wanted was to drive her insane with pleasure for granting me rights to touch her.

I was diving into my desire for her deeper than I'd ever hoped to go, and I vaguely feared I'd never come up for air. I unleashed every last ounce of wanting I possessed into the kiss, my hands grasping at every part of her I could reach. She met my every kiss and grope with equal ferocity. If I kept her here, with her breasts flattened against my chest, hips rubbing frenetically against mine, mouth and mind occupied by my sensual assault, nothing bad could ever happen to her.

Then I felt it. The connection Emma had identified so quickly. Seeking Emma's presence inside myself, I found her pleasure wrapping around my body like a blanket of energy, electrifying and exciting me further. My mouth migrated away from her sweet, tantalizing mouth to taste and explore the delicate skin along her neck, scraping my teeth along it, alternating between using just the tip of my tongue and completely sucking on her flesh. I was fascinated to discover what made her moan, what made her jerk, and what forced wetness between her legs. I felt the ghost of her reactions heating and tingling my own sensations.

Captive to my exploration, Emma first grasped at my hair then ever so gently clawed down my chest. I had lost my fingers through her tangled tresses at the base of her skull. Firmly tugging her head, I granted myself full access and control of her mouth. She whimpered, her hips pumping forward. It was a small aggressive act on my part, but her ghostly pleasure spiked inside me. It had turned her on. I could feel it, the biofeedback loop made me so hard, I could hardly think past devouring every inch of skin and marking it as mine.

Emma's hand reached the hem line of my dirt-covered shirt. Thin, partially broken fingernails scraped up my torso just above my pelvis, sending an intense shiver through me. The blood that had already been traveling south rushed like a shot to my quickly hardening length.

"Yes," she gasped. Knowing full well what she was doing. Then pushing my shirt up over my abs, she moved back to pull it over my head. As she stared at my exposed chest and abs, I felt the blanket of her pleasure shudder around me in anticipation.

I allowed her to take her time perusing my body with her eyes, but I felt my muscles coil like a tiger's, ready to spring at any moment.

"Jesus," she breathed. "This will never get old." Her fingers traced my body from my clavicles down my chest, tracing the indents of my abs and pausing again just above my pelvis causing me to shiver this time. "I think I have to make sure you never eat pizza again to preserve this ripped bod. Do you have any idea how ridiculously fucking gorgeous you are?"

"You would deprive me pizza?" I asked, a sad note in my voice that made her smile.

Emma's eyes were hooded with lust, as if it was a struggle to focus. "Maybe I'll give you a pepperoni here and there." I leaned back in toward her mouth just as she said. "Perhaps a square of chocolate, if you're good."

"I'm done with being good," I said, then grabbed her hips and ground them into mine as I overtook her mouth once more. The sounds she made. Oh gods. The blissful, sensual sounds purring from her throat made me want more. I had to have more.

I grabbed the tank top that had been practically torn to shreds and pulled it over her head. Her breasts were easily covered by my palms but they bounced as I pulled the shirt away. My balls tightened almost painfully. She quickly unlatched her pants and sat back to push them off her legs. When she rolled back up onto her knees, I couldn't help but immediately press a finger through her soft curls, seeking the point I had once found that made her keen in pleasure. Without the confines of her clothes, I could smell her desire and I began to pant like a dog, hungry to devour her.

"Calan," she breathed, pushing my hand away before pushing at the hem of my own pants. Pausing my exploration of her sex, I made quick work of kicking my pants off. Before I could get back on my knees, she pushed me onto my back, hovering over me. My sex strained long and hard between us, begging to seek refuge between her legs.

Emma wetted her lips as her delicate fingers encircled me before firmly grasping it and sweeping from base to tip.

My hands flew to her shoulders. "Stop," I ordered, my teeth gritted.

A sly smile spread across her face. A war of imminent pleasure and deep desire to make this last as long as possible had my face screwed up in concentration.

With a shaking hand, I brought it up to her cheek then used my thumb to caress her bottom lip. It was moist and swollen, like I was sure her lower lips were.

"Emma," I said, my voice catching. "Since the moment I first saw you, I have loved you. Everywhere there is darkness, but it is you that are the true light. I will never betray you, never turn away from you, and love you to my dying breath."

Emma closed her eyes as if my words had physically laid into her. Tears started to drip from her lashes before she opened them again, smiling in a way that confused me as she cried. "I love you, too, Calan. After all you have done, after all you have been through, I just want you to have a life you can believe in again."

My other hand came up to frame her face. Afraid I would break her with my intensity, I fought to keep my grip light. "The only life I could ever want is with you."

Emma reached for my manhood and stroked harder, pushing me back with her other hand until I was lying flat. She covered me with her body and the hot, liquid of her sex slid against my hard, muscular thigh. My inner beast howled. All I wanted to do was grab her and slam her down onto my hard length. Though I had never known the actual experience, I ached to know now, my hips instinctively bucking toward her.

Instead of giving into my direction, Emma disappeared and I found myself swallowed into the impossibly scorching wetness of her mouth. I grabbed at the ground, seeking purchase and control and everything in me threatened to snap.

"Oh gods, Emma." I cried out, not sure if I was begging her to stop or continue. I reached down and was more careful to grasp at her hair, needing another point of contact to focus on other than her mouth. She engulfed my hardness, though she could only fit half in her mouth, before she sucked her way back up. Releasing the tip, she dove back down trying to take even more of my length down her throat. Finally she brought her hand to wrap around the base to cover that which she could not take into her mouth, and I bucked under her with a deep groan.

"Please, Emma," I begged, still not sure what I wanted but knowing she could give it to me. She let me go with an audible wet smack from her mouth that was almost my undoing. Emma paused and I knew, whether from the look on her face or our unique connection, she was soaking in the sight of me with the feminine pride of bringing a man to his knees. I was on my back, but I would have done anything she asked me.

When she crawled on top of me, I lifted my knee until it firmly set between her legs. Emma threw her head back and groaned, grinding harder and harder back onto my thigh. Her wetness ran down my thigh and I knew my pleasure had been hers, and she too was on the verge. We were desperate to both give in to what we wanted, but also to make it last. Her body wriggled wantonly against mine until she raised herself slightly. When she reached down to touch herself, my mouth dropped open in shock as she pleasured herself on me.

Lost in the moment, she seemed to barely notice me but I knew I was the true source of her pleasure. I clenched my fists to keep from grabbing at her, mesmerized by her building orgasm. Emma's back arched forward as her eyes snapped open. Her emotive, honey-brown eyes met mine in an expression of pure shock and elation and I felt it all. Her body was engulfed in a trembling, rolling orgasm that swept all rational thought away.

Closing my eyes and steeling myself against the sensation, I let her ride it out above me. The moment she slowed, I rolled her over, hovering over her body, my tip nuzzling her dripping wet folds. The silver light of the moon filtering in through the cave entrance, finding its way to the top half of her face. It perfectly lit her glassy, lust-filled eyes.

I couldn't believe she wanted me, except I knew it with every fiber of my being.

My back arched and my balls drew up into my body, wanting nothing more than to penetrate.

"Calan," she moaned, the friction reigniting her desire all over again. Ever so slowly, I began to push into her until the head was swallowed by her tight sex.

"Calan." She said my name sharply this time, and it felt like a cold bucket of fear had been thrown over my body. When I opened my eyes, her eyes were screwed up as if she was in pain. I'd heard that it was painful the first time for a woman, and instantly stilled, my body afraid of hurting her. Then a fraction of my senses returned to me and I saw what gave her pause.

Her face was no longer bathed in the silvery light of the moon. Instead, it was illuminated in a sickly green hue. Trying to make sense of it, I looked up and saw the slugs had not altered from their blue glow. Then I looked through the cave opening which was angled perfectly to give us view of the moon.

Emma's words were so faint, I almost didn't hear them. "When the night sky becomes ill…"

The moon had taken on a bizarre, unnaturally sick shade of green.

I didn't want to believe it. It was hard to concentrate, partially immersed in her, and though I mourned it, I didn't fight Emma when she pushed me back and out of the heaven I sought.

Before I could speak, she licked her hand and reached down grasping me in her hand, pumping me with vigor. I tried to protest, but the sensations overwhelmed me. She needn't have lubricated her hand, because the sweet nectar of her sex had already freely flowed on my length making it slippery for each tight pump that brought me closer to my own orgasm.

"Emma," I pleaded, wanting her to stop, desperate to be inside her, but at the same time unable to stop the building crest of my own orgasm. She wouldn't stop, building the rhythm to an almost frantic pace.

She leaned down to my ear and whispered, "Come for me, Calan." With that she dropped down and swallowed as much of me as she could and sucked.

Her words coupled with her mouth hit me like a shot. All the tension I'd been holding in exploded and my back lifted off the ground, arching almost to my breaking point as I came. The hot seed shot out from me so hard and fast, my vision blurred and I couldn't breathe.

When awareness returned to me, I felt Emma dropping kisses on my neck and chest. She murmured over and over in between kisses. "I love you, I love you, I love you."

I wrapped her in my arms tightly, my voice hoarse from the exertion. "It's not true. It's not true, Emma. They are liars. None of it is true."

She nodded against my chest and said, "Shh. Everything is okay now."

Between her soothing words and the force of my orgasm stealing my last bit of energy, my thoughts slowed. I couldn't tell if my chest was wet from our sweat or from her tears as she buried her head against me. I was about to ask her but it was then my mind drifted away to deep, dreamless sleep.

CHAPTER THIRTY-SIX

I reached over to pull Emma closer to my body, she was too far away. Even in sleep, I felt cold and empty without her, as if the world was terribly wrong or sick. Her presence could fix it.

My arm landed on the rapidly warming soil of the cave. Blinking my eyes that had crusted together in sleep, I tried to find Emma. Knowing the cave was relatively small, she couldn't be far. She'd know it was too dangerous to venture outside of it without me. Pushing up from my side, I looked around. Sunlight streamed in through the cave's entrance, and the blue tint of the slugs was barely visible now, as if they'd dissolved into the rock itself.

Perhaps she had stepped out to quickly relieve herself. I wanted to peek outside, but figured I'd give her a minute of privacy to finish. I stretched and slowly stood, shaking sleep off of my sore and bruised body. Once again, I was forced to hunch over.

That's when I felt it. It pounded through me like a fresh raw wound. Guilt. It washed over me in continuous, near-overlapping waves.

I'm sorry. I'm sorry. I'm sorry.

Had I gone mad in the night, and never been with Emma at all? It felt as if my heart and mind were being dragged along by some greater force.

Coming to my senses, I realized the strong feelings pounding through me were not my own. They were Emma's.

My heart stopped in my chest, constricting with sheer panic.

She wouldn't have. There was no possibility she would do such a thing.

I hurried outside into the throb of morning heat, looking around our cave for signs of her. There was none. Irrationally I searched up past the trees for the cause of this madness, but the green-moon had disappeared from the day-lit sky.

"Emma," I called out though it was unwise to attract the attention of the jungle. The creatures, dark and dangerous secrets created by the Luxis, would be ready to swallow me up in an instant. Yet I couldn't keep silent. "Emma, come back. It's okay. You don't have to go. We'll figure this out together." My feet smashed through the foliage as I searched a wider and wider radius hoping against hope I was wrong.

The guilt pulsating through me like blood in my veins began to lessen. She was moving further and further away from me. I had to find her, *now*.

When I found her footsteps, my body completely numbed. It was as I had feared. They led back in the direction of the Temple of Lux. I ran back to grab my sword and threw on my pants, leaving my tattered shirt behind.

I ran through the woods until my lungs burned with white fire. They threatened to give up all together, if my leg muscles didn't do so first.

I'm sorry. I'm sorry. I'm sorry.

It was fainter than before. I was losing her. Panic constricted around my chest and throat. I refused to lose her.

There wasn't a plan other than to bust in there and pull her out. Wrap my hands around those delicate shoulders of hers and shake her until sense returned. Who cares if the night sky became ill? It could mean anything, it could mean nothing.

You don't believe that, a voice inside me countered. *It was just as they predicted. The time of darkness has been named.*

"No," I ground the word out between my teeth, trying to audibly drown out my thoughts. The Luxis were wrong. Emma didn't need to die.

By the time I raced up to the Temple, I knew I should have a plan. Barging in there was just going to get me thrown into the room of corrections or worse, disposed of. Yet, I could not stop my feet from slapping loudly up the stone stairs up a side entrance. I didn't bother to approach with stealth, they'd know I was coming for her.

"Emma," I cried out once inside the cool stone walls of the Temple.

She was here. I could feel it. The guilt weighed me down so heavily, it became difficult to move. My need kept me pushing through the inertia.

Then the weight disappeared so suddenly I almost tripped over myself from the sudden shift within my heart and body. Catching myself, I searched inward for any trace of the guilt that plagued Emma. I was alone, plagued only by my own panic and urgency.

Gooseflesh painfully pulled at the skin across my whole body. "Emma, I'm here. I'm coming for you." My voice bounced off the walls, reverberating back to me as I ran through each room, each one as empty as the last. The interpretation of the sacred text had been removed, and no one had been left behind for me to question. They knew if they'd left anyone I would have extracted information out of them using any means necessary.

Coming to stand in the middle of the large hall where I'd last seen my Masters, it finally sank in that she was gone. They were all gone. They'd stepped through a portal and disappeared. A dry wheezing laugh escaped me, as my fisted hands fell open. Blood rushed back to my fingers with a painful wash of invisible pins and needles. It was nothing compared to the roar of an ocean of fear and pain that slammed into me with a finality ending so silently I thought I'd been deafened. They took Emma with them, and I would never find them as long as they didn't want to be found. I knew it with absolute certainty. After all, they had taught me that particularly trick.

CHAPTER THIRTY-SEVEN

The last rays of daylight warmed my face, but inside I was cold as stone. The fresh scent of pine stung my nose with over exuberance, as birds chirped in the towering trees a half mile out from here. It was as if they knew to keep their distance from me. From the fourth floor of the unfinished building in Smoky Badger, I had a perfect view above the Colorado forest of the sunset. The sky was lit with deep golds and soft oranges, but I wished the sky had been painted red. It would have been more fitting than this picturesque serenity.

I'd finally learned in town that they had lost funding for the construction, which is why this place remained an abandoned skeleton, half built. The wine bottles had remained untouched in the corner where I'd left them. A thin layer of golden-yellow, chalky pollen now covered them, evidence spring was nearing. Things were still, fixed here as though nothing had moved in my absence, but I had gone further than I'd ever dreamed. The last time I was here, I was a man who knew his mission. No, not a man. A force played by someone else's hand. I had voyaged for what felt like a lifetime only to return to stand at this precipice.

It had been two months since Emma left to do what she'd thought was the right thing. She thought the order of Luxis was going to help her save the world and surrendered herself to them. Whether it was Gatsby or another Chevalier they called upon who created a portal to move the entire order, I never had a chance of catching up.

My hand barely touched the exposed metal beam holding up the roof, while the front half of my feet hung over the edge. I sucked in more of the fresh, pine air, hoping it would ground me. I was free. I was my own man, my soul to wield as I saw fit. Yet, with all that freedom I felt like little more than a flailing babe, screaming to the heavens for help while my insides had frozen into a paralysis I could not name.

No, that wasn't true. My paralysis was fear. Fear of decision, of choice, of having to lead myself. It left me incapacitated.

Is this how everyone felt? All these years, I had passed by civilians who seemed to face each new day with assured calm as they poured onto the streets, walked to work, to restaurants, to meet with their friends and family. Those people I'd seen serenely sip coffee outside a café, those who danced on the sidewalks singing with abandon in the middle night with their friends after imbibing. I had once looked forward to knowing my place amongst them, but now I knew the truth of the perfected blank mask everyone affixed as soon as they woke up. It covered up the truth I had come to know. It covered absolute and utter terror.

In possessing my soul, I was free to choose, but there was no way of knowing whether I was doing the right thing. At times I suspected I knew the truth, but was never certain. I only knew one person who was fearless looking into that frozen tundra of fear every day.

After overcoming my initial denial that Emma was really gone, followed by the complete lack of ability to do anything about it, I considered maybe she was right. Maybe she was meant for sacrifice all along, to save the world. I roamed the empty halls of the Temple of Lux, haunting it for weeks. I would stalk about the reading room, staring at the books willing them to give me the answers until the smell of their aging pages offended me back out again. Several times, an unbidden rage swelled in me until I could no longer contain myself. I would grab books off the shelf, hurl them across the room, rip them in half, try to destroy the tools that were useless to me. There was nothing left there for me.

The trials had nearly killed me as a child, but walking through the jungle a second time, I was a changed man. I still didn't have my powers, but I had an iron-will to find Emma no matter the cost. Gods help the creatures I slaughtered who got in my way. When I finally arrived at a village equipped with a modicum of modern technology, I discovered I was in a country called Tajikistan. I'd never been instructed on its geography, only told it was the home to which I should always return by way of portal unless otherwise instructed.

Between guidance from the locals and the currency I took from the unguarded Temple, I was able to move around from city to city, watching and waiting. I eventually made my way into Beijing where information was abundant. Though I could not read, I'd already been trained to speak in thirty-seven languages so I could properly observe wherever my mission took me. There was never a moment I was far from a radio, or television. I even learned to use the computers in the local cyber cafés with the help of some children who had taken a liking to me, despite the warnings of their parents who seemed to detect the rage behind my eyes.

The green moon had thrown scientists into a tailspin. While most described the event as a beautiful mystery they were eager to study, for many it quickly became a phenomenon, fading into the background of their day-to-day lives. However, a small percent of people around the world recognized it for what it was. A portent evil was coming. They carried posters proclaiming, 'The end is near.'

Then I got my sign. An earthquake of unprecedented magnitude made national news. It shook the small town of Smoky Badger until the earth's crust ripped into a gigantic crack, and everyone had to be evacuated.

Where the earth breaks, the dark lord shall journey in a fortnight's time to set his deathly foot upon the dirt of the earth.

It made sense. We had to go back to the beginning. The soul eater broke ground when he stepped onto our plane and his Dark Lord was going to follow the path.

I had found my way to an airport and crossed my first ocean, which gave me ample time to think. Who was I to stop Emma? It was her life to choose what to do with it, just as my life was my own now. Could I stop her from doing what she believed in? It forced me to ask the question, what did I believe in now? Did I believe the Luxis? Did I believe any of the Orders? Did I believe the end was coming? Did I believe in myself to fight it, if it came to that? I could never meet the endless litany of questions with any semblance of an answer, and thus I flailed. Flailed for guidance, direction, from someone, anyone who wasn't me.

My thoughts easily fell to Emma, always procuring deep stabs of loss. Her expressive eyes, the delicate slide of her fingers against my knuckles before she took my hand in hers, the concentration of her scent I'd found where her shoulders and neck met. Yet she was so much more. The way she walked into a room demanding attention and respect, no matter who thought they knew better. Where I was once blinded, she uncovered the lies around me one by one.

After all you have done, after all you have been through. I just want you to have a life you can believe in again.

Standing there on the fourth floor, watching the sun finally disappear, the last rays shooting up into the sky illuminating thin trails of clouds into purple rocket trails, it finally came to me. It came as effortless as a breath. Looking down, I was hardly surprised to see my palms were glowing. Humming with power, I felt it vibrate from my toes to my chest. It was different than before. The energy felt purer, almost clean in comparison to the magic I had wielded in the past.

I didn't know what I was going to do, but I knew I was capable of doing whatever was needed now.

Closing my eyes, I reached out with my senses into the forest. Like water lapping at a beach, it sought for any disturbance as it flowed out. I opened my eyes. They were almost here. All of them.

CHAPTER THIRTY-EIGHT

When I first locked eyes on Emma, my body surged of its own volition, almost jettisoning me from my hiding spot high up in a tree. My hands wrapped around nearby limbs so tightly my knuckles went white. I forcibly stilled the straining, tense muscles in my body, choosing to watch, carefully taking in as much information as I could. The pinprick tips of the pine needles brushed against my back and arms as if soothing me. *Soon, you'll get your chance soon.*

The seemingly endless deep chasm was less than a quarter mile from Smoky Badger Liquors where it had all begun with the soul eater. I'd reached the unnatural fissure before anyone else. Climbing up near the tree line, I got a vantage point of the chasm at its widest yawn of eight meters.

My breath caught over the lump that had formed in my throat. Emma wore a white dress, similar to the one the Order had put her in when I'd first taken her to the Temple of Lux, except this one had sleeves and was made of heavier material to fight off the bite of evening chill in the mountains. Her mother's necklace hung around her neck as always. The white gemstone caught the light of a torch and winked at me with a twinkle. Her eyes were wide and I caught the glisten of her lips as she repeatedly licked them in what seemed nervous anticipation. Her hair was wet and slicked back, as if she'd just bathed. Of course, they would want to anoint her before sacrificing her, I thought with disgust. My muscles tensed again with all the rage of the feral beast I'd been twisted into by lies and manipulation. I didn't want them touching her, blessing her with their deceit, before sending her to her death.

This is what she wanted, a voice inside me parried. *You came to enact her will, whatever she may choose.*

Licking the front of my teeth, I tried to rid myself of the sour taste that unexpectedly flooded my mouth.

Emma pushed her thick pink glasses up her nose. She must have retrieved them when she returned to the Temple. There was tape on one corner, holding the frames together. She was surrounded by an escort of ten Order members who were leading her toward the fissure. They held torches to light the surrounding land. The green moon added its own sickly cast making me as uneasy as when I first saw it. The ground was a blanket of browned pine needles with patches of grass that had resiliently pushed its way through in places. The layout was a stark contrast of dark robes, hoods covering the faces of each member, to Emma's feminine frame in white, billowy material.

This is what she wants, I insisted once again to myself, but it felt wrong. Everything about this was wrong. I had to find a way to make her aware I was here. I needed her to know I was here for her, no matter what she chose to do, but it was too soon to reveal myself. It was unwise to charge in blindly. My body coiled further into the tree in preparation as her escort spread out in formation, giving her more space.

Emma's head whipped around, looking between each Order member, now biting her wet lower lip. One hand picked at the nails on her other hand. It reminded me of when we talked after she'd pulled over the car on our journey to rest. It ended with her confessing her mounting attraction for me, and I foolishly spurned her advances, thinking I was saving her.

My brow furrowed. She looked scared and unsure. This wasn't at all the confident woman I knew. Even when she'd made hard decisions, she found certainty in them. Like when she resolved to take the harder path by my side rather than return home. Like when she left me to do the right thing. Though I had come to realize I'd never once thought for myself, I had been in awe of her ability to know what was right. Even when she'd left me in that cave, I knew she was resigned to what she must do, though I hadn't reached that conclusion with her. Now, she looked like cornered prey, seeking a way out.

You just want that to be true so you can run in there and save her, I assured myself. *Don't move. Don't do whatever foolish thing you think you need to do.*

That was when I saw Master Wu walk out into the clearing to stand just outside the circle of order members. His deep blue robe was encrusted in jewels for the occasion, I observed bitterly. Closing his eyes, he raised his hands as if in prayer and mumbled words just out of my hearing range. The Order members remained still as stone except for one who twisted slightly to glance at Master Wu. It was brief, but I caught sight of the order member's round face under the hood. Travis.

I bristled in enmity, sizzling blood flooded my face causing my breath to come in short hot bursts. It was his fault. Travis was the one who had made Emma go away. The cowardly weasel insisted she needed to die to save the world, and for the first time, I wished it was him who would die tonight. I grasped more firmly at the ridged, layered bark but ceased when it audibly crunched under my grip.

I still didn't see anyone holding any kind of sacrificial blade to take her life and Emma didn't hold anything to take her own life with. I wondered if that came later.

Emma's eyes searched the darkness outside the circle of light, as if looking for something. Her hands continued their agitated dance. I was desperate to be with her, to soothe her. Desire to know what she was thinking flooded me. If only I knew....

Of course. I *was* a thick imbecile. I closed my eyes and searched inward. My anxiety to find her -- the anxiety wasn't just my own. I felt Emma around me, in me, intensifying my emotions with her trepidation. Emma's eyes were probing the darkened forest, searching for someone. She was looking for me.

That was all I needed. Quickly and quietly I slunk down the tree, focusing on the bark scraping against my legs and palms, steadying my breath the whole way down to keep from bounding down and toward her. The moment my boots hit the ground, a blade met the vulnerable flesh of my neck before I could even straighten. I froze, waiting to see if the knife would continue its journey into my jugular. The muscular arm that wrapped around my neck stayed firm but still.

"So glad you could join us, brother," Gatsby hissed into my ear from behind me.

Gatsby led me out into the clearing, my hands carefully raised in surrender. He had repositioned the blade behind me, keeping it expertly pressed between my third and fourth rib, ready to strike at my liver if I made any rash moves. Though I could not see his face, I could sense his smugness over getting the drop on me.

"Look who decided to bless us with his presence," Gatsby called out to Master Wu. Emma whipped around. When she saw me, her face was a mixture of relief, surprise, and sadness, no one single emotion winning out. I couldn't help but notice Travis's hood rise to catch sight of me, but I didn't spare him a glance. He had chosen his path.

Master Wu's robes swept forward as he drew near. He appeared to glide rather than walk. Ferocity gripped his features in a twisted expression of pleasure. "If you've come to stop us, I'm afraid that won't be possible. We anticipated your attendance."

Gatsby nudged me with the knife again, causing me to lean away from the pressure so it wouldn't puncture through.

"And what are you doing here, Master Wu?" I asked smoothly. I spoke to Master Wu but kept my eyes on Emma who seemed to be silently pleading with me. Even searching the lines of our connection, I knew she wasn't even sure what to hope for. There was so much conflict in her, I couldn't determine what it was she wanted me to do. Part of her wanted me to send me away, another part desperately wanted me to stay, and it all covered up a deeper conflict that raged inside her.

I finally turned to Wu. "I was under the impression the Propheros was here to make the sacrifice of her own free will." I glanced at the circle of Luxis members. "And even if not, you sent enough of an escort to make sure she wouldn't change her mind."

"Indeed," Master Wu smiled. His pointed teeth, gave him the appearance of a malignant hyena when he grinned. I had the thought in the past, but immediately squashed any irreverent thought I had toward one of my Masters. Now, I let the unflattering comparison soak my impression of someone I had once respected and obeyed without question. Malice flashed behind his dark eyes. "Though this may be dangerous ground to stand on when the time comes, I assured the others I needed to see this through to the end."

So there was no chance of him leaving. The bigger part of me wondered if he weren't here to see me to my end. My disobedience had beyond incensed him.

"Are you to take her life personally," I asked, "or were you going to hand her the blade to do it herself once you see the darkness coming?"

Master Wu's eyes narrowed in smug triumph, knowing something I did not. He kept his lips sealed.

Emma said in a thin, reedy voice, "It's not that kind of sacrifice." She cleared her throat to make her voice stronger, "The sacrifice is—"

"Silence," Master Wu's words snapped in the air like a mighty whip.

Emma's lips immediately thinned away and a shudder of fear rippled up my spine. It wasn't my fear, it was hers. He had done something to make her afraid of him. Fury rippled through me.

"I am not here to make trouble," I announced. I gripped a fist to keep my powers at bay. The light tingled inside my right palm. I hadn't needed to form a sacred sigil with my hands, nor chant words to focus my energy. It came easily now. A need to defend myself against Master Wu threatened my logical thinking and calm demeanor. I had to focus on my objective. "I am here to protect the Propheros."

"You have betrayed your Order and the Light," Master Wu's nasal voice boomed as if he were making a proclamation. "You shall be used as an observance of darkness and sent back to the Stygian, where you belong." His smile was full of promise of unimaginable pain to come.

Gatsby dug in me with the needle point knife again, this time piercing through my shirt and flesh. The warmth of blood trickling down my back got my attention. The cut from the tip of his knife stung, but I didn't give him the pleasure of even a grimace.

"You were relieved of your duties, brother," Gatsby said. "Without your powers or your dignity, you can't possibly be of any use. *I* am the one chosen to protect the Propheros."

For a moment, a deep sadness welled inside of me. Gatsby's voice was harsh and full of spite. I knew he took umbrage with me, but in that moment I realized how much.

"I knew you resented me brother," I said softly. "I don't think I realized how much until now."

He snorted.

I said in a flat tone, devoid of emotion, "Ironically, you were the one who had the most sense of us all."

That gave him pause. I could feel it, though he was behind me and I was unable to see his face.

"You want to ask me, don't you? It's on the tip of your tongue. It's what made you better than the rest of us, and the reason why you were punished the most. Your innate curiosity."

"Gatsby," Master Wu's voice cracked like a whip. "You will hold the rogue Chevalier until the prophecy has been fulfilled. Do you understand?"

There it was again. That slight hesitance that urged Gatsby to ask more, but instead he led me back and away to the outskirts of the ring of order members.

Emma watched me with wide eyes as her hands came up to rub either arm against the early night chill that had set in. The wet hair couldn't be helping her body temperature.

I'm glad you're here.

I heard the words inside my own head but they were Emma's. Though I wasn't sure how she had done it, I focused on solidifying the words in my own head and tried to send a message back to her.

To the end, my love.

Emma's mouth quirked on one side, the barest hint of a smile disappearing before it barely began. I didn't know if she heard me, but I sent one more message to her.

Are you sure?

My heart pounded in my chest so hard, I could barely hear over its thunderous beat in my ears. Part of me, sure I would throw myself back onto Gatsby's knife myself if her answer was yes. If I had to watch her take her own life, I surely wouldn't survive. But I would never do that. I had to protect her life and would in whatever way she chose, even if it killed me to do so.

For a long time, I watched Emma rub her arms and stare at the ground. She did so for so long I doubted she had received my psychic messages at all.

Then she reached up with both hands to slip off her glasses, shakily closed the frames, then looked up at me. Her smooth white throat convulsed under a hard swallow. Travis's head rose several inches, and I noticed he was watching her too as if sensing a shift.

Her answer came through crystal clear as her eyes met mine.

No.

CHAPTER THIRTY-NINE

"Gatsby," I said, under my breath, well out of earshot of Master Wu, who'd begun loudly chanting in fervent prayer. "Did they tell you why I was no longer fit to be Chevalier?"

"Attempting to take the virginity of the Propheros seemed like a pretty good reason," he said in a bored tone. If he didn't have the knife stuck in my back, I was sure he'd be cleaning underneath his fingernails with its razor tip.

"Do you really think I'd take something so sacred for myself? Do you think I would just turn on the Light like that?"

Gatsby didn't respond. There was something about his pause that I didn't understand but felt I should have.

"Temptation is real brother, yet the Chevalier must be cleansed of it." His words were tight, and I could tell he was hiding something, but I didn't have time to probe for what.

"Yes well, when have you known me to succumb to temptation, brother? Ever?"

He didn't respond.

"Admittedly, Emma is unique and I have had to fight baser instincts I'd never known before, but do you know why I finally turned against the Luxis, brother? It wasn't because temptation had overcome me."

Again, that static hum around his silence. He wanted to ask. His curiosity wriggled and prodded him to ask. I couldn't speak it until I knew he was ready. I had to rely on his knowledge of my previous devoutness. How could he forget when it disgusted him so all these   years?

"I think you knew," I added in a low voice. "On some level, I think part of you had always known the truth, which is why you had to suffer the most." I closed my own eyes against the pain of my blindness.

The pressure of his blade lessened ever so slightly off my ribs. "What truth?"

Though I inwardly crowed in victory over that chink in his armor causing him to ask, my jaw tightened and my chest constricted as I explained.

"We were never soulless. They told us that so we would bend to their will. Our only objective was to exhibit absolute obedience, and they worked out a brilliant plot to demand just that. Convince us to work toward a redemption we never needed in the first place."

Gatsby gave a slight snort, and I couldn't tell if he was amazed at how well the Order's ploy worked or if it was because he could never truly conform to the obedience they demanded. I counted on it being the latter. That way he would come to the truth sooner.

"We've been lied to and used." Though I was speaking to Gatsby, I kept my eyes trained on Emma who rocked back and forth between each foot. Her glasses hung off the neck of her dress now. She held each arm, and though she wasn't pacing, she was clearly agitated. Though no one could blame her, waiting for her death. I wasn't sure if Master Wu could sense the change of Emma's mind. Even if he hadn't been present, the number of order members would easily prevent her escape if she decided to leave before the darkness came.

"Which is why we must act now." I kept my voice low enough that I couldn't be overheard.

The forest stilled of every bug chirp and twittering bird. It happened so abruptly, even

Master Wu's words died off his lips. Perhaps I was too late. Perhaps the darkness had come and I couldn't save Emma. Energy pulsed through me, begging to be released but I held my ground. If I was going to fight, I needed to know I could win. Between Gatsby and Master Wu, I wouldn't get two moves into a spell without them both stopping me. Maybe my new-found power was strong enough I wouldn't have to use a spell though.

As I debated whether to try to use the brute force of my magic, figures emerged a quarter mile out past the fissure. Green light illuminated two familiar faces. Phillip and Regina stepped from the woods and into the clearing. Both wielded katanas. The long thin blades caught the light of the green moon, causing the weapons to glint with menace.

The Luxis pulled blades from their robes as if sharing the same breath, all except for Travis who fumbled to pull his out. In contrast to the Veritas, our order members carried claymore swords, the original medieval articles made in Scotland. The handle scooped downward over the blade.

Master Wu seemed irritated, but not alarmed. He knew the two agents would be easily overtaken and he wouldn't even have to bother to lift a finger.

Fifty more agents stepped out from the trees to join my biological parents. Master Wu's irritation now pulled his lips down into a disgusted sneer.

The house of Veritas erupted in a battle cry and charged across the clearing toward the chasm separating them from their enemies.

The agents had to round to either side of the chasm where it was narrowed in places enough to jump the crack. The Luxis order members fanned out in both directions. It wasn't long before the clang of blades reverberated in the night. Emma instinctively took several steps back, away from the melee. Blood spattered the ground near her from an agent of Veritas who was dead before hitting the ground, Emma turned to face me, ready to run into my arms.

Master Wu stepped in between us. I couldn't wait any longer. I launched forward, but Gatsby grabbed my arm and used my momentum against me to throw me to the ground so I landed on my back facing up toward him.

"Please Gatsby, we need to protect her," I pleaded, propping myself up on my elbows.

Tucking away his needle point knife, Gatsby grinned down at me. "I am," he said before throwing a hard punch to the side of my face.

I kicked at his stomach with both feet, but Gatsby was quick to draw back. My face stung, already swelling from the blow. Jerking my lower half, I jack-knifed into a standing position. "Gatsby, didn't you hear me? You can't defend the people who have lied to us our whole lives."

Gatsby wasn't listening. He didn't want to kill me, but he was ready to express a lifetime of resentment and anger to me. He threw several more punches at me that I quickly dodged, though my head swam with hot prickles from his earlier blow.

With a quick glance behind me, I saw Master Wu gripping Emma's arm as she tried to twist back and away from the battle behind them. Claymore against Katana, the swords clanked, punctuated every once in a while with the groans from the wounded or dying. The agents of Veritas had bottle-necked on either side of the chasm. The servants of Luxis held them at bay, but soon the numbers of Veritas would overcome them.

As I rolled to avoid Gatsby's punch, his boot caught my gut, causing vomit to jettison up my throat. I had to still the urge to vomit from the sudden, unexpected hit. Instead, I rolled away before he could get me again.

"Gatsby," I rasped, bile still stinging my throat. "You have to stop. Listen to me."

He didn't and he wouldn't. Before I could speak another word, Gatsby's hands poised in two L-shapes. They lit up as he chanted then he pointed them at me, sending two blasts of power at me. I rolled and escaped the first blast, but the second connected with my back as I ran away. I fell forward, my body momentarily paralyzed as it processed the white-hot pain that licked up the muscles from my lower back and up my right side. A gush of blood rushed down my back. My cheek connected hard to the pine-covered ground but I could barely feel the multitude of prickly pine needle ends.

"That's it, Chevalier," Master Wu cried victoriously to Gatsby. "Destroy him as he would do to you."

My breath returned to me, and my back now screamed in pain, but my brain could process again and I had to get up. Rolling onto my side, I saw my brother come to stand over me. Even if I managed to get to my feet, I couldn't run from another power blast with him on top of me like this.

Gatsby's hands were bright white, a strange red tinge at the edge of his power I'd never noticed before. Large chunks of hair had escaped his pony tail and wildly framed his face. His light gray eyes seemed almost whited out from the reflection of his light. His shoulders heaved from the adrenaline flooding his body. I knew he had always wanted to be on top, and with me out of the way for good, I was one less point of comparison to cause him strife.

My eyes moved past him and Master Wu to Emma whose mouth was open. She looked like she was screaming, but I couldn't hear her.

Like a wound being sliced open, a tear opened behind Emma. It was like a portal, but this was forced, wrong, and looking at it made me sick. It was like watching some kind of surgery as it started as a sliver several feet above Emma's head then slowly ripped down, opening like a ripping membrane, into the Stygian.

CHAPTER FORTY

When I couldn't bear to look at it anymore, I focused up at Gatsby who had yet to end me with his force.

"What are you waiting for?" Master Wu screeched. "Obey me at once. Kill him before he kills you."

The glow in Gatsby's hands dimmed and I could see the conflict in his eyes now. Before I could consider the possibility my words had finally penetrated, Gatsby turned toward Master Wu.

"You see, the problem, Master Wu," he said with deadly calm, red lightning jumping in his hands and eyes. "Is that Calan would never destroy me given the chance. That is, unless you had ordered him to under no uncertain terms. Just as you are doing so to me now."

Master Wu straightened, his lips thinning until they disappeared. "Chevalier, I demand you obey me at once. If you do not obey me, you will never receive your lost soul. Do you want to put your soul at jeopardy?"

"That's the thing. Calan here says we are in possession of our souls and have always been so." The lightning flashed brighter as if to intimidate Master Wu.

It was strange to see. Even discovering the Order he believed in was a lie, Gatsby still had his powers. In lieu of realizing the Luxis were deceitful and manipulative, Gatsby seemed more powerful than ever. How could that be? I asked myself. Then again Gatsby always struggled to obey, it was probably true it was never the Order he unfailingly believed in like I had. It made me wonder, what was his belief so strongly grounded in?

The clash of swords could still be heard in the background. No one had yet noticed the tear in the world. I pushed up to my feet, secure that Gatsby had moved his attention elsewhere. Yet Master Wu and Gatsby still stood between Emma and me. I hoped she knew not to run into the fray. Behind Wu's shoulder, she paced back and forth, recognizing the dog fight she didn't run to get in the middle of.

Master Wu's face hardened and I caught the side of Gatsby's humorless smile. "So the old boy is right after all? See the one thing I do know is Calan is infuriatingly decent, so who am I to doubt his word? If your most loyal dog won't heel, I've got to think you may have done something to betray his trust. Your word on the other hand...." he trailed off before releasing a blast of power at Master Wu.

"Emma, look out," I cried.

With quick fortitude, Master Wu threw his hands up and with an invisible force, the blast was redirected long enough for Wu to duck out of its way. Our Masters used magic but their powers were no match to that of their wards. For our Masters to cast, it required great preparation and the combined efforts of our Masters to call powerful magic forth.

Emma gasped and stumbled back toward the tear she had not yet seen. As if sensing something unnatural was near, Emma slowly turned toward the open wound that led to the Stygian. It glowed red and what looked like poisonous gas seeped out from the torn membrane between planes. I had to get to her.

Undeterred, Gatsby rushed forward, throwing punches at Master Wu. Wu ducked this way and that, taking most of Gatsby's hits. "Did you lie to us? Did you tell me I was a little monster, then beat me when I wouldn't play your made-up game? Tell me." He was screaming now while pouring out all the anger he possessed. Wu began to resort to using small bursts of his power to fight Gatsby off. Blood vessels immediately popped in his eyes from the magical exertion. Gatsby held his hands up in an L-shape again to power up.

"No, Emma, no," I cried, but as if in a trance, Emma stepped closer to the tear. I tried to get by Wu and Gatsby but another errant blast sent me face first into the ground. I scrambled back up, but then I saw it.

A grotesque, black, stick-thin limb stepped through the perverse portal before it was joined by the rest of its twisted body. The demon had to duck to get through the tear then straightened to a dizzying height of fifteen feet.

When the soul eaters appeared on our plane I was familiar with their accompaniment of sulfur rot and a disconcerting mist of both hot and cold. The Chevalier detected the presence of evil more acutely, the better to hunt it. The demon lord's presence almost knocked me over. It wasn't just hot and cold. The air froze as it burned. The smell of rotting meat and illness was overpowering.

Its body sickly glistened, tar-like goop dripping off in places. The thought of it touching Emma made my stomach turn over. The torso was considerably thicker and seemed to pulse and contort. For a moment I imagined I'd seen a hand press against its stomach from the inside out but when I looked again the impression was gone.

Emma's head slowly tilted up until she met the burning eyes of what I could only surmise was the demon lord the prophecy has predicted. The coming darkness. The demon lord didn't destroy souls, it enslaved them in the burning torment in its body, a perfect reflection of the Stygian embodied.

"Save the Propheros," I heard Regina cry out distantly and the clang of swords increased with fury as the agents of Veritas made their way through the bottleneck.

Master Wu stumbled back from Gatsby but saw the agents running toward Emma. He almost missed Gatsby's next assault which would have fried his scalp off. I tried to run by them again, but another blast shot in front of me, singeing my shirt.

"What are you waiting for, brother?" Gatsby yelled back at me.

With impatience I cried, "For you to stop trying to blow me away."

With that Gatsby forced Wu back in a different direction clearing the path for me.

The demon lord had caught sight of Emma and was transfixed. It was as if it were a dog that heard a whistle no one else could. Its eyes blazed in excitement and it beckoned her forward. Emma took a couple hesitant steps toward it. I felt her uncertainty. She didn't know what to do, but faced with the darkness that had been prophesied, she knew there was no running.

The setup smacked me in the face. This is what the prophecy meant. She was to sacrifice herself to the demon lord and it would destroy the darkness. The Luxis told her to walk to the darkness when it came for her.

Emma took another step.

She's going to do it. Oh god, she's going to do it.

I had to stop this. I straightened my fingers, igniting my own powers to fight the demon lord off. The magic came easy again, without having to focus with gestures or chants. I channeled my magic through the belief I held to my core now. Gatsby had kept out of the way, resorting back to a physical skirmish with Wu who now sported bloody lips and a swollen eye. Gatsby wasn't shooting to kill anymore. He wanted Wu to suffer. As always, Gatsby lost his focus on the bigger picture, reaching for the low hanging fruit of revenge.

I ran straight for Emma. She said she didn't know what was right anymore. She didn't know what to do, but I did. In a world where I had nothing left to believe in, I had absolute and total belief in her. My hands heated with liquid sun until it was almost painful, as I focused on my belief in Emma. I took two more sprints toward her, close enough that I could strike the demon lord with my powers. Maybe I could hit it until it tumbled down into the hellish crevice it had created with its coming.

A sledgehammer slammed into my chest and I was thrown back twenty feet. My ribs crackled as I took in a gasping breath, not remembering my journey backward, it happened so fast. Looking around, I caught sight of Wu's enraged face. The skin around his eyes had grayed and black veins pulsed visibly on his face. It cost him to send me that blow.

Gatsby stepped in again, bearing down on Wu who had gone nearly limp from his assault on me. The demon lord held out its spindly hand and Emma lit up as if in a spotlight. She was lifted off the ground, her hands splayed out on either side. The demon began to sip on the light surrounding Emma. Where I once thought I'd seen a hand press against the demon lord's stomach from the inside out, I now watched as the torso nearly tore itself apart, several seemingly whole humans trying to push and claw their way out from the demon lord as it feasted on Emma's essence. Her light began to wane.

I pushed past the mind-numbing pain in my body, forcing myself to stand. On my screaming legs, I ran harder and faster than I'd thought possible. It would not drink the last drop of Emma. She would *not* die for a prophecy she did not wholly believe in. I would not, could not, believe the world would be a better place without her in it. She brought light and if she were dead, I was certain the world would be plunged in darkness.

I leapt off the ground and into the air. Grabbing Emma, I knocked her from the demon's hold. With my arms wrapped around her, we rolled away from the demon. My ribs crackled under the impact of each roll. I couldn't breathe or think, the pain was so sharp.

The demon lord let loose an inhuman cry but I barely noticed. Pushing up onto an elbow, shielding Emma from the danger behind us, I poised myself over her.

"Emma," I said, giving her shoulders a slight shake. "Come on, wake up now." Emma's lips were bloodless, her body limp against my light shaking. The pendant stuck under her left collar bone. Trying to reposition it, I found it stuck to her. I pulled it off with a small sucking sound. The pendant's star design had been burned deeply into her flesh. "Come on, Emma, you've got to wake up. I need you. The whole world needs you. I believe it. I believe you need to live. I believe in you above all else." She didn't open her eyes.

Sending a look over my shoulder to see if the demon was coming to finish the job, I saw the house of Veritas had overtaken the last of the Luxis, and rushed toward the demon with battle cries. I caught sight of my mother and father hanging back, her hands emitting a green glow again.

As if coming out of a trance, the demon lord took a step toward its assailants and stumbled momentarily. It seemed disoriented, and worked to keep its balance.

Twenty agents circled around the demon lord. Half of them raised their hands, emitting various jeweled colors of magic light, while the other half gripped their swords. The demon's head whipped around observing them surround it before throwing its head back and giving a monstrous scream. At first, I thought the cry was born of anger or fear. In the next few moments, I'd learn it was in joy.

The agents rushed the demon. Katanas hacked away at its stick legs, splattering ichor everywhere, yet never cutting through. The other half threw their magic at it. Its torso lit up like a Christmas tree and the skin there sizzled and smoked but its flesh did not break. They were like flies buzzing around it, simply annoying the dark creature.

The demon raised its arms and with it twenty wispy white souls ripped out the tops of agent's heads. The bodies collapsed like sacks of bones. The demon lord plucked the souls out from the air and shoved them down its maw until its torso began convulsing again, with souls trying to push their way out of their new prison. My parents backed up several steps along with the handful of remaining agents. They were the second wave, but what could they do that the first wave hadn't already done?

"Back to hell you go Demon Lord," Wu bellowed, approaching the demon lord. Blood dripped from his eyes. His visible flesh had gone entirely gray and the black veins now traveled down his neck, disappearing beneath his robes. Gatsby was nowhere in sight, and Wu had drawn heavily from his life force to fight us off. He was also about to get himself killed.

I focused on the opportunity that afforded us. We had a shot to get out of here.

I turned back to Emma. "Emma, you have to wake up, we have to go." I leaned down to listen to her heart beat. I pressed my head against her hard, avoiding her scalded flesh, and stopped breathing so I could hear.

There was no gentle thump against my ears. Emma was dead.

CHAPTER FORTY-ONE

I grabbed Emma's lifeless body, pulling it against me.

It can't be. She can't be dead. I believed in her above all else. She was the one who knew light and truth.

Tears burned my eyes until I couldn't see, then they released in a torrent as I rocked Emma's body back and forth, her limp hands dragging against the pine needles. Anguish seemed to blow me into a million incoherent pieces. If I had been faster, quicker, smarter. If I had grabbed her the moment I saw her and ran for our lives, even if she'd protested....

Wu screamed behind me, and I heard the same sickening rip as when the demon lord had taken the souls of Veritas.

The darkness had come, destroyed Emma, and would continue to reign down terror. She died for nothing. The one thing I had ever truly loved was destroyed and now I didn't care if the whole world burned.

I clenched my eyes shut, staving off more tears.

That wasn't true. Emma wanted to save this world, and though Emma was gone, my love for her burned hotter than ever. I would always love her. Always. If she were still alive, she would have me save this world. It was why she left me and returned to the Luxis. She was driven by doing the right thing, just I was. I brushed the hair back from her forehead, and wished I could see her big brown eyes open one last time. Emma was my last guiding light, and I wouldn't fail her now. I knew what had to be done. When I was finished, I wouldn't have to mourn for Emma any longer. It was unlikely I'd survive. Emma gave her life, so if it took the last drop of my life-force to exact her will, I would do it. For her.

Gently laying her back down, I ignored the futile war cries of the remaining Veritas agents. I briefly wondered if my parents were among them. I got to my feet. Time seemed to slow around me, as if I were moving through water.

I turned around to face the demon lord advancing on the remaining fighters. Two of the Luxis members still lived and had joined the agents of Veritas to fight the common enemy. Though it did not speak, I understood the creature. It was about to swat the remaining insects who dared think they could defy it. When it was done, it would walk forth and destroy everything in its path, ripping the whole world asunder.

There was nothing to stop it.

Nothing, except me.

"Hey," I yelled at the demon lord.

It swiveled around, recognizing it was being called.

"You want a tortured soul." I raised my arms out in offering. "I've got one right here for you. It's full of power no one else here possesses. You like power? Come get it."

The beast took several steps toward me. Unlike the corporeal soul eater, this one didn't make a noise as it moved, which was more disconcerting. Two of the agents of Veritas charged it from its left side. Without even looking it smacked them away. Their bodies flew away into the forest.

The tears on my face had gone cold, but I reached into myself and touched the thing that warmed me beyond my comprehension. Emma. My love for Emma and hers for me. She was gone but I could still believe in our love. It was the truest thing I'd known.

The skin along my palms shuddered as light infused them. I closed my eyes. I remembered Emma slipping her hand along my bicep and leaning into my ear outside of the motel massacre as she said softly, "Try again." I had blasted the soul eater away, but this demon was so much more powerful. If it took my soul and my powers there would certainly be no stopping it, but I had to save this world. For her.

As it approached, the souls in its torso began to squawk and writhe again. Emma was in there. Stopping myself from thinking about that, I focused on my belief in her. My body hummed, then buzzed. Light engulfed my entire being as I fed my powers with my love for Emma. I waited for my powers to stop fueling when they'd reached capacity, but it didn't happen. My hands burned brighter, my energy peaked past anything I'd known.

The demon lord stepped in front of me and poised its hands, ready to rip my soul from my body. The soul Emma had seen all along, even when I couldn't.

I closed my eyes. It wasn't his. My soul was hers and nothing would ever change that.

"Run," Phillip yelled out.

When I opened my eyes, I realized he wasn't talking to me, he was talking to those who remained. I looked down and my whole body burned with incredible white light, and I couldn't help but squeeze out a few more tears with a small smile. Emma would have loved to see this. I'd be with her soon.

A blistering, icy heat fell on my skin then sank deeper inside. The demon. It was like a feverish sickness sank into me, sure to kill me any moment. Yet, I was still encased in the bright tingling of my own powers. The demon's long spindly finger poised in the air before me, touching my soul. Its finger flicked upward. I felt something at the root of my being yanked at, except nothing pulled free. My soul hadn't budged from my body. I was unmoved as it tried a second time.

"Calan, do it." I heard Emma's soft but reassuring words. I imagined her right behind me.

I squeezed my fists tight letting the unprecedented ocean of power crest. My heart beat wildly in my throat as I took my last breath. Opening my hands, I let it all go. It felt as though I was dropping from the sky, plummeting toward the ground. Wind rushing my back, I was certain if I opened my eyes I would find myself flying, but I didn't. I kept them closed, holding the image of Emma in my mind. The day she accidently met my eyes over the colorful book she'd kept her nose in, her glasses slightly askew on her face.

I'm coming, my love.

With my powers, went all my energy. Then, like someone blowing out the candle of my consciousness, everything went dark.

CHAPTER FORTY-TWO

Emma's face hovered over mine when I opened my eyes. It took a lot of blinking to beat back the blurriness of my vision. Though I hadn't moved, my body was wracked with aches and pains which were set aflame with each breath I took. The world shook around my body as if I was in a continuous earthquake. Each bump and shake made it harder to think.

"Are we in heaven?" My voice was low and hoarse. "Is there pizza?" Despite the flare of pain, I reached out to grab the angel's wrist.

Emma took my hand and held it between both of hers, dropping kisses on my knuckles.

Tears swam in her smiling eyes. "No doofus, this isn't heaven, but you were superman so I'll see about getting you a pizza."

It was then I noticed the tape holding the corners of her glasses together and the warmth of her hands on mine. I moved to sit up but was hit by a wave of dizziness. Greasy nausea welled up my throat, so I stayed lying down.

"Where are we?" I asked. With that, another bump caused my body to jerk hard. I heard rushing wind over my head and Emma's hair was tied back but the little flyaways were flapping wildly in the wind.

"It's not Emma's jeep, but it's got wheels." Travis's faint, disembodied voice came from over my head.

Looking around, I realized I was lying down in a truck bed and Emma sat next to me, hovering like a mother hen. Travis was driving and he had yelled over his shoulder out the small open window that led to the truck bed.

"Travis," I growled and tried again to get onto my elbows, determined to tear him into pieces.

"Whoa there, Terminator." Emma stopped me with a hand on my chest, firmly pushing me back down. Weakened as I was, it didn't take much force on her part to push me down. "Travis also helped save the day."

"He's a part of the Order," I growled again.

Emma tucked a flyaway piece of hair behind her ear and again I noticed the freshly burned imprint of her pendant under her left collarbone. "He's redeemed himself just fine. Sure, he was a big ole douche-nozzle who joined an Order that wanted to sacrifice me King Kong style." She shot a dirty look at the back of Travis's head.

"I heard that," Travis yelled from inside the truck cab.

"But," she added with distinction. "After you melted that demon down like a hunk of tar, releasing a bunch of scary screaming ghosts into the night--"

"Nightmares for the rest of my life," Travis mumbled.

"You collapsed. The order of Veritas high-tailed it but your mother and father rushed back." She looked down. "They were coming for me."

"But, but you died," I said, still not sure I wasn't dead. The details of her story were too much when I still hadn't yet processed the fact she'd survived.

She shook her head and cupped the side of my face. The feel of her thumb caressing my cheek, made my eyes flutter close and I wanted her to never stop.

"That evil sonofabitch was draining me. Sipping me like a damned fine cognac. When you knocked me out of its path it took me a while to recover. My soul, or whatever it was drinking from me, returned since the demon didn't finished the job. I'm sure if it had fed on me for any longer, I'd be stuck inside its creepy distended stomach."

I opened my eyes to catch a shudder ripple through Emma. "When I woke up, you were glowing, like an archangel." She smiled softly.

I wanted to kiss the corners of her soft pink lips. The way she looked at me, with such reverence, I had always shied away from it feeling undeserving. But now, I knew I deserved her love. I could allow it to enter me, accept it with all my heart.

"It was you then," I said in wonder. "I thought it was the ghost of you speaking to me, but it was really you."

Her smile broke into a full grin. "Yeah baby, that was me."

"Baby? Yech," said Travis.

"Shut up, Trav, I'm trying it out, okay?" Emma snapped. There was no real annoyance in her words, but she blushed.

Emma continued to explain my parents had returned to end me in my weakened state before grabbing her and running. Before they could get to me, Travis emerged from his hiding place – he hid once the demon had arrived, not a shock - torch still in his hand. He set fire to the robe he'd been wearing and threw it at Regina. In the time it took Phillip and Regina to get the burning cloth that engulfed her off, Emma and Travis had dragged me to the truck he'd brought around, then we tore off like banshees from hell. My animosity toward Travis drained in lieu of his readiness to keep Emma and myself safe.

When Emma finished telling me everything, I felt I had enough strength to sit up. Once repositioned, I pulled her onto my body. Emma instantly molded herself against me and I sighed, trying to process everything.

"So, the Luxis's interpretation of the prophecy was wrong," I said at last. Wanting it validated outside of my own head. It would finish all this for me. I could walk away from my life with the Orders without looking back.

Emma tilted her head up at me, worry filled her eyes and her mouth was set in a serious line. "I don't think so anymore."

Before I could ask how she could say such a thing, her hands squeezed me as if needing an anchor. "It was so close," she said quietly, her words almost lost to the rushing wind sweeping by the truck. "When the demon was feeding off me, I felt it weaken. As if something in me was like a delicious poison it couldn't stop drinking."

I remembered how the demon lord had stumbled after I pushed Emma away. Perhaps she was right. My head started to hurt.

"But you destroyed it, Calan," she rushed to say. "So I don't think they were wrong, but they weren't right either."

Travis yelled back to us. "Except with Calan's way, the portal to hell is still open."

Emma's lids lowered. "Yeah, there is that." She licked her lips, again, something she did when she was anxious. I wanted to kiss her but I had more questions.

"The tear in the planes is still open?" I asked, alarm trying to flood me with adrenaline, but I was all tapped out.

Emma slowly nodded. "We saw it still open as we left. Your parents still believe I am the key and they want me to go through that crazy ritual thing."

I grabbed her tight against me and lowered my head capturing Emma's lips for the first time in what felt like an eternity. She was the most delicious, sensual, lovely thing I had ever tasted. Pain ebbed away from my body as she healed me with her touch. Though I was out of adrenaline, she still managed to excite me with a kiss, her fingers skimming down my chest while the other grasped at my waist. She eagerly met my kisses, and I fell into them whole heartedly.

Abruptly, I pulled away. "We have to stop it, you know. Who knows what is escaping the Stygian and entering our world every moment it is open?"

"I know," she said, sounding as grim as I felt.

"I don't know how," I confessed.

"We'll wing it," Emma gave me a crooked smile.

"Wing it?"

"You know, improvise, make it up as we go."

I leaned back against the truck cab, exhausted from our passionate kiss. I pushed back the flyaways behind Emma's ear. "But first, I need something,"

Emma's face became very serious. "Anything. Are you okay? What do you need, big fella?"

"Alright, I need two things. One, don't call me big fella ever again."

A smile threatened to crack her serious façade but she nodded.

"And second," I said, closing my eyes, pulling her in close me again. "We need to go on a picnic." Ease flooded through me with Emma curled against my chest as I finally remembered the word which had evaded me for so long.

"A   picnic?"   she   asked,   not comprehending. "Is that like code for some secret order, Chevalier, magic powers business?"

I opened one eye to look at her, "I thought it was that thing where you ate on a blanket outside together." I closed it again, my voice becoming wistful. "I've never been on a picnic. Since the first time I laid eyes on you, it became my fantasy."

Emma's mouth brushed up against my ear. "Oh, we are going to level up your fantasies real fast, but sure, we can start with some food on a blanket." Her hot breath caused my skin to prickle in delighted excitement. I had a feeling I was going to be harboring many more fantasies than I could handle soon enough.

Here's an excerpt from the next exciting installment of the Five Orders Series, coming June 2019.

Soulless Son

By Holly Roberds

CHAPTER ONE

I don't know if I screamed when Travis slammed on the brakes to avoid hitting the man who appeared in the middle of the road from out of thin air. I'm not even sure if I made a sound when the truck flipped. Time slowed down as every cell in my mind and body dilated to take in each individual second. My stomach zinged up like the carnival game where you smash a mallet into a landing to make the ball go as high as possible. I reached for Calan who sat next to me, but then time sped up as the truck crashed back into the road. We rolled, bone crunching sounds exploded all around me. The momentum of the vehicle threw my body and arms any which way it pleased, and away from Calan.

Blinking, I realized I must have blacked out because the truck was now right side up again except I was staring into the ditch and the roof of the cab brushed against my hair. My hands were braced against the dashboard and it took another moment to register the trails hot tears on my face. If Calan and I had still been in the truck bed, we would have been instantly killed.

"Emma," Calan murmured next to me. His large hand closed around mine.

Despite the tear trails, and the ringing in my ears, I felt eerily alert. "I'm okay. Are you?" I turned to see blood trickling down his temple from his dark curly hair, but other than that, his ridiculously handsome face was unmarred. His deep blue eyes anxiously searched me too, looking for any harm. His eyes slid past me, and alarm tensed his features. "Travis."

Travis was slumped over, but I could see his face had smashed into the steering wheel. He must have broken his nose because blood poured from his nostrils, dripping onto his pants. I put my hand on his back, panic constricting my throat. It took a second but then I felt the rise and fall of his ribs. He was still breathing. Relief was brief as I was hit in the face with the cloying stench of gasoline.

"We need to get out of the truck, now," I said, feeling the blood rush away from my face.

Already depleted from using the entirety of his powers to kill the demon lord who had tried to eat my soul, it took Calan several long moments to get steady enough to exit the vehicle. He held out a hand to me to help me out. As I was about to take his hand, Calan retracted it, his head snapping toward the road.

Perhaps it was the car accident that left me woozy, but with his profile in view all I could think of was how this man was my own personal superman. Clark Kent had nothing on Calan's chiseled jaw, cerulean blue eyes, and sculpted warrior body. Since I'd met him, it had been nothing but a series of dashing heroics, defending me from evil spirits and demons. I almost forgot I needed to get away from the gasoline leaking car. Yep, probably slightly concussed.

"Stay here," he said before stalking off to the road.

Ignoring his warning, I pushed myself out of the open passenger door, following him, though I stumbled several times. It took another minute before my vision stopped spinning and then I saw the serious shit we were in.

"Did you really think you could run, dark one?" Master Ylang's voice was even, but the knuckles wrapped around his staff were white with rage. The ends of his thin, waterfall whiskers brushed the golden rope that cinched the middle of his black, velvet robe. He reminded me of an evil wizard from a fantasy book I'd once read.

"Pretty much. That was basically our plan," I supplied, peeking over Calan's broad, muscled shoulder, even though the question wasn't directed at me.

Calan shot an exasperated look back at me, but he should have known better to think I'd let him go into any fight alone.

"Emma," Calan's low voice cautioned before he moved to further put himself between me and his former Masters from the Order of Luxis. "You failed," Calan announced to them. "Emma is of no use to you now. Leave us be."

Though I'd only spent two months with the Order of Luxis, I knew enough about Master Ylang to see that the dude was seriously pissed. His bald, knobby head looked likely to start pulsating any minute, and his strange, foggy blue eyes pinned us like needles. The two Masters behind him shared the same sour-faced displeasure. They also wore ornate black robes and carried the same staff as the one Ylang held; a long, twisting, ancient piece of wood topped with a murky, green gemstone.

A muscle in Master Ylang's jaw jumped as his eyes narrowed at Calan. "*You* failed us. If the demon lord had feasted on the soul of the Propheros, the demon would have perished and the gate between dimensions would have closed with her sacrifice. You have defied your Order and the Light. With the gate open between our dimensions, and dark creatures from the Stygian are escaping onto our plane. You've unleashed hell on Earth."

"Who knows if sacrificing my soul to that demon would have worked anyway!" I shot back, still trying to meet Ylang's eyes over Calan's shoulder, but I was too short. I brushed my fingers against Calan's lower back, taking comfort and strength from the contact.

To be fair, after the demon lord sucked out a generous swath of my soul, he seemed a bit wobbly on his feet. Maybe if he'd finished the job, gobbling up the rest of my soul, he would have died and the tear between dimensions would have closed back up. But I sure as hell wasn't about to admit that to these douche nozzles.

"Besides, chuckles," I added. Ylang's foggy eyes still managed to flash dangerously with ire. "You guys lie about ninety percent of everything else. You snatched Calan from his crib, lied to him about not having a soul to make him your slave. You didn't teach him to read, then filled his head with whatever convenient fictions best served you. Who knows what you people really want? Maybe the Order of Luxis wanted the gate of hell open."

It was then I noticed another man off to the side. He had been the one who had appeared in the middle of the road by using a portal, sending us flying off into the ditch. If he could make a portal, it meant one thing. He was a Chevalier, a Knight of the Light, basically a lap dog for the Order of Luxis, just like Calan had been before I came along.

This Chevalier was as tall, broad, and herculean as Calan. This one's pale, almost translucent green eyes bore a striking contrast against his cocoa skin. Those near colorless eyes made him appear cold, calculating, and as indifferent as a brainwashed soldier. Even when Calan had been playing the obedient son, I saw desire, warmth, and nobility in those soulful eyes. Which I found ironic, since the Chevalier were told they were soulless beings so they were more easily controlled by their Masters.

Master Violetta's black and grey-streaked hair was pulled back into a tight bun, giving her hawk-like features a makeshift facelift. "We seek to serve the light. That is our only purpose."

Calan squared his shoulders. "You wanted to sacrifice the Propheros to save the world, but if you knew this woman for any amount of time, truly knew her," his deep, soulful blue eyes slid over to me and my breath hitched under his intensity. "You'd know there is no possible way this world could be saved by her demise."

It was strange to hear these guys talk as if they were in ye olden day, but as Calan described it, they lived in a world between worlds. I had to explain to him that a hidden temple in Tajikistan didn't exactly count when there are literally other dimensions.

I glanced back to where Travis was still unconscious in the truck. At least he wasn't awake and

dissolved into horror-movie proportion hysterics. Then again, he'd grown a lot since fighting off a number of demons. Then when the world split and the gate to hell opened up, he swooped in to help me get Calan in the truck and slammed on the gas to get us out of there.

"Can't you just make a portal for us?" I murmured to Calan.

Calan gave a slight shake of his head. I couldn't tell if that meant no, or not right now, but I clamped my mouth shut. We'd been through worse and I had every bit of faith in him that he would get us out of this. I just needed to trust Calan's lead.

Calan's powers were still depleted, but what could the Masters do? Calan was far more powerful than them, even without his magic. It was the other Chevalier I was worried about. But we'd been through worse before, and we'd get through this, too.

Master Ilsa, who sported two large white-blonde braids that trailed down her back, leaned in toward the cold-eyed Chevalier and said something I couldn't hear. Immediately, he did an about face and walked away across the road and disappeared into the woods on the other side. I should have been glad to see him go, but inexplicable fear gripped my chest. Why did he leave? What was happening?

Master Ylang closed his eyes, as if in pain. "I must admit that I am experiencing a great deal of disappointment," he spoke to Calan. "You were one of the most promising Chevaliers we had ever seen, which makes your fall all the more tragic." When he opened his eyes, remorse seemed to drain away from him until someone devoid of mercy stood before us. "But you have made your choice and now you both will face the consequences."

Out of the corner of my eye I saw Calan's palms light up, and my heart took off at a gallop. He'd activated his supercharged powers and was ready to blow these bastards away.

I wished I could help, but the reality was I wasn't the one with superpowers. I'm sure I had other things going for me.

It felt like someone had my heart in a tight grip. It took me a moment to realize I was experiencing Calan's anguish. We shared a psychic connection that transmitted our heightened emotions to the other.

Calan was about to fight Ylang, the closest thing he had to a father, and it caused him pain.

I briefly touched Calan's back, letting him know I understood and he wasn't alone, then I stepped back. It really sucked not being able to help.

As Calan raised his arms, taking aim, all four Masters thumped the base of their staffs into the ground and everything seemed to stop. No, not everything, just Calan. His arms had frozen, aimed toward the ground at Ylang's feet. A green glow surrounded Calan's body, like the tops of the staffs that were lit up like Christmas trees.

"Calan?" I reached out to touch his back but as my hand dipped into the light I recoiled with a hiss. It was white-hot. Sweat beaded under Calan's dark curly hair and began to run in streaks down his face and his jaw was clenched.

"What are you doing?" I screamed. "Stop it!" I couldn't get to Calan, so I had to stop whatever it was they were doing. I charged past Calan at the Masters, not caring anymore if I didn't have super powers. I would beat their asses.

Hands grasped around my arms. I jerked back to find two plain-robed Luxis servants, holding me back. How the hell did they sneak up on me?

I flailed and kicked, but I couldn't break free. Unlike Calan, the only combat training I had was from reactively fighting off demons the last couple months.

Master Ylang and the rest of the Masters closed their eyes and chanted together in a slow, haunting, ethereal echo. When Ylang's eye snapped open they were illuminated with the same green color that encircled Calan's body. Master Ilsa and Violetta continued to chant and sway.

All I could do was continue to yell at them to stop. My next cry died in my throat when I saw Calan's feet had lifted off the ground and his frozen body was held mid-air by whatever force they were using. He looked like he wanted to scream but his jaw was clenched shut.

Ice cut through my stomach, as I realized more and more how screwed we were. Maybe Travis would come back and interrupt whatever creepy spell this was. Maybe the other Chevalier would change his mind and come back and save his brother.

Master's Ylang's voice was harsh, reverberating from the throes of concentrated energy. "You see, Calan," he said the name Calan had chosen for himself, like it was made of acid. "Though you've been in possession of your soul, that has only been through the grace of our will. Just because you have a soul, it does not mean we are incapable of taking it from you."

I realized why they had sent the other Chevalier away. They wanted him to maintain the belief Calan didn't have a soul and this sure would blow that lie wide open.

The Masters thumped their staffs against the ground in unison once more. "So now, we shall take the soul you have used to serve the Dark, and then we shall take the Propheros and repurpose her into something useful by the same means in which we shaped you."

Though Calan could not move, could his face was contorted, his eyes sparkled with rage, and his mouth had curled into what looked like a soundless snarl. He looked like a trapped, feral beast ready to rip out their throats given the chance.

What did that mean? What were the means in which they shaped Calan? I knew little about Calan's upbringing, but what I did know, I wouldn't describe as warm or fuzzy. Again, I whipped my arms about in a frenzy trying to get free.

Ylang's head fell back and the rest of the Masters followed suit. They pursed their lips and emitted a low-whistle in unison. It was simply a whistle, but the organs in my body shivered as if someone had dragged a gigantic nail down a chalkboard.

Calan's limbs snapped out to the sides and his jaw unclenched. His eyes went wide, and the dark circles hanging under them from lack of sleep deepened until his eyes looked hollow and haunted. It as if he was looking into the Stygian itself.

"Calan!" I screamed, trying anything I could to break the Order members' hold, but I was utterly and completely hopeless to help him.

White, smoky light tunneled out from Calan's eyes, nose, and slackened mouth. I screamed as I felt something ripping out of me. I didn't remember falling to my knees, but I vaguely felt my knees digging into dirt as I convulsed against the pain.

I had seen this before. When a soul eater had attacked a motel, it sucked the souls out of people, leaving behind putrid bags of decaying flesh. It sounded like an inverted wind-tunnel as Calan's soul continued to funnel out of his body and toward the gemstone set in Ylang's staff. They were killing Calan and a part of me was dying with him.

This couldn't be. Even as I lay writhing on the ground, I knew something was going to stop this. Something or someone always showed up to save us. Maybe Calan's other brother, Gatsby, would pop out of somewhere to protect Calan. Maybe Travis would wake up and provide a distraction. Maybe Calan could break their hold. He was the strongest person I'd ever known.

Those deep blue eyes managed to turn down toward me and time seemed to stop around us. In an instant, I read all Calan's agony and regret. Even as he died, he was still worried about me. Tears streamed down my face and I couldn't breathe. As abruptly as it started, the pain ceased, the green light disappeared, and Calan hit the ground. I sucked in a deep, desperate breath. It no longer felt like I was undergoing surgery sans anesthesia, but an aching emptiness remained in its stead.

The Order members had released me so I could roll in agony on the ground. Taking advantage of the freedom, I hurried to Calan's still form. I pushed him over until he was facing the sky. The dark circles remained etched under his closed eyes. I shook his shoulders, flashing back to only a few hours ago when I thought he'd died saving me from the demon lord. It felt surreal, like a dream of a dream. I shook his shoulders and called for him to wake up. To give me any sign he was alive. Then it hit me all over again, my world was ripped apart and my heart couldn't do anything but howl inside my chest. I was barely aware of my hysterical sobs.

Knobby fingers touched my shoulder and nausea slithered in my stomach. "He will live," Ylang said gently in my ear. Getting a hold of my sobs, I wiped my face and looked closer. Calan's chest rose and fell with each breath. My sobs renewed with relief this time.

The fingers tightened on my shoulder, digging in painfully, until I grimaced. Swallowing hard, I looked for the last time at the face of the man I loved. I knew this would be the least painful touch I would know for a long time to come.

About the Author

Even as Holly grew up writing romantic fanfiction for the Terminator, Matrix, and anything Joss Whedon, she would have never presumed she'd end up a professional writer.

Holly lives in the Denver area with her husband whose handsome looks are only outdone by his charming and supportive personality. She is supervised by two surly house rabbits who make sure she doesn't spend all of her time watching Buffy reruns.

For more sample chapters, news, and more, visit www.hollyroberds.com